I0583731

COMING HOME

A NOVEL

COMING HOME

A NOVEL

Edward K. Mackendrik

IMPERIUM PUBLISHING
CREATE YOUR STORY

ISBN: Soft Cover – 978-1-64318-051-9
ISBN: Hard Cover – 978-1-64318-052-6

Imperium Publishing
1097 N. 400th Rd
Baldwin City, KS, 66006

www.imperiumpublishing.com

CHAPTER 1

Arnold Barkley had just finished his first cup of coffee. It was only 6:00 A.M. on July 7th 1955, and already the temperature was 74 degrees heading for 98 in Calumet, Oklahoma. Outside the window of the cafe, headlights turning off of Calumet Road cast circles of light against the building and the pickup trucks in the parking lot. The sun had not risen yet, but a morning twilight was beginning to spread a pale yellow behind the clouds in the eastern sky. One of the two waitresses on duty that morning refilled his coffee cup. He smiled a distracted "thank you," lifting his cup slightly towards the window in a toast to the new day.

At 29 years of age, Arnold was a sizeable man. He didn't think of himself as handsome, but he was manly, six feet, four inches tall and two hundred forty pounds naked. He had deep blue eyes and a large, welcoming smile. His large feet encased in size 12EE boots balanced his stature. He definitely took up space wherever he walked. He was a friendly and optimistic man at heart. His smile came easily. He was also an emotional man, one that cared deeply for those he loved. Looking back now though, it seemed that all his relationships had been complex and frustrating as well as emotionally and financially costly. Nevertheless, he had never been able to avoid them.

He was planning to steer clear of them now though. The shrapnel from his divorce from Charlene had injured him deeply. Arnold's marriage to Charlene had ended in a bitter divorce that had damaged his self-confidence and almost wrecked his finances. Charlene had taken a lover while they were married, a deceit Arnold could not tolerate. So, he had stepped into the legal battlefield and fought for the right to keep his assets. Fortunately, they had no children to fight over or the conflict would have been more intense. He had won the battle for his assets, but the experience had taken an emotional toll on him, draining him of his trust and peace of mind.

Arnold continued to love his ex-wife, but he could not accept her back into his life now. He was a divorced man, a free man, but a hurt man. He had decided that he would never consider marriage again. He knew he would need sex. Afterall, he was a healthy man, but he would refuse to become attached, no relationships, no responsibilities. This presented some moral and emotional conflicts for him because he was well trained in the values of his father and mother to "always do the right thing." Somehow, somewhere, and at some time, he felt he would have to deal with this issue of sex and relationship. Could he separate them? Charlene apparently could, but she had remarried already. He often thought of her and her lover, creating intimate settings in his mind, playing them again and again, cutting up his own heart and head. He thought he was going crazy.

Frustrated that thoughts of his divorce continued to haunt him, Arnold got up from the table, paid his bill for the coffee at the cash register, left a tip on the table, and stepped out into the early morning sunlight.

Going through the door, he almost bumped into a wiry man with red hair and leathery skin that looked very familiar. They looked twice at each other.

"Arnold," the shorter man smiled.

"Ray," Arnold took his outstretched hand. "I haven't seen you in ages. Where have you been."

"I'm still cowboying on local ranches," said Ray.

"Married? Kids?" asked Arnold.

"No. Still just in love with my horse," laughed Ray.

"I'm divorced and heading out west myself…starting fresh," Arnold said.

"Good luck man. Stay healthy. I miss the old days of riding with you and the fellas when we were kids, free, running free. Man, you always loved that quick little pony of yours, what was its name, Stormy?"

"Yeah. I did love that little horse and those days. You take care too, Ray."

Arnold moved on past his old friend and folded himself onto the bench seat of his well-worn 1949 Chevy pickup.

He smiled when he thought of the days on the farm when he on Stormy, Ray on Kicker, with Billy on Half Nut would ride the roads and hills all over the county seeking adventure.

In those days, he thought, *all three of them had harbored a strong love for their ponies. Ray still did. Billy had died in a car accident five years ago. Me, I'm alive, but sadly horseless, homeless, and wifeless.*

"This divorce," he whispered to himself as he turned the ignition key, "cannot dictate my future."

Five miles down the road, he turned the truck into the driveway of the simple white three-bedroom house on McKinley Avenue that he rented. All of his possessions, besides the investments that continued to make unbelievable and unexpected profits were stored in the large attic of this 40-year old house. Arnold had sold everything else.

His plan was to travel the United States in the guise of a poor man, one that had no money, no relatives, no friends, no job, and no responsibility for anyone but himself. He was a free man. At least this appeared to be the case. However, this was only partly true. In truth, he had significant assets. Assets that he would be leaving behind, today. He was leaving the money behind because it had served to attract people to him, like Charlene and her lover, who tried to take it from him. He had resolved not to let that happen.

He was seeking change and new experiences. He had always been good at making money. He had always been responsible and self-motivated. Even in his early years, Arnold had been more serious than most young men about learning things, always seeking knowledge in business matters, investments in mineral rights, real estate and stocks and bonds. Lately, he had achieved considerable success resulting in very large profits. Now, as difficult as it would be, he was going to pretend he had no money, not touching any of his investment dividends.

It would not be quite so hard to pretend he was alone. Arnold had no living relatives with whom he communicated. He had many uncles and aunts and cousins, but no children of his own, and all his own immediate family were dead. His parents and all five brothers and seven sisters had died of various sicknesses. There was no one he needed to visit. He was free of responsibility and planned to keep it that way.

As he packed his one bag and tidied up the bedroom he had used, he considered the one big question he had left: *Where he would go?*

Highway 66 might be a good choice, he thought. Although he had never driven the route, he knew from his geography class in school that Highway 66 had passed through Calumet when he was a child, but in 1933, the highway route was moved to the south.

As he grabbed up a map of the United States, patted his pockets to make sure he had the house and car keys, he wondered who he would meet in his travels and what would he see? He ignored the swirl in his stomach that could have been either excitement or fear. He would let his experiences answer those questions, he decided.

As he drove away from the house, he looked back for one last view of the residence where he left many memories and tons of emotions, along with boxes of photographs stored in the attic. For the first time, the reality that he was completely alone began to take form in his consciousness; however, he forged ahead, taking comfort in the familiar surroundings of his truck, the well-worn leather of the seat, the sparkling dust motes on the dash, and the tiny metal cross that hung from the rear-view mirror.

On his way out of town, he made one last stop and pulled into a local real estate agency. There he signed a rental agreement so he could continue to store his possessions in the house on McKinley. He planned to forward his mail to the address of the real estate firm and claim his mail from there periodically.

As he drove away, he was conscious of how little he had with him, one suitcase, one map of the United States, and the signed an agreement with the real estate firm to take care of his property. He had not brought a thermos or even a box of cookies.

Arnold headed south toward U.S. Highway 66, which would lead him somewhere—he didn't really care where.

He asked himself, "should I turn left on Highway 66 and go to Chicago, then on to Washington DC or make a right turn and travel to Los Angeles, California?"

The sun, directly overhead, behind a thin curtain of clouds, gave him no help with direction for it had not begun its own descent from the midpoint of the sky.

Rotating the steering wheel to the right, he chose.

Just like Will Rogers said, he thought. *Go West Young Man.*

"It is West then," he spoke out loud to himself.

CHAPTER 2

The sky had been overcast all morning, but the weather forecasters had thought it would clear up. It never did as Arnold drove West towards New Mexico. There were indications of rain and Arnold felt tears forming and his breathing constrict as his old life disappeared from view.

At first, he thought his dismal feeling was due to the gray rainy day, but rain and clouds had not made him sad before now. No this was homesickness combining with panic. He realized he was picturing Sarah in his mind. Sarah had been his rock. She was the woman who had comforted him all during the terrible days of his divorce from Charlene. As emotion welled up in him, making it hard to breathe, he pulled the car over to the side of the road and made a U turn instinctively returning to home. He was facing East now and parked on the shoulder with his emergency blinkers flicking on and off. Squeezing his eyes tightly closed, he lectured himself again about attachments and relationships.

Sarah with her blond hair, soft hands and soft blue eyes that looked steadily into his would not be easy for Arnold to forget. He couldn't just forget because he felt guilty about the way he had treated her; that, and he needed her comfort. She had listened to him by the hour during his divorce as he wrestled with anger and grief over his lost marriage. She had also sat by him and held his hand when the judge granted his divorce. She had pleaded with him to always remember his parents and how much they meant to him. Sarah was a beautiful person. She probably loved him, and right now, Arnold felt he loved her. But he was committed to taking this trip alone.

"I must go on," he said to no one. "I must find out who and what I am."

Arnold turned the truck around once again, kicking up loose gravel from the shoulder, and drove west again on Highway 66. For a while he drove at a faster speed than he had before and, tears ran down his cheeks, soaking into the legs of his jeans. He wondered why it had taken leaving for him to realize that Sarah was more of a friend than he first believed.

As the miles passed, his grief subsided, and he was able to appreciate the beauty of Highway 66 as it lay across the landscape like a ribbon to the horizon. There was a lot of highway ahead of him, and he wanted whatever experience was ahead waiting for him. The thought came to him that he could drive for a long time without deciding where he would stop. Why then, he asked himself, did he feel unhappy? It felt good to drive and dream and be free of worry or concern.

Suspended on the road he had chosen to take him West; Arnold drove for miles without a break. He crossed the border into Texas before he began to feel hungry and a little lightheaded. He remembered that he had not eaten breakfast. The coffee he had drunk was long gone. Hunger and thirst began to plague him. He must have been very preoccupied earlier to forget to eat breakfast. Eating was one of those necessities, that he rarely overlooked. It was mid-afternoon. He began to look for a town ahead, his eyes alert for a cafe or diner along the road.

Arnold soon pulled into the parking lot of a roadside diner. He did not know the name of the small Texas town he had pulled into. As he entered the diner and visited the men's room, he noticed the waitress.

She brought Sarah to mind. Her blond hair and serene smiling blue eyes made her seem kind. As soon as he sat down at the counter, the waitress offered a menu, water and a smile. He detected a perfume that enticed him to think of other necessities of life beyond food. Begrudgingly, he ordered food and waited for her return. When she placed the plate on the counter, he could not help but notice that the fingers on her small hands were ringless. She seemed to look only at him, and her smile was radiant.

Women had always found Arnold attractive. He did not really know why. Maybe it was his size, maybe the strength hinted at in his broad shoulders, or his smile, his tan, or his clear blue eyes. He felt warm under her regard and ate every bit of his meal. He would have liked to leave the waitress a big tip. But given the limited funds he had allowed himself to bring with him, and his determination to live as if he were rock-bottom poor, he paid only for the meal. He did not leave a tip and quickly left the diner.

It embarrassed him not to leave a tip. But he told himself that now was the time to begin this effort to live without money, and without pride.

"This is going to be difficult," he said to the wind shield as he turned the ignition to start the truck.

As night fell, Arnold knew that he needed to look for a place to sleep. He had been moving forward all day without planning or thinking of the necessities of living. When this thought hit him, he began to see how totally new and different this way of living was for him. He liked it.

Amarillo, Texas was the next town and it was coming up quickly along the highway. At the edge of town, a sign blinking "vacancy" came into view. Arnold pulled into the parking lot, got out and entered a tiny lobby. No one was at the counter, so he rang a bell placed there with the palm of his hand. A pale freckled man came out of a back room. Arnold noticed that he had the tattoo of a mermaid on the inside of his forearm.

"May I help you?"

"Yes. How much is a single room for one night?" Arnold asked.

The night attendant looked over the top of his glasses as he answered.

"A single room is four dollars a night."

"Is there any work I could do around here in exchange for the cost of the room?" Arnold asked.

"Maybe," the night attendant replied.

Arnold waited for the man to say more, but he said no more about the type of work he needed done. Motioning Arnold to follow, the attendant accompanied him to the first room down the hallway and opened the door.

"The bathroom is down the hall on the right. I'll be back in a while and tell you what to do," the night attendant said.

The room was small with a wooden floor covered by a worn rag rug with a single bed and no radio.

Arnold undressed and went right to sleep unconcerned about the task he would be asked to do. Whatever it was. He could do it. Awaking after a brief sleep, he discovered that he was not alone. He could see the outline of a man in the corner of the room. In the light that filtered through the worn curtain from the parking lot, he could see the man was fondling himself. A strip of faint light caught briefly on the tattoo of a mermaid as the man's arm moved and he knew the man was the same freckled night attendant who had given him the room for the night.

Was this how he was expected to pay for his room? Arnold wondered.

"What do you want?" Arnold asked warily.

The night attendant did not say anything. He kept up his self-fondling in front of Arnold. Arnold thought the man must need someone to watch him while he manipulated his sex. The whole thing seemed ridiculous. But he watched and found that he was becoming aroused himself. He wondered if this behavior was common among men. He decided to go along and see where this experience went.

14

Once he and the silent night attendant whose name he did not know had each achieved their own satisfaction, he fell into a deep sleep, deeper than usual. Later, the night attendance tried to awaken him again, but he refused to acknowledge that he was awake, keeping his eyes tightly shut.

Very early the next morning, he woke up alone and thought it all might have been a dream. He thought of how cold it all had been, no names, no touching, just the exploitation of the other as an object in the night. He rolled over and returned to sleep. Later when he was up and had washed and shaved in the shared washroom down the hall, the episode seemed like a dream. Arnold knew that he had run into his first weird experience and had participated in it in exchange for a place to sleep. He knew what his father would think, "It is an abomination for man to have sex with man."

There was no one at the front desk when he left. The sun was up and shining. He made his way to his truck and departed the motel satisfied, feeling that he had avoided spending money, but not so sure he had done what his parents would have defined as "Right."

CHAPTER 3

Arnold pulled out onto Highway 66 noting the beauty of the brown hills and vegetation he could see behind and between the buildings along the road. Hot black coffee and a large breakfast were on his mind. For the first time ever, he faced the dilemma of how to get breakfast without money. His experience the night before at the motel in Amarillo taught him that getting even the basics of food and rest without money left him vulnerable to the demands of his benefactors. He was confused by his own participation in the encounter and did not want another experience like it.

Seeing the sign for a diner ahead, before he had left the city limits of Amarillo, he pulled his truck over into the parking lot of the Flying Cow Diner. Inside, Arnold sat down at the counter, setting his hat brim side up on the chair beside him, hoping a young waitress would serve him. He wished for a sympathetic one with little or no experience. His hopes were dashed when a short and rotund middle-aged man asked if he wanted coffee.

"Whatever is free," he responded.

The man looked at Arnold blankly as though he had not heard him and walked away only to return with a cup of black coffee. Arnold began to wonder if the man would return for the rest of his order.

An older lady appeared instead and asked, "What would you like to eat?"

"A large breakfast at no cost," Arnold replied.

"I'll see what I can do," she responded.

She returned with a large breakfast and a receipt marked "no cost." After eating his fill, Arnold retrieved his hat and departed the diner without leaving a tip or paying anything for the meal. He had tried to say "thank you" but no one seemed to be around. He sadly wondered if the woman who waited on him had any money herself or if she had nothing but a kind and generous heart. He was grateful but felt guilty too as he drove away.

Unexpectedly, Arnold began to be bothered by the way he was living. He tried to enjoy the gorgeous scenery, but he could not forget the waitress and her kindness.

"Maybe I should go back," he thought out loud.

He drove his truck onto the side of the road and stopped. He thought about returning to the diner. After a while, he discarded the idea of turning around and continued to drive West.

Two hours later, he began noticing road signs alerting him that he was about to cross over the state line between Texas and New Mexico. His eyes were getting heavy and he found himself shutting his eyes occasionally to "rest" them as he was driving. Fortunately, the road was not busy for he caught himself dozing a bit and swerving. He decided to take a nap at the first rest stop he came across.

Arnold was relieved when a rest stop near the border came into view. It was none too soon. He pulled over and parked beneath the shade of a short tree that had been distorted by years of wind. With his window open to the strong breeze, he dropped quickly off to sleep. Deep into his sleep, he dreamed of his night encounter at the motel in Amarillo.

When he awoke and pulled back onto the highway mostly refreshed, he couldn't explain to himself why he had dreamed about the sexual encounter when all day his conscience had beat him up over cheating the waitress and not for the sins of the previous night. The interior dialogue had gone on for miles, like two old lawyers, Defense and Rightly, discussing right and wrong over a cup of hot coffee.

Defense would whine, "A poor man does not have money to spend on tips for a free meal."

Rightly would counter, "But your poverty is chosen. Your assets were set aside voluntarily, not lost."

Defense, "When I have money, people only see it and fail to see me."

Rightly, "When you are yourself and you have your money with you, you always help people who need

it. Now, you have deceived...and cheated a poor waitress."

Defense, "Maybe she was not poor."

Rightly, "Does this sound like an action your father would think is the right thing to do?"

"Oh Lord," Arnold signed.

His feelings toward the confusing sexual encounter the night before involving the tattooed attendant in the motel room had not felt like guilt. In fact, he had woken from the dream in the rest stop rigidly erect. Thought of the man in the motel aroused no guilt in him. But then, the man had got what he wanted as payment for the room. The sex involved was merely part of his new experiences. He accepted that. He was thankful that he would probably never meet that man again.

A hot wind blew in the open truck window and over the hairs on his arm where he rested his elbow on the ledge. The scenery swept by in stripes and blocks, tan sandy soil, red bluffs, and dried out greenery.

Far off, he could see hills and places where cliffs and rock formations had formed exposing layers of colors laid down over time.

Considering that he was traveling with little money, he thought that maybe he would camp out tonight. He had his camping gear in the back of the truck, a tent, a bedroll, some rudimentary cooking tools. He could get by.

He saw a sign for the Canadian River and Conchas Lake as he came into the outskirts of Tucumcari, New Mexico. Although the road took him a little off Highway 66 to the North, in a half hour, he found a likely camping spot near a stretch of the river. The river was shallow. The water sparkling clear and reflecting a blue sky. Each bank was edged with sage brush, juniper trees, and large flat stones. He parked near the river and looked for a quiet flat spot to lay out his bedroll. He found one near a fire pit that someone had used recently. The only serious dilemma he faced was lack of food. Weariness consumed him. He prepared his bed on the ground, laid it out where no rocks would poke him in the night and fell soundly asleep. Tomorrow he would worry about breakfast.

Early the next morning before dawn, he awoke to find he had company. Around him were campers who, like himself, chose to sleep under the stars. As he looked around in the partial darkness, he saw that most of the sleepers wore few clothes. Very near him, a beautifully shaped nude woman was stretched out on a blanket. He could see her skin gleam where starlight reached her. He enjoyed looking at her. As if feeling his eyes on her, she opened her eyes and smiled at him, inching closer in invitation. His arousal was rapid and his resistance to her was weak. She eyed the evidence of his arousal. Closing his eyes in frustration, he thought to himself. This is the beginning of my struggle with the values taught to me by my Father. He slowly reached out to touch her, but stopped, pulled his arm back and did not complete the action. She frowned at him and made an irritated huff as she turned away. It took him a while to get back to sleep.

He awakened late the next morning. The sun was up and shining brightly. The campers were gone. He wondered about them. Who were they? What were their names? Living without knowing names, living with strangers was different for him. Although strangers, they had not exuded menace or did him any harm. They were free, like a flock of wild creatures that had come and left. For no reason he could explain, he sensed a goodness in each.

Realizing he had not showered in days, a need to be clean grew in him. He was unpleasant to himself and surely was unbearable to anyone else. He scouted around the area he was in and found a secluded place where he could wash in the Canadian. Playing in the water, he found small waterfalls and pools where he could bath. He had no soap, but the feel of the water was most enjoyable. He scrubbed with his fingers through his hair. Sitting on a rock, he dried in the sun.

Late that night, he packed his camping gear back in the truck and drove on down the road, so he could drive while it was cooler. He had only gone a short way when he noticed that the gas gauge was near empty and that it was 1:15 AM. He began searching for a filling station with some urgency. He came upon a tiny town named Cuervo. There was one filling station, but it was closed. To avoid running out of gas on the empty highway, he parked adjacent to a gas pump and fell asleep.

Around daybreak, the car began to shake, and he woke immediately. A highway patrol man was standing by his car. A cruiser was parked in front of his truck, blocking his escape, should he attempt to make one.

"What are you doing fellow?" The officer asked.

"Oh! morning Officer," Arnold said through the window of the pickup, startled out of sleep.

"I am almost out of gas and wanted to stay close to a gas pump so that I can get more when the station opens."

The officer grunted in reply and started to leave,

"Could you give me some money to buy gas?" Arnold asked.

"No. I cannot," said the officer. "In fact, I should arrest you for not having any money."

"Wait!" Arnold said, and pulled five dollars out of his pocket and waved it out the window at the officer.

"I am not completed out of money. I just don't have enough for a full tank and breakfast."

The officer got back in his cruiser and departed with a growl and a shake of his head.

It was not long before the station attendant arrived. He greeted Arnold with a nod and set about unlocking the door.

Arnold followed him into the station.

"Are there any odd jobs I can do in exchange for a full tank of gas?" Arnold proposed.

"No. I'm sorry fella," the attendant refused.

He changed his mind when he entered one of the station bathrooms to clean it. He turned around and saw Arnold was still by the pump.

"Hey. You. I found something you can do for gas," he called.

Arnold grinned, crossed the lot in a few short strides and with a smile, took the bucket, mop, and rags from the attendant and went to work. He had just finished the ladies' room when a woman entered to use it. When she departed the ladies' room, she left it once again in a mess. He cleaned it again.

He filled his gas tank, thanked the attendant, and resumed his journey to wherever he would end up next.

CHAPTER 4

Arnold's next stop was not far down the road, a Methodist/Catholic mission facility for the homeless in Santa Rosa where he would be able to get a night of restful sleep, a shower and a free breakfast the next morning. The building might have been a converted grocery store. The front was windows. The big room behind the windows was filled with low cots and simple bedding. A Mexican American woman greeted him as he entered and pointed out a cot for him to use. She said her name was Annamaria.

"There are bathrooms and showers in the back," she said as she pointed to saloon-type swinging door at the back of the room. "And, we serve breakfast at 7:00 AM at the tables along that wall." She pointed out a row of tables along the wall to his right.

"Thank you," Arnold said as his gaze followed her finger.

"You are welcome here," she smiled as she spoke and turned away to greet another man coming in the glass doors at the front of the building.

Arnold surveyed his surroundings. The building was made of cinderblock walls that were painted white, a white that was chipping in many places showing the grey beneath. The place did not have much color, everything was shades of white or grey. The color came from the people. As other trickled in from the outdoors in their blue denim wranglers and checked shirts or their cotton dresses and colorful scarves, the place became livelier.

Since Arnold had washed in the river that morning, he decided to wait until morning for his shower. He stretched out on his assigned cot and rested until dark approached and he actually fell asleep.

During some early hour of the night, he was awakened by a disturbance between a man and a woman fighting over one cot. They were fighting over the cot right next to him. Sleepily, he offered his bed to the woman, and she accepted with an offer to share. He agreed, rolled onto his side, and went back to sleep.

The next morning, he awoke as the woman who shared his bed rolled off the cot and got to her feet. She smiled at him when she saw his eyes open and mouthed 'thank you' without making any sound. He saw that she was very young, perhaps a girl of sixteen or so and very attractive but very slender. During breakfast he observed her eating habits which were picky at best.

Over the rim of his cup of coffee, he asked what she was doing living at the mission.

She replied, "I am homeless. Where else can I go?"

"You should eat more breakfast," he encouraged.

"Are you my protector?" she asked.

After that, he minded his own business and did not engage her in any further conversation.

When he was done drinking his fill of the hot, but weak, coffee, he wrapped 4 buttered biscuits and a few extra pieces of bacon into a napkin and left the mission, striding across the parking lot to his truck. The girl hurried out after him and followed him to his truck.

"Can I have a ride?" she asked.

He inquired, "To where?"

"I want to go with you wherever you go," she replied firmly.

"Let's go then," he said as he cleared articles that had collected on the front seat of the truck during his travels so far. "My name is Arnold," he added.

She sat down and said, "I'm Julie."

"Where are you going today?" she asked as he drove out of the parking lot.

"It is so hot, I'm going to check out a swimming lake, the Blue Hole. I saw a sign for it earlier as I came into town. It is right beside the highway. The sign said you can dive and swim there."

As he drove back through the outskirts of Santa Rosa, he began to think about how he had just might have given up his carefree existence. He had gone from being totally relaxed without responsibility to accompanying, rather transporting, a young Mexican woman whom he did not know. He considered turning around and leaving the young woman where he picked her up, but he did not.

As he retraced his drive from yesterday, he saw a sign come up for the Blue Hole and turned right onto a dirt road.

The pool, or blue hole, was not far from Route 66 and exactly what he would have expected. It was crystal clear and blue and aqua. It was rimmed by desert rocks and a few people were already diving into the water and swimming. As he and Julie got out of the truck in a small lot where other vehicles had parked, he noticed a sign that said the Blue Hole was an artesian well where the water stayed at a constant 62 degrees. The pool was 80 feet across and the top, but 130 feet at the bottom.

"I'm going for a swim," Arnold said.

"I am too, but it will have to be in my underwear," Julie said and ran to the edge of the rocks, stripped off her outer clothes and jumped off, splashing as she hit the water below.

Arnold laughed and followed.

For an hour or so, the two swam and floated around in the crystal-clear water.

When they got out, they laid on the rocks to dry off out of the way of the most heavily trafficked area because they were after all in their underwear. Julie trotted part way around the pool in her underpants and undershirt to get their clothes after a bit and they dressed. Arnold could not help noticing that her underclothes were not new, grey, thin, almost transparent.

They walked out into the red hills on faint paths until they got hungry and headed back to the truck for biscuits and bacon and apples.

As he unwrapped the biscuits from their greasy napkin and folded bacon into the buttered sides, he asked "Do you have any identification or a driver's license that can confirm who you are and how old you are?"

"I am 22 years old; no driver license and no identification," she replied.

Ah. He thought. Now, the trouble begins.

"I am from Santa Fe," she continued. "I would like to go home to Santa Fe to find my parents if that is possible."

"Santa Fe is not on Highway 66 anymore, but it is kind of on my way," Arnold said. "It is maybe 200 miles ahead. Have you ever camped beside a fire?"

"No, but I am afraid of the dark," she replied

Keeping to his mission of not spending any money, Arnold did not want to spend money for a motel that night, so camping was his only option.

He moved them down the road to Park Lake where there was an established campground. They explored the lake and a spring that shot water out of the desert until it was evening.

They built a fire, but there was nothing to eat so they laid down to sleep side by side on his bedroll. Arnold's curious mind remained alert

He wondered if she was really 22 years old.

As they lay together, staring at the moon and stars, which were very bright out there in the desert plains, Julie spoke.

"I have a son, a baby boy who is a year old."

Arnold's mind and other parts of him began working overtime. Julie turned towards him, ending her star watching. He wondered what he was going to do. His erection was becoming obvious and Julie was not helping the situation, snuggling in closer to him. Every movement caused him more concern. What was right? Julie touched his manhood and pressed it against her body. For Arnold, that decided it. He did not resist his instincts any longer.

Even as he let down his moral boundaries, he argued with himself, On one hand I don't know her at all or plan to marry her, or care about her future, she is much younger than I am, but she is not a virgin, she is a mother, and she is willing. He turned to her and the two of them wiggled out of their remaining clothes, hers wrinkled and thin, his stiffer cotton and denim. Beneath a thin sheet that was part of the bedroll, with only a mat between them and the still warm earth, they explored each other's bodies. Sexual tension built, until together, they found satisfaction.

Arnold did not know how many times they came together during that night camping on the ground. In the morning, the sun and the sounds from the other campsites woke them up. They each visited the campground bathhouse and silently loaded their few belongings into the bed of the Chevy.

They stopped at a café in Santa Rosa, a café called the Club Café, and Julie managed to talk a waitress out of two cups of hot coffee for the road. As he drove, West out of Santa Rosa, he took Highway 84 towards Santa Fe.

Sipping her coffee, Julie informed him she was three months pregnant. The news came out of the blue. He wasn't sure why, but this made him feel cold. He did not want a child. She was already with child so there was no problem of her being pregnant by him, but the idea that she became pregnant so easily left him anxious.

The highway to Santa Fe was much quieter than Highway 66. Julie directed him to her parent's home, a small home of wood and clay, not unlike, but better kept, than some of the ones they had seen abandoned beside the highway. Arnold thought that at one time, this road was Highway 66, until the route was straightened so that it went directly into Albuquerque from Santa Rosa.

As he dropped Julie off in the dirt driveway in front of her house, he got out briefly to acknowledge her parents, Enrique and Maria Arroyo. He did not go into their house, and they did not invite him in. It was obvious that Maria and Enrique had been worried about their daughter, but he could tell they wanted to talk to her, or scold her, or worse, now that she was safely home. Arnold and Julie's parents spoke briefly, their conversation about the hot weather and need for rain. They thanked Arnold for bringing Julie back to them.

Arnold wished Julie well and excused himself. Neither seemed inclined to hug or touch each other this morning, even in farewell. With a sense of relief, he resumed his journey, heading out of town towards Albuquerque to work his way back to Highway 66.

Arnold examined his conscience. His resistance to a very attractive and young woman had been rather weak. For some reason he did not fret about it like he would have expected. Like the episode with the man with the tattoo in the motel in Amarillo, he accepted his night with a woman who was possibly a child of 12 instead of a woman of 22 as another experience that he did not want to repeat.

With the truck careening down a long hill, leaving Santa Fe far behind as quickly as he could, Arnold noticed that Julie had neglected to take her belongings. They laid on the seat where she had left them. Driving with one hand and his eyes half on the road, he riffled through them. Rolled in a long sleeve blouse, there was a small purse with what felt like a few coins in it, a black and white picture of a baby that was torn on one corner, a band aide, and a postcard from Cline's Corner. Not stopping, swerving only a little, he threw the shirt out the window over the top of the truck and followed the shirt with the tiny purse, postcard, pictures, and band aide all in one handful.

He did not see any identification.

He never did ask her baby's name.

He guessed that all was well with her in Santa Fe. He had returned her to her home.

CHAPTER 5

Being a free person with concern for himself only was a good thing, Arnold thought. He enjoyed thinking about the people he had encountered along the way and wondered if he had seen the real person or someone putting on an act, like the one putting on. He was not sure he even knew who he was trying to be. Confused, he focused on driving and reading road signs. Did he want to travel further west or turn north toward Colorado? He concluded that he would turn North and maybe someday make it to Wyoming and see the Tetons, someday maybe, not now.

He drove north on Highway 285 then turned off on the smaller State Highway 68 at Espanola New Mexico toward Embudo, for no other reason than the name Embudo intrigued him. He had driven about three and a half hours through the Sangre De Cristo Mountains through villages with names like Questa, Buena Vista, and Costilla. He crossed into Colorado when he noticed an abandoned house, or one that looked abandoned. He stopped out of curiosity to investigate. A barbed wire gate was strung across the dirt road leading to the house. He could not figure out how to undo the gate, it appeared to be wired shut, so Arnold pressed the top wires down, threw one long leg, then another over the fence and walked the few hundred feet to the house.

Before he had walked very far, he was met by a small mixed breed dog, that appeared vicious, scratching the earth with his feet, bouncing up and down on stiff legs, barking and acting as though he did not want Arnold near the house. Ignoring the dog's show of aggression, he picked the dog up, noticed an abundance of fleas in the dog's fur and promptly put him down. He pressed onward towards the house, all the while watching and speaking to the barking dog. The dog became somewhat friendly, but he seemed scared to let Arnold touch him. Maybe he was a she, Arnold thought. The dog became friendlier as he continued to speak to it.

He approached the front porch of the house and observed that the entire house was in poor condition and in need of repair and paint. Walking around the house, he observed another porch similar to the front porch but in better repair. An elderly gentleman exited the house onto the porch.

"What do you want?" asked the elderly man.

"I want to talk with you about a job," Arnold replied.

"Come on up," the man said, going back into the house for two chairs. When he came back, he gestured for Arnold to sit in one.

The gentleman was very tall, perhaps five inches over six feet, yet very slender, weighing perhaps one hundred sixty pounds. The two men studied each other for a moment or two.

"You are over-weight sir," the old man stated abruptly, "how much do you weigh?"

"Two hundred thirty-five pounds," Arnold replied with a grin.

"How much do you want to be paid for an hour of work?" the elderly man asked placing his broad brown hands on his knees as he leaned towards Arnold.

"I'd like, maybe, $5.00 an hour, or whatever you can pay, Arnold replied, "depending on the type of work."

"Horses and cows, feed and water; that kind of stuff; also, treating castrated bulls that may have become infected." The older man listed the work and showed him what appeared to be a survey of his property.

"Can you hold it up to the light?" Arnold asked. "I'd like to get a better view of that."

"Surely you can see it. I apologize for not noticing your eyesight. Mine is perfect," the elderly man replied, and he handed the survey to Arnold.

"The ranch is four thousand acres. It includes this house and several ponds over the hill to the west. I have 400 cows and calves, and they need care every day."

"Where are your horses?" Arnold asked.

"They will show up here around 4:00 PM," the elderly man replied. "If I need them for the next day, I put a rope around their necks and tie them to the house." He went on, "I have six horses, all of them quarter horse mares. They are broken to ride and drive cattle."

"Do you live all alone?" Arnold asked.

"No. I have a sweetheart that lives with me, the older man smiled serenely."

"Brenda!" He called in the back door of the house. "Come on out Sweetheart and join us on the porch and bring a chair."

The woman that walked onto the porch and welcomed Arnold was a beautiful woman, with dark blue eyes, and free flowing reddish hair with curls streaming over and down her shoulders. She was rather tall, and she smiled at Arnold warmly.

"What is your name, sir?" she asked.

"Arnold. Nice to meet you." He told her and removed his hat pinching the crown and setting the hat brim up in his lap.

"Do you want a job here?"

"Yes."

"How long do you plan to stay?"

"A couple of days, maybe three," he replied. "I need a little money."

"We pay $5.00 per hour for eight hours a day. No room, no food, no water, nothing but the $5.00 per hour. You may start tomorrow if you like."

Arnold could not take his eyes off her, and Brenda was having the same trouble. She smiled into his eyes, forgetting everything else around her.

"Is your real name Brenda? Or, is it Sweetheart?"

"Arnold you may call me both names as I love hearing you call me Sweetheart and Brenda, especially when we are getting better acquainted," She answered boldly.

"Do you know anything about horses, cows and calves?" Brenda asked.

"Yes. I know about all three." Arnold replied.

"And, do you know about women?" she asked, her eyes dancing with mischief.

Arnold flushed, and less sure of himself, responded, "I can always learn more than I know today."

"That is good," Brenda responded in turn. "I will be the teacher."

"That too is good. I am willing to be the student," Arnold said.

"When would you like to start working?" Brenda asked.

"I'd like to start early tomorrow," Arnold said.

"Where are you going to eat and sleep tonight?" Brenda asked.

"I could go back to Santa Fe but that is a long way," Arnold said.

"If you go back to Santa Fe, I would like to go with you and buy some groceries for my Father and me," Brenda said.

Arnold felt himself perk up when he heard that Brenda was the daughter of the older man. This was music to his ears.

"Sure, I'll take you into Santa Fe," Arnold readily agreed. "Would you tell me your Father's name?"

"His name is Henry," she said. "Henry is my Father, and he is getting up in years and needs help doing the ranch work he once did by himself. He is a wonderful Father, and I love him more than you can know." Brenda said. Almost without pausing, she continued, "I have a story that is somewhat of a secret to tell about my Father. My Father sometimes walks in his sleep and one night at about 2:00 AM, he got out of bed and walked to the corner of the porch where he had tied his mule and proceeded to mount him. However, when he tried to ride away, the mule refused to pull away from the porch. He wakened me with his yelling at the mule to back up. I came to the rescue and led Father back to bed."

Laughing she continued, "Breakfast the next morning was exciting because Father denied it all. He may deny it, but I get to tell the story, and it is not one I can make up. Deep in his heart, Father really knows it is true."

At the end of her story, Brenda asked, "When are you planning to leave for Santa Fe?"

"As soon as you are ready," he replied.

Brenda jumped up eagerly, "I'll get dressed and get some money from Father.

Five minutes later, she was ready to go. She had money in her hand, but no purse.

Arnold drove back to Santa Fe with Brenda sitting in the truck beside him. They located a grocery store and purchased a little under $100.00 of groceries.

While they were driving back to Brenda's home, she asked, "Where are you going to spend the night?"

"I brought my camping gear and will sleep outside, under the moon and stars where I communicate with God. Sleeping under the stars provides a new experience every night, a wonder not available when you sleep inside. The twinkling of the stars is remarkable, and as I said, it is different every night. Because it is so thrilling, I miss it when the clouds cover the stars. I sleep under the stars frequently because I enjoy it."

"Even if you enjoy sleeping under the stars, I have to apologize for not having better accommodations for visitors, she sighed.

"How do you plan to attend to your obligations to me?" She asked.

"As of now, I do not have any obligations to you because I don't really know you."

"We know each other's names, what more do you need?"

"You could be partially correct on one level." he agreed.

Brenda stood straight and tall in the evening light and Arnold stood beside her looking down at her.

"You are as beautiful as you are tall," Arnold spoke softly.

"Is that all you have to say about size?" Brenda asked.

"That is all unless we are going to start showing and telling." Arnold said ending on a laugh.

Brenda looked up at him. They grinned crazily at each other and laughed.

"Good night Brenda," Arnold whispered.

"Good night Arnold," Brenda returned as quietly.

CHAPTER 6

The next morning came sooner than Arnold would have liked. The horizon lightened and the sun was just peeking over the rim of the eastern horizon enough to entice early risers to get started. Arnold started a campfire under the pot of coffee that he had set out and prepared the night before. It only took a few moments and the coffee smell was letting everyone know it was time to get up and smell the coffee and then do other things. He took the pot of coffee to the kitchen door of Henry's and Brenda's house.

Four horses were tied to the corner of the house. He wondered why four horses would be needed but was content to wait for Henry to tell him. In the kitchen, he served Henry and Brenda a cup of his brew. They both came alive under the influence of his coffee and welcomed him to their clan.

"Arnold. Are you going to stay for a day or two?" Henry asked curiously.

Arnold noticed Brenda had fixed a large breakfast.

"You have outdone yourself Brenda with the huge breakfast," Arnold said.

He eyed the home-made biscuits and honey in particular.

"I recently captured that honey from the bees myself," she smiled. Arnold ate more than his fair share.

"That was delicious," Arnold said. "Your cooking skills are exceptional."

Brenda blushed when he complimented her and turned back to begin cleaning the stove, her bold demeanor not showing for the moment.

"Perhaps you would join us for dinner," she invited.

"Well, I'd love that, but my day is being planned by Henry. If he says it is okay, I would surely be there." Arnold promised.

"Arnold, I have the horses tied up outside." Henry said. "They are good solid quarter horses, but they had not been ridden for months or maybe even years. They are all skittish and jumpy. Come outside and look them over. You pick the one you want to ride."

Arnold put the saddle on one of the horses and he bucked for ten minutes trying to get it off.

Arnold decided to change horses. While he was in the process of changing saddles and horses, Brenda came out of the house.

"Arnold," she called. "The horse with the white stripe on its face always was a gentle pony and will not try to get rid of his saddle." So, Arnold changed horses again. This time the horse was fine, and he climbed into the saddle.

"I'll show you where the cattle spend the night," Brenda volunteered. This horse can accommodate two riders."

She climbed on board and sat in front of him in the saddle. There was really not enough room for the two of them, but they made it work. Brenda did not seem to even think about what her riding astride between his legs might be doing to him. At least she did not comment while Arnold struggled to contain himself. He hoped he had not become obvious.

"There they are," Brenda pointed out the herd of cattle.

"It might be difficult to get all the cattle from where they are to where your Father wants them to be because they are rather wild and not accustomed to being driven by cowboys," Arnold commented as they approached the herd that became more agitated the closer they approached.

"Do I look like a cowboy?" Brenda chided

"Nope. I've never seen a cowboy that looks like you," Arnold flirted and lowered his nose into her hair, "Nor one who smells like you or walks like you either. I will never again refer to you as a cowboy."

Then Brenda asked, "since I don't look, smell, or walk like a cowboy, would you describe what I do look like, smell like and walk like?"

"Someday I will answer your question, but right now, I am on the clock as an employee of Henry, your father. You will have to wait for another time to hear it."

"Well your work ends at 4:00 PM. I'll remind you then," she smirked.

Soon Henry came riding his mount, bare back, to join them.

Arnold asked about what strategy Henry wanted to use to roundup the cattle and drive them to the house.

"Watch me and follow along." Henry said.

Henry rode to a point in front of the herd and began to call them in some language Arnold did not recognize. The cows got in line about 6 or 7 across and several cows deep and followed Henry as if he owned them, which he did. They followed him right to the house and stood around waiting as if for the day to end. Henry opened a sack of caked meal and began throwing it in front of them, and they ate it like it was the best food in town.

Henry rode up next to Arnold and Brenda. "I'll feed them again in the morning, inspect them for any injuries, like broken bones or cuts, and then return them to their favorite pasture.

The three riders tied their horses to the corner of the house, took the saddles off, and put them on the porch.

He really looked forward to his campsite, and the comfort of his bedroll was exactly what he needed. It had been a long two years since he had ridden a horse and the last 8 hours had given him blisters on blisters, which Brenda said she would doctor with rubbing alcohol if he wanted her to. A part of him, said okay. But another part said no, not this time. While he would have liked Brenda playing with his butt, he didn't think he could stand the fire she would start, nor resist the temptation she presented.

"I will have to head to my campsite and sleep tonight. The pain in my butt is not to be taken lightly."

As he laid in his bedroll waiting for sleep to overtake him, his thoughts turned to Brenda. There was no doubt that Brenda liked what she saw in him. Arnold thought that she was the kind of lady that was eager to learn about men. Maybe she read about sex and men in books and magazines, but she did not have actual experience.

Maybe she heard things from her Mother.

Maybe her Mother had told her, "Get to know your friends, especially your male friends because they want what you have, and they are committed to getting what you have."

Or, her Mother might have told her "Because of your beauty, they will be persistent. When they succeed one time, they will become more persistent."

Her Mother probably would not have told her that some women would also want what she had, but she could have learned that from books she had read.

Brenda was a very caring person especially when it came to her father, Henry. He occupied a special place in her heart. Arnold admired the way she cared for him daily and protected him. Still thinking of her, he fell asleep.

The next morning, the riders would repeat the same steps backward and again be ready to go to work. Arnold hurt from one end to the other and found it difficult to move. His long strides had been reduced to small steps taken slowly.

After a few stretching exercises and a cup of hot coffee, he began to move without so much pain. However, his butt had not recovered. He wondered how he was going to sit in the saddle today when the workday started.

Henry, though elderly, was already taking care of the horses when Arnold approached the kitchen doorway. Brenda had already prepared breakfast. This was a welcome event because he was ready to eat. Brenda invited him in and yelled to Henry that breakfast was ready. Everything was delicious. She served hot biscuits, sausage gravy, sausage patties, eggs with butter, jelly and plenty of coffee.

"I think this would be a good start to the day, don't you?" Arnold asked as he gave Brenda a warm hug. "Thank you for preparing this food.

Brenda surprised him by hugging him back enthusiastically. She topped that off with a kiss on his lips, to which he responded appropriately.

It had been a long time since a beautiful, young lady kissed him. He hungered for all that he had missed and instantaneously longed for more.

"Well, Arnold. I'm not going with you today unless you insist. I've got some housework to do," Brenda stated.

Henry explained Arnold's work assignment for the day. "I really want you to look for the castrated calves today and make sure their wounds are healing well. If not, give them some medicine."

"Do you have a rope for me?" Arnold asked, assuming he would be roping calves.

"I don't have a rope," Henry said. "You can could catch a calf and throw him to the ground and it will produce the same result. I don't own ropes any longer, haven't for over twenty years. I've lost the ability to use it properly."

Arnold asked. "Henry, how long has it been since you tackled and threw a steer to the ground?"

"A long time," Henry responded. "That is why I hired you. I thought I might be able to get Brenda to do it, but she refuses." Henry chuckled at his own joke. Brenda gave her father a look that only a woman can give, and Henry got the message, giving his daughter a wink.

Arnold gathered his gear and headed for the horse that was standing at the corner of the house where Henry had tied him. Carrying the disinfectant and the yellow stuff for doctoring the calves while riding was going to be interesting, but he would manage, he thought.

As he climbed on his horse, Brenda handed him a sandwich of biscuit and sausage.

"This will taste good around noon time," she said. "I do not have a thermos for coffee though."

"Don't worry Brenda, Arnold assured her. "I am well equipped with coffee- carrying gear and the coffee will taste good around noon and a couple of times before and after.

"Is your thermos the size of a 10-gallon can?" She asked.

"No but I have two; one for early and the other for later in the day."

She placed her foot in the stirrup and jumped up unexpectedly to give him a warm and passionate kiss.

"Do you think that will last you all day? She questioned.

"No. Only 3 minutes," he joked.

"In that case, you should probably not leave," Brenda grinned back at Arnold.

He tipped his hat to her and turned the horse away from the house.

CHAPTER 7

Arnold headed for the west side of the ranch well equipped for a day of work. The sun was already working overtime, and it was getting warm. Despite the heat, he thought summertime was the best time on a ranch.

Henry did not tell him his horse's name, so he called him "Henry." It seemed to work for the horse, so he used it. He noticed several calves that had been castrated and looked to be healing as planned. There were seven or eight others that required medical treatment, and he smeared them with sufficient medicine to guard against further infection. Two were suffering enough that when he approached them, they did not run or walk away. When he threw the calves to the ground and tied their legs, they did not resist. He opened the wound and applied the medicine and the calves laid on the ground for a while before getting up and walking away. He also put a yellow stripe on each calf so he would know which ones he had treated and apply more medicine the next day. He was glad he got to them in time to prevent their deaths.

The constant motion of the saddle and horse reminded him of the day before and the effect of riding all day. He gritted his teeth against the pain of his saddle sores and continued to ride.

Now that Brenda was not along to talk with him, he realized he had a lot of time to think about things. His travels to date and this employment were already giving him new things think about, providing a fresh outlook, and helping him forget the pain of his divorce. He wanted to scrub some of the bitterness out of his soul. He recognized that when he left Oklahoma, he had not known what he was getting into. He had taken off with no plan for where he was going. He was just traveling where his nose led him.

When in his car and driving, he thought of beautiful women and camping and seeing beautiful scenery. Providence would have it that he always encountered the beauty he dreamed of. In camp sites, he found beautiful women when he looked for them and beautiful scenery like that of this ranch with its cattle and horses. Now he needed to learn to enjoy both the women and the scenery.

His thoughts turned first to Brenda, this morning. She was without a doubt one of the most beautiful woman he had ever seen. She was about 5 feet 10 inches tall, and probably weighed about 120 pounds. Her eyes were a deep beautiful blue. Her smile was quick and warm. In his mind's eye, he could see her long narrow fingers on his shirt sleeve when she touched him.

Arnold knew he was not going to be able to resist her bold advances for long. He was going to violate his Father's admonition "to him to always do the right thing." He was struggling with this idea because Brenda was special to him. He liked everything about her: her friendly demeanor, her progressive outlook, and her good sense of humor. He could find nothing wrong with her and he wanted to take advantage of the opportunity she presented to him in the right way. She was so nice that he did not want to do anything unacceptable, although she was really tempting. This was new for him. Usually, where women were concerned, he took what he wanted without guilt. He didn't know how long he would be working for Henry therefore he was reluctant to go very far with Brenda.

He liked the freedom this job at the ranch gave him. He could leave whenever he wished. He could camp and camping was a great joy for him. Out here on Henry's ranch, he camped and never tired of the stars and their nightly presentation. He could look out on the open prairie where there were no trees, nothing to harm anyone and plenty of fresh air and sunshine. Henry gave him an area wide enough to allow for a small fire so he could make coffee in his coffee pot. He got water from Henry.

What more could I need?" he thought.

As long as he stayed disciplined and did not allow his natural drive to cause him to stray sexually with Brenda, he thought he would stay in the good graces of Henry, and Henry would keep him working.

Sitting his horse, watching the cows moving around the pasture, his hat tipped down over his nose to block the glare of the morning sun, his thoughts wandered over what his life was like now compared to what his life had been like a few days ago when he left Oklahoma.

Life was good now. He was at peace now. When he left Oklahoma, he was at war with himself over who he was, what he did to Sarah by leaving her, what he was doing to himself, and where he was going. The divorce from his wife as devastating as it was, was in the past. Now, today, none of this mattered. He fully realized that his good mood might be temporary and that one of these days he might be back in a bad mood, thinking about all the things that had gone wrong in his marriage, but not today; today he was sitting in a saddle atop a nice saddle pony watching over several cows and calves and there was no indication that even one natural enemy was present.

This, Arnold thought, was 100% natural peace of mind.

Amidst his dreaming, he heard the muffled foot falls of an approaching horse. Brenda rode up beside him. He did not raise his eyes from the cattle immediately. He knew that now he would be tested again. He hesitated to look at her for he knew from memory that her beauty was awe inspiring. Those blue eyes, her red hair, and her beautiful smile were almost more than he could resist.

"Arnold, are you doing okay?" Brenda asked bending over in the saddle to peak beneath the brim of his hat.

"Brenda, I am doing fine. And may I ask how you are doing?"

"Arnold, I was sitting around the house listening to my father complain and decided I needed a different kind of company. So here I am, and I brought iced tea and cookies. Care for some?"

He dismounted and walked around Brenda's horse and gestured for her to dismount.

Brenda swung down from her horse right into his arms and hugged him and kissed him with enthusiasm. He could not resist and responded wholeheartedly. They kissed and hugged several more times. He knew Brenda was innocent and sweet, but he did not know her age. She did not volunteer it. So, he did not ask. They stood close to each other and everything seemed to go rather smoothly as they did nothing but stare into each other's eyes and grin. His bucket of discipline had a big hole in it and was leaking profusely, leaving it less than half full. At that moment, he did not care. He thought to himself, just let it leak.

"Is it your time for lunch yet? Do you have time to eat?" Brenda asked.

Arnold looked at the sky and said, "Almost."

"Let's eat then," Brenda suggested. "And let's have some tea. I brought a couple of blankets that we can spread out and use for a tablecloth,"

Arnold agreed and began helping her spread the blankets on the ground. He then removed his sandwich from the saddle bags. Brenda unpacked a jar of tea. The tea was delicious. Arnold thought Brenda was pretty delicious too as she helped herself to him again, leaning over to give him teasing kisses between bites that he did not refuse.

After eating and drinking some tea, Brenda and Arnold laid back on the blankets and enjoyed each other's company, letting their food settle. Brenda asked him numerous questions:

"Where are you from?"

"Oklahoma," he replied"

"Where are you going?"

"I don't know?" Arnold answered truthfully.

"How long will you stay and work for my father?"

"Until your father says 'leave'," Arnold laughed.

"When do you want to get paid?"

"When Henry gives me money," Arnold grinned, enjoying her interrogation.

And then, she asked the big one, "when will you make love to Brenda?"

"When Brenda thinks the time is right." Arnold said more soberly.

"The time is right now," Brenda said. "We are wasting time every time we delay."

Brenda reached across the blanket and put her arms around Arnold and hugged and kissed him for a long time.

Then she said, "the time is right because we are where God can watch us and no one else will know except the two of us, and we both want us to do what we are doing, so we will not object."

Brenda laid back and pulled him onto her, asking "How do you like the way things are progressing?"

For his part, Arnold began to explore Brenda's body with his big hands, and she helped him. She felt great.

"Do you have any form of birth control?" Arnold groaned.

"No." Brenda said. "What should I use?"

"I don't know, but I'm as fertile as any male, and I do not want to take a chance on making you pregnant," Arnold said as he pulled away from her far enough to look her in the eyes.

"That is a pure shame." Brenda stared back at him. "I am exactly the right age to have a baby. I want a baby. And, I want you to be the father of that baby."

Whew He thought to himself unable to look away from her sincere gaze, I am a lucky guy.

To Brenda, he said, "You would make a beautiful mother, but we need to refrain for now."

"Okay," Brenda said letting a big sigh escape her lips, "but I get another kiss," which she managed to do for the next two hours.

Between kisses, Brenda and Arnold discussed a wide range of subjects. He learned that she was 28 years old, had graduated from high school the same year her Mother died and since, had felt obligated to take care of her father who was now 93 years old and fast losing the ability to care for himself.

"My father has had at least two strokes that we know of," Brenda confided.

"He refuses to seek care from a doctor and in my opinion also suffers from stomach ulcers," Brenda said.

"How do you pass the time?" Arnold asked.

"I read a lot, listen to the radio and worry about my father," Brenda said. "Father owns the ranch, but after my mother died, he has not taken care of the legal issues affecting transfer of ownership of the property when he dies."

"Are you sure he owns the ranch so that it would transfer to you when he dies, as in joint ownership with you?" Arnold asked.

"Father owns it jointly with my mother. It has never been changed," Brenda replied.

"Do you know how to get that changed?"

She said, "No."

"I think we should discuss this with your father and take action to get it changed." Arnold said.

"Will you take my father and I to the county seat to get that changed tomorrow?" Brenda asked unexpectedly. "I would be happy to do that," Arnold replied.

"I am going to ride to the house, fix dinner for the three of us and talk to Father right now." Brenda said. "We will plan to go tomorrow."

Do you know where the county seat is?

"Yes. It is in Alamosa."

"We will go early and have plenty of time then," Arnold said.

Brenda gave him more final hugs and kisses, mounted her horse and rode to the house, waving as she disappeared over a rise in the prairie.

CHAPTER 8

When he arrived back at the ranch house at the end of the day after evaluating the cattle, he briefed Henry on the status of his calves. He had enjoyed the day he had spent sitting in his saddle dreaming and the lunch he had spent with Brenda.

Henry was pleased with his work and asked, "When do you want to be paid?"

Arnold replied, "Anytime you want to pay me. As long as you feed and water me, I will not be in a hurry."

Henry reached for his wallet and paid him $5.00 an hour for the day. Arnold put the money in his shirt pocket.

"How far is it to Alamosa?" he asked Henry.

"About 80 miles," Henry said.

Henry then asked, "Would you take Brenda and I to Alamosa to take care of some important business? How much would you want for taking us?"

"I don't charge for being friendly to good people." He smiled as he spoke.

Henry smiled too, "Can we go tomorrow? Brenda says she has important business to take care of. "

"I would be pleased to escort Brenda to Alamosa, and you can ride along free of charge," Arnold replied.

Henry opened the conversation after dinner in their small living room.

"I'm particularly pleased that Brenda wanted to modify the owner-ship of the ranch to include her," Henry said. "I've worried about that a lot. As I have become elderly, I don't always remember the things I need to do. I have been concerned about my daughter's future considering the house needs repair, and when I'm gone, I don't know what she plans to do. I often wonder if she plans to run the ranch or leave it. We have no living relatives. I have sort of assumed she was going to run the ranch, but it is nice to have this confirmed by her interest in the ownership."

"Brenda, come in here and answer a few questions for me," Henry called to his daughter who was working in the kitchen washing dishes.

Brenda came into the room and offered Arnold a cup of fresh coffee and her father a cup of hot tea, each with cookies, freshly made. She sat down on the couch next to Arnold and replied, "What do you want to know?"

Henry asked, "When I die what do you plan to do with this ranch?"

"I plan to operate it much the same way you do," Brenda replied. "I'll hire someone to help me do those things I cannot do."

"What do you plan to do with the house?" Henry asked. "It is need of much repair and not worth the cost of repairing it."

"I have no idea. Maybe I should bring in a mobile home, mount it on a foundation, move what I want out of the house into the mobile home, and then, burn this house to the ground."

"Since I have had two or more strokes, did you ever take out life insurance on me and yourself?" asked Henry.

Brenda said, "Yes, I have $100,000.00 of life insurance on you and the same amount on me, which I took out about 15 years ago. That reminds me, I need to apply for Mother's life insurance benefit, which should be substantial because I purchased the same amount for Mother. I will check on how to apply for it tomorrow when we are in Alamosa."

"So, daughter," Henry began, "when are you going to start dating the boys?" He gave a little wink towards Arnold.

"Father, hush," Brenda said. "I have had few chances, and the ones that have been possible were not desirable from my perspective; however, if that comment includes Arnold, then I think he knows how I feel about him. If not, I will clear up that matter completely as soon as he and I have some privacy. I am very impressed with Arnold."

Henry laughed, "Sweetheart, I totally agree with your judgment, and I think I will put Arnold on our payroll forever just to give you adequate time to convince him you are the one for him."

Brenda got up and asked around the room,

"Arnold would you like more coffee?"

"Father, would you like more tea?"

"A fresh cup of coffee would be great," replied Arnold. When Brenda reached for the cup, he gave her a quick kiss.

She smiled and blushed a little pinker.

Following dinner, Arnold helped Brenda with the dishes, and she made a list of groceries to purchase when they were in Alamosa. He was surprised to learn that they did business with the Alamosa bank. He knew some of the people there. Brenda also told him that they filed their income tax with the bank's secretary because she was recognized as the best in the country.

"Do you want to sleep in a bed tonight…with me?" Brenda asked Arnold.

"You know I would love to, but you and I must be careful to avoid a pregnancy. I am very tempted to throw caution to the wind and do just the opposite."

"Do you have a condom with you that you could use?" She asked. "I've never had sex before. I don't have anything, but I'd still like to have sex with you."

"I do not have one, but we can try to be careful if you want."

Brenda grabbed him around the arms and hugged him. "I want you now, not after a while and not later." She said. "We can go to my bed now or, if you prefer, I can join you at your camp site. Which do you prefer?"

"I think you will be more comfortable the first time in a bed," He whispered since she had him pinned so close to her.

Her bed was soft and clean, and their loving was wonderful. Brenda was curious and eager to learn everything about him. If was very difficult for Arnold to honor his Father's teaching, 'to always do the right thing.' In the midst of petting and kissing, RIGHT had so many definitions. Brenda felt great to him and they pleased each other without him penetrating her. He felt like a teenager again.

"Brenda, I don't think I can do this again. Resisting was too hard," Arnold admitted. "I can not accept you getting pregnant and that might very well happen."

"I understand… somewhat," Brenda said.

"Do you know what also makes me feel good?" Brenda rolled over on her side and rested her cheek in her palm as she studied him.

He replied, "No."

Looking directly into his eyes, "I have someone I can trust with exactly what I am thinking. I have never had that before, and it is good to feel that I can do that with you."

Arnold rolled over on his pillow to face her and then said, "You told me last evening you had never dated before, and I find that difficult to believe."

"You have a choice whether to believe it or not, but it is the truth. And now, since I met you, I do not want to meet or date anyone else. You are the most kind and thoughtful man I have ever known. I need to know more about you. So, tell me about you. Everything."

"Brenda, I will tell you everything that is important. I was born in Oklahoma. I was raised on a wheat and cotton farm then a dairy farm. I was one of 13 kids, but none are alive today. My parents are dead and buried in the United Methodist Church cemetery located south of Calumet, Oklahoma. I was married, then divorced."

Beth looked concerned at that, but Arnold continued.

"It was a bitter and ugly divorce. I may tell you about that someday, but I am not in a hurry, so do not rush me on that subject. I was employed in a job where I made a lot of money, invested it in securities that produced great revenue, then the stock split three times in four years, and now I have sufficient income that I do not have to work.

At one time in my life I worked 16 to 20 hours a day. I got burned out. Now, I have a difficult time taking on anything that requires me to be responsible for the outcome. I do not want to be responsible for anyone or anything. However, I must stay busy or I'll go nuts, or crazy, so to speak. I am driven to accomplish things. You might say I am addicted to a sense of accomplishment. For example, I love helping your father and I love helping you. Just like I helped with doing the dishes last evening, Tomorrow, I'll take pleasure out of helping you and your father change the ownership of the ranch back to the way you want it to be. I am a good businessman under this rough exterior. This is my disguise."

Brenda giggled at his 'rough exterior' comment. "I guess it is my turn."

"Yes, I've given you a lot of information about me. Now it is time for you to give me your story."

"I'll begin with my early life on the ranch instead of my birth," Brenda said. "When I was in the eighth grade, I decided to become what the students called a book worm and study everything I could. I made straight A grades and excelled in speech, history, math, and geography and current events. I was not like the other students. I did not participate in sports or after school activities because my father would not allow me to and because I had to ride a bus to and from school.

When I was a senior in high school, everyone wanted to know what college I was going to attend, and I told them I was going to take care of my parents.

No one believed my story, but it was true. My mother was a kind and friendly lady, but she was always ill with something and the doctors could not determine what was the matter with her. She died about a year after I graduated from high school. Father and I buried Mother on the ranch and placed several large rocks at the head for a headstone.

Father tried to help, but all he could do was weep. He cried himself to sleep for several nights after Mother died. One night I went to his bed side and comforted him with a back rub and a cup of hot tea. He eventually went to sleep telling me he loved my mother. I knew he loved her as I did. I returned to my bedroom that night and cried for a long time too, asking God to help me and my father. God helped both of us because I did not hear Father cry again except one time as he was tying the horses to the house. I went to his side and comforted him again.

After that we began talking about Mother and how good she was to us. Father liked doing this, and I always listened. Since that time, all I have done is help Father take care of the ranch. I've had no boyfriends and really no girlfriends. There are things Father cannot do any longer, so I have stepped in to do them. For example, when Father tried to help the veterinarian work on the calves or inseminate the cows, he just could not do what was required so I helped the veterinarian do the work. I hated castrating the calves, but it had to be done. I liked inseminating the cows because I knew a calf would be the result. Maybe the cow would have preferred a bull, but it worked, and we didn't need to do it a second time so who can complain. We also got over 200 calves that we can now sell for money."

Arnold listened intently and put his arm around her one more time. She smiled at him and gave him a hug and a kiss.

"I'd better go back to my own camp site now," Arnold said. "Tomorrow we go to Alamosa."

CHAPTER 9

Early the next morning, Arnold, Brenda, and Henry, set out in Henry's car for Alamosa, the county seat. Arnold's truck was not big enough for all three of them to travel the 80 miles comfortably. Arnold drove. After about 20 miles, they passed through the tiny town of Las Mesitas, which was little more than a post office.

"What is the address for your ranch?" Arnold asked Henry and Brenda.

"Las Mesitas," they both replied, "but it is for mail only."

"As you can see," Brenda pointed out the window as they passed through the town, "Las Mesitas, had nothing except the post office. The government has tried to close the post office several times, but the citizens complain, and it never gets closed. That is good," Brenda said.

The drive to Alamosa took them through flat high desert farm and ranch land with the craggy mountains of the Sangre De Cristo Mountain range looming over the road.

When they got to Alamosa, they found the building that housed the insurance company without much trouble. Brenda presented herself to the life insurance representative along with her identification.

"My mother had a policy and I am the beneficiary," she said. I'd like to know how much the benefit from my mother's life Insurance policy will be."

The representative a round man with a bald spot on the top of his head went to a filing cabinet. pulled out a file and made some quick calculations.

"It will be $100,000.00 plus approximately $20,000.00 in paid up premiums that have accrued since your mother's death."

"It looks like you are the only beneficiary," he said. "You will receive a check in about two weeks."

Brenda confirmed her mailing address and social security number for the check.

On the road back to Henry's ranch, Henry fell asleep in the back seat.

"How do you feel about getting your business caught up?" Arnold asked Brenda.

"I'm happier than I've ever been, and I want to stay that way. Thank you for knowing what to do," she said.

"Some time you should take me to see where your mother is buried," he said.

"I'll show you where the grave is. Father wants to be buried beside Mother and that is my plan," Brenda said.

Brenda gave Arnold's arm a squeeze as he drove. "Would you like to operate my ranch for me?" She asked.

Arnold looked sidewise at her for a moment then returned his gaze to the road.

"That is a question that will take a lot of thought before I answer because I do not want to give you an incorrect answer," replied Arnold after a while. "I have some property that is being managed in Oklahoma and someday, I believe it will be worth a lot of money. Much more than I have now," Arnold told Brenda.

They were silent for a while as they drove home.

"Brenda, would you like to go to Santa Fe, New Mexico for a week vacation after the cows are sold?" Arnold asked.

She smiled and asked, "Really?"

He said, "Really. I will rent a motel for you, your father and me at a resort. We will eat at a nice restaurant and enjoy the sights, including a musical."

"Do we have to wait for the cows to sell? I would like to go today."

"I take that as a 'yes'," Arnold chuckled

"You are so good to me and my father," Brenda murmured.

Brenda's comment set Arnold to thinking.

While he had a history of being an outstanding citizen, always wanting and trying to do good things for people, his presence in Brenda and Henry's house begging for a job, eating their food and sleeping on their land did nothing to show his past nature to Henry and Brenda. In fact, he appeared to be just the opposite of the self-assured successful man he had always been and that was beginning to bother him.

Arnold wanted to talk with Brenda about how she felt toward him but was afraid of what she would say. All he brought to the table was a couple of days of work and a ride to and from Alamosa; hardly a recommendation for a deeper relationship. He was convinced he needed to do something for them that would to show them who he really was. His pride required this.

I hate mooching off Henry, Arnold thought.

I hated not paying a tip to an elderly waitress who probably needed the money a hundred times more than I do."

When they arrived at the ranch, Brenda fixed the three of them a good home-cooked meal.

Arnold helped Brenda wash up the dishes and then when he was heading out to his campsite, Brenda asked him if she could join him.

He replied, "Absolutely you may."

Arnold put his arm around her with a blanket, and she smiled at him and gave him a hug and a kiss. They watched the stars for a while in silence.

"I'm going to return to the house if you do not invite me into your bed for the night," she told him.

"Someday," he said. "I'll ask you to stay."

"I am not sure I can wait," she laughed, "so hurry."

Brenda returned to the house leaving Arnold to think about that comment all night.

Arnold laid in his make-shift bed under the stars and all-night long thoughts ran through his brain.

Here I am a healthy man doing without a female mate when one that is truly good, truly beautiful, and truly willing is close at hand, and I say 'no' to her. I am staying true to my values, he thought.

That should make me feel good instead of ridiculous and confused. I've traveled from Oklahoma alone wanting to find peace of mind, and now, I have the chance of a lifetime to do just that, and I say 'no'. What is wrong with me? Am I so bitter about the past that I cannot forget it and have future happiness? Can, I not live for the present with confidence?

Brenda is good, Arnold thought, and exudes that quality from her core, so why hesitate? I must come to my senses and wake up to reality and make a smart decision, a decision to welcome Brenda into my life. Together we can make a future for ourselves.

Currently Brenda is committed to taking care of her father, which is a wholesome, caring thing to do that reveals Brenda's true caring and beautiful nature. I cannot simply ignore this and move on to a new place without her. This would be a serious mistake that I may not recover from. I need to let her know that she and I should go forth together and make a life of our own.

Now I need sleep. I know what precisely I should do in the morning. Or, should I wake her now and tell her? I will wait until the sun comes up and then tell her.

In the early morning, when the sun had not yet peeped over the horizon, Arnold was exhausted, restless and afraid. He was hopeful and tried to remain confident of his decision even in his exhaustion. He wanted to carry through with his convictions.

Thoughts continued to roll through his mind, but at a slower rate, probably from pure exhaustion.

I don't want to hide any longer. What if I have delayed being myself to Brenda for too long. Perhaps she slept well and will accept him and his plans for them this morning.

It was early, but he needed a cup of coffee. He pushed out of his blankets and set about making a pot. As the coffee was perking but not yet ready, Brenda walked from the house with two cups of coffee and gave one to Arnold. She sat beside him on his make-shift bed and each enjoyed their coffee.

Arnold could not hold his thoughts back any longer. He put down his coffee cup, turned to Brenda, took her coffee cup and set it in the dirt, and grasped her face in his large hands.

"Brenda, I have fallen deeply in love with you and I want to make a good life for both of us."

Brenda beamed with happiness and wordlessly embraced Arnold. They fell over backward on the bedroll and Arnold kissed Brenda repeatedly, trying to talk through his kisses.

"You are so good, so beautiful…," Arnold whispered.

"Hush," Brenda said, smothering his words with her lips.

The sun was up and shining when the two realized it was time to eat breakfast. Their laughter was open and loving as they walked to the house arm in arm and there, enjoyed a delicious breakfast together.

Henry joined them and looking from one to the other, asked

"What is going on with you two?"

"We are going on vacation for a week after the cattle sell, and we want to invite you to go with us," Brenda said.

"I will drink to that," Henry said and lifted his coffee cup in a salute to show his appreciation.

Standing next to Brenda at the kitchen sink while she washed up the breakfast dishes, Arnold said, "I'd like to talk more with you Brenda, but I have to get to work first."

"Maybe I should go with you today to take care of the calves and we can talk as we work," Brenda suggested.

"Yes. I'll saddle a horse for each of us. Join me when you are done here." said Arnold and left the kitchen

As they rode out to find the calves, Arnold talked about his plans for the vacation.

"I've never been on a vacation to a motel," Brenda said, "or been away for even as much as one night. I have no idea what to do on vacation."

"We can stay in a motel. Do you think Henry would be okay with us staying in one room as long as there are two beds in the room for a week?" Arnold asked.

Quickly she said, "I plan to go, and I do not need to ask for permission, but I want to make sure Father is comfortable with all of this."

"Brenda, we should insist that it is absolutely necessary, that Henry go with us. He should go along and enjoy the vacation too," Arnold replied.

Brenda smiled. "I'll talk to him. Be patient."

Arnold circulated through the cows and calves and noticed one that needed more attention as he showed evidence of an infection. This time, Arnold roped the calf, tied his legs to avoid getting kicked, and treated the infected areas where the testicles had been removed and around the naval opening.

Soon Arnold noticed another calf with the same kind of infection and treated it the same way.

"You are a very good worker," Brenda said. "You have saved two calves today. Father will be very pleased."

Brenda dismounted and placed a blanket on the open prairie. Arnold rode over to her.

"Do you need any help?" He asked.

"Yes. I need you," she responded tilting her head to look up into his eyes where they were shaded by his hat.

Dismounting from his horse, Arnold joined Brenda on the blanket.

"Lie down," she requested. Then, she joined him, wrapped her arms around him and began hugging and kissing him very passionately.

"I just wanted to remind you how much I missed you and how often I needed you. Now you can go back to work," she teased.

"You cannot get away with such a short reminder," Arnold laughed and grabbed her forcefully, but carefully recalling his strength and began his own hugging and kissing. He laid his body over hers as if he intended, and maybe he did in that moment, to do more than kiss, and make love to her.

Brenda kissed back as good as she got and arched her body into his.

The two horses stood close by.

After a long while, Brenda came up for air, "I think we have an approving audience right here," she said nodding to the two horses.

Arnold only smiled

They had forgotten to take sandwiches with them when they left the house in the morning, so Arnold decided the cattle did not need additional attention today. They quit for the day so Brenda could discuss the vacation idea with her father.

When they got back to the house, Brenda fixed sandwiches for everyone.

"Father, I have an important subject to discuss with you." Brenda said

"I'm available anytime." He responded.

"Arnold thinks his job with the cattle is done, and he has proposed that he and you and I go to Santa Fe for a week. What do you think of that idea?"

Henry replied instantly, "Sure I will go with you or I can stay by myself, and I hope you have a great time. Just tell me how much money we will need so I can go to the bank; and, just as a reminder, the cows will be picked up by the cattle trucks the day after tomorrow and will be sold. You might want to tell them good-bye."

"Arnold will pay for the entertainment and motel," Brenda said.

Arnold overheard that part of the conversation and pulling Brenda into the kitchen, reminded her that she was bringing the entertainment with her.

"I hope so," Brenda said, and the two laughed like high-school kids on a date while Henry looked on over his coffee with a secret smile.

CHAPTER 10

Arnold asked Brenda when she wanted to leave for the vacation in Santa Fe, and she said, "In the morning as soon the cattle have been loaded and sent to the market and as soon as you are awake enough in the morning to drive."

Arnold, Brenda and Henry departed for Santa Fe, New Mexico early the next morning. They drove Arnold's big Ford Fairland Crown Victoria because it had room for Harold in the back seat and their luggage in the trunk. They had forgotten to eat breakfast because they were all so excited to be going on vacation. Arnold had made coffee though, so they had that, and on the way, they talked about their plans.

While driving down the highway Arnold saw a rest stop and suddenly drove into the place for cars and stopped.

"Why did we stop?" Brenda asked.

"For this. I could not wait any longer," Arnold said as he gathered her to him and kissed her soundly. "We are on vacation."

Brenda giggled and kissed him back. Arnold pulled back out on the road with a grin on his face, and Henry gave a cowboy whoop from the back seat.

An hour later, Henry was sound asleep in the back seat and Brenda said softly, "There are so many things about you I am having a difficult time waiting for, but I keep reminding myself it will be worth the wait. Please don't take too long finding a nice motel. We need to make good use of our time. We only have one week."

Arnold replied, "Your attitude makes me happy."

Arriving in Santa Fe, Arnold stopped and inquired at a nice-looking motel and rented two rooms for a week. The attendant at the desk provided copies of the current programs and shows playing in town.

Arnold and Brenda accompanied Henry to his room to make sure everything was okay. They decided they would rejoin each other in the lobby downstairs in two hours to find a place to eat and review what was available to do.

Five doors down from Henry's, Arnold and Brenda found their room. Arnold stepped inside first, then Brenda wrapped her arms around him in a bearhug, pulled him the rest of the way into the room and looked up into his face smiling broadly.

Arnold quickly closed the door.

"Finally," Brenda breathed.

Arnold grinned at her in the half-light of the room, managed to free one arm enough to reach his hat and set it on a nearby chair before Brenda pressed her lips to his.

"Oh girl," he groaned as he pulled his arms out from under hers and wrapped her round in his warm and strong embrace.

His hand tangled in the back of her hair as he pressed her lips into his. His lips traveled from Brenda's lips to her chin, cheeks, eyes, brow, and neck taking hungry little bites of each part of her he found.

Brenda groaned and followed his lead, exploring his face with warm kisses and tiny touches of her tongue.

Arnold pushed Brenda's coat off her shoulders and once free of it, she reached for his jacket and pushed it down off his shoulders as well.

They had to step away from each other to let the garments fall to the floor.

Brenda reached for Arnold's shirt buttons and smiled up into his eyes as she undid them one by one. Her fingers sneaking into the opening to touch the sensitive skin and hair on his chest as she pulled the shirt opening apart.

Arnold's mind went blank. There was no thought of right or wrong as his hands massaged her shoulders and skated down over her waist and buttock. He watched her explore him with her eyes and hands as his hands wandered over her still clothed curves.

When Brenda reached Arnold's belt and Levis, she hesitated for a moment. She skimmed her hands over the hard ridge that had formed under the denim.

"Ah!" she said. "Arnold," she huffed as he kissed her neck and pulled her hips into his. "Remember, I've never done this before. You're so big and hard."

Arnold pushed her hands aside and undid his own belt and jeans, releasing his penis into her hands.

"Big, but still flesh and blood Brenda, still just flesh and blood."

Arnold gritted his teeth with pleasure that was much like pain as her hands touched his bare skin. He reached for the buttons on her blouse and dispensed with them clumsily. He dispatched with her jeans in no time and then unsnapped her bra so that she stood before him in panties only.

In the dim room he could make out the outlines of her beautiful white breasts and with his calloused hands gently outlined them and his rough thumbs brushed her nipples which were already button hard. His hands traveled to her hips. Then, he stepped back from her caressing hands and removed the last of his own clothing and she followed suit with her panties.

They stood naked for only a moment studying each other. Then, their eyes locked, and Arnold picked her up and deposited her on the bed, following her down.

Brenda clung to him as he caressed her body that was now completely naked. Arnold could tell her desire was building as her body arched up against his seeking what she didn't really know. He kissed her neck as he parted her thighs and his long fingers explored the soft folds of her womanhood, finding the little knob that when he touched her there made her cry out and buck against his thighs and hips.

"Arnold," Brenda whispered.

Arnold groaned as he felt her moisture and arched her over his forearm. Sitting back on his haunches, he lifted her, so she was poised against his chest and the tip of his penis stroked the wet petals that protected her vagina.

Her eyes were slits as she stared into his eyes breathing hard. He lowered her onto his hard member. She bucked against him and he thrust himself up into her, penetrating past the bit of flesh that guarded her virginity and deep into the hot recessed of her very center. He gasped because she was so tight, he almost spilled his seed immediately.

"Ahhh," Brenda cried out a bit in pain and then in something else that shortened her breathe to short pants and she shuddered against Arnold as he moved within her.

Arnold watched Brenda through half open eyes for a few beats, perhaps seconds, until his body took over completely and he pressed and pulled within her tightness, his strokes becoming harder and faster as his body fought his mind for release. He wanted to be gentle. He wanted to be slow, but the days of fondling and looking without satisfaction had added up and his ability to hold back shot out the window.

Lost in desire the two moved together until Arnold released his sperm into Brenda in hard shuddering thrusts that slowed once the climax of his control was reached. He could feel the tiny quivers of Brenda's body tight around him.

He laid her back down then onto the bed, and his big body followed hers, completely covering her smaller one. He pulled the spread up from the sides since they had not taken the time to pulled down the spread and wrapped the heavy fabric around their bodies. He pulled a pillow down and lifted Brenda's head so he could place it under her.

That was all he could do before he laid his head on her collarbone and shoulder and fell into a deep satisfied sleep.

When he woke, Brenda was watching him quietly. Her hair was spread on the pillow and glistened in the tiny bit of light.

He hardened again as she smiled and moved beneath him.

Cocooned in the bedspread, they began to move slowly against each other. Slick flesh slid easily over slick flesh.

They breathed through parted lips. Brenda's hand moved lazily over Arnold from shoulder to hips. His hands for their part gripped her as he lowered his mouth to caress her softened breasts. Under the slow sweeps of his tongue, her nipples hardened again, and she arched back as her body woke up and began to demand more.

Arnold was happy to comply and this time it took a little longer for their mating to be complete and by the time they arrived at the last powerful thrusts, Arnold into Brenda and Brenda upwards against Arnold, the bed spread had flopped back and their hot naked bodies cooled slowly in the room air.

They fell asleep once again entwined.

When they woke, it was dark in the room. Henry was knocking on the door.

"Hey! Arnold. Brenda. Are you coming up for air? I'm hungry. Get dressed and meet me downstairs."

Arnold looked at Brenda with one eye closed and one open.

"Holy cow," he said. "I don't know if I can move. What happened to us?"

Brenda giggled and if the room had been lighter, Arnold would have seen her flush deep red.

"Let's shower," Brenda suggested, "together." She tried to push Arnold off her and laughed out loud happily when he refused to move and held her down.

"Give us a half hour Father." She called out.

They could hear Henry groan outside the door.

When they finally arrived in the lobby, it was 7:00 PM. Henry was reading through the show materials they had been given when they arrived.

He eyed their relaxed, smiling demeanors and grinned.

All he said was, "Finally."

"Let's eat," Arnold said.

Brenda and Henry both said, "YES!" at the same time, and gave each other silly smiles.

"Do you prefer steak and potatoes with salad or Italian food with a lot of choices."

Brenda said, "Steak and potatoes with salad."

Henry said, "Steak and potatoes with salad."

Together, they walked down the hall to the dining room and enjoyed a delicious dinner. Arnold ordered steak and sweet potatoes with butter and pecans. When Henry and Brenda heard Arnold's order, they asked to have the same thing.

Brenda whispered to Arnold, "I have never eaten a sweet potato fixed that way, but it sounds delicious."

"It is delicious, but not as delicious as you are," Arnold whispered back.

Brenda smiled and squeezed his hand on the table.

All three ordered wine with their meal and coffee after.

"I'm too full to eat desert," Brenda complained.

"I'm too full too," said Henry. "We will have to plan better next time and eat desert first."

The hotel had quite a lot to offer and the three of them wandered down the hall where they could hear the live entertainment.

Peaking in at the dancers, Henry said, "I am going to bed."

"Sleep well," Arnold said.

"Sweet Dreams Father," Brenda said, kissing her father on the cheek before he left them.

Brenda and Arnold returned to the large room filled with live music, dancing, and comedy sketches by three very talented and funny comedians. Brenda was apparently awestruck with the thrill of it all and sat quietly just looking around for a while.

"How much does all this cost," she asked? "I've never seen anything like this."

"The cost is irrelevant," Arnold informed her. "This is my treat."

She laughed at the comedians and tapped her foot to the music.

"I will remember this day forever," She yelled over the orchestra.

She clung to Arnold; her eyes moist.

"I can't help but think of my mother and father. They never had the opportunity to enjoy anything like this or even anything close to this. I wish my father had been able to stay awake," she said wistfully.

"I understand. I felt the same way about my own father. They worked so hard and received so little pleasure."

Arnold noticed that a special live musical production was scheduled to start in twenty minutes.

"Maybe we should take a short break before the next show starts," Arnold said.

He steered Brenda down the hall to the powder room.

When she returned to the doorway and he started to lead her back to the entertainment, she asked, "How much will it cost?"

Arnold replied, "It is free for us."

"Hmm," Brenda said as she raised an eyebrow and looked him in the eyes. "Well thank you Arnold for being so generous and thoughtful."

Arnold said, "You deserve the best of everything, because you are who you are."

That evening they returned to their room. This time when they entered, Arnold turned on a bedside lamp and made down the bed. He turned and smiled Brenda as he lowered his lips to hers and lifted her up to lay her on the bed.

As new lovers do, they made love several more times into the night.

The next morning, Arnold asked Brenda how she felt.

"A little sore," she smiled, "but very happy."

It was then Arnold realized that he forgot to use a condom.

CHAPTER 11

Every night for the rest of the week in Santa Fe and sometimes in the morning or afternoons, Arnold and Beth would make love, flirt and talk.

Arnold drove Brenda to sites around Santa Fe in Henry's Fairlane. Henry was often with them, but sometimes he stayed behind to rest or walk around the neighborhoods near the hotel. They watched Indian dances and bought silver and turquoise jewelry from round Indian women sitting on blankets outside the Governors' Palace. They visited beautiful churches and walked along the downtown looking in all the shops.

At one shop, Arnold purchased a new dress, shoes, and purse that Brenda picked out.

Tears well up in Brenda's eyes as she tried to express her appreciation to Arnold.

"Your husband is obviously proud of you." The store attendant advised.

Brenda smiled at the woman and said, "Today, I will approve of everything he does."

As the attendant moved to her position behind the counter, Brenda whispered to Arnold, "I also approve of the comment about you being my husband, which I also approve of."

As they drove to another part of town, Brenda commented, "the trees, green grass, and mountains are so beautiful here, I wish we I could live in a nice place like this."

"Sure, it is beautiful, but not as beautiful as cattle and horses roaming on the open prairie."

"You are right," Brenda said. "But it is nice to have both."

"I'm not sure how I can get and manage both yet," Arnold replied.

"The solution is not readily available," Brenda agreed.

They tried, including Henry, to see every show in town and eat at every great restaurant, sampling several dishes that none of them had ever tasted before. Arnold went so far as to purchase a camper freezer that would keep food frozen for several days and would fit into the trunk of Henry's car. They purchased different dishes to take back to the ranch.

"I thank you from my heart," said Brenda, "Father will so love to sample these meals again when we get home. My cooking is okay, but not as spicy as this."

After having such a wonderful time Arnold, Brenda and Henry departed for the ranch. Henry and Brenda slept most of the time. Arnold concentrated on his driving and on formulating his plans for the future.

His plans for the future were troubling Arnold.

When he returned to Henry's ranch, what would he do? He worried. The work was done, the cows would be sold before he got back, and he needed to make plans for tomorrow. The confusing part was Brenda. She was not his responsibility yet. Did he want to make her his responsibility? Everything about the idea sounded good. Brenda is good. Brenda looks good. So, why not?

Arnold continued to drive and think.

He simply did not know what to do. He decided to take it one day at a time and fall back on the plan he had when he left Oklahoma, 'Let his experiences tell him what and when to do the next best thing, and do not take on responsibilities that were not his to have.'

Soon, they turned into the driveway of the ranch. A barbed-wire gate with a large post at each end needed to be opened and closed for each entry or exit. The driveway was little more than a thin two-track road with a little gravel on it and grass and weeds growing on either side. Arnold parked near the house as Henry and Brenda began to wake.

Brenda sat up with a jerk. "Home already," she yawned.

Getting out of the car and stretching, Brenda was welcomed by her dog. Henry headed for the mailbox, eager to determine that everything went fine with the sale of the cows and steers. He thumbed through the mail and read it carefully.

"Brenda, we have received enough money to purchase material and hire employees to build a corral," he said.

"Excellent," Brenda said. "How much money did you make?"

Henry said, "$57,000 for 300 cows and 50 calves. The hauling of cattle and sales commission equaled $7,000. The expenses subtracted from the gross sales left us a net of $48,000.00."

Henry then surprised Brenda when he requested that she come into the house for a private discussion. Brenda quickly went into the house not knowing what to expect.

Henry turned to Arnold and said, "Arnold, would you join us?"

Once inside the kitchen, Henry said, "Brenda I think we should sell the remaining livestock including the horses. Then, sell the ranch and relocate to a nice place in town for the two of us to live. Considering the amount of life insurance that you collected from your mother's policy, $120,000 plus the $9,000.00 from the sale of cows. I have calculated that we would get approximately $9800.00 if we sold the cows and horses.

We would be in a financial position to purchase a house wherever we would like to."

Brenda said, "Out of the $137,000.00, how much will we have to pay in income taxes?"

Arnold thought, she did that calculation in her head.

Henry said, "about $40,000.00 leaving us about $97,000.00 to spend on us."

Brenda asked, "How much would you receive from the ranch if you sold it?"

"Approximately $30,000.00; however, it would rent for around $2.00 per acre annually and that would be 4,000 times 2.00 equals $8,000.00 per year for six years, which equals $48,000. So, I would try to rent it to have an income."

Arnold kept quiet during the family meeting. After the meeting, Brenda and Arnold unloaded the car, and Henry wrestled with his dog. It was difficult to determine who was the happiest, the dog or Henry.

Brenda said she would prepare food for dinner that evening and went into the kitchen.

Arnold was thinking of Henry's proposal to Brenda, and he knew that Brenda and he needed time in private to discuss the ramifications of Henry's proposal.

Before he went to his camp site, Arnold suggested to Brenda that she and Henry discuss going to Santa Fe again.

Brenda said, "With everything Father said, about selling out and moving to town, I am wondering when he wants to do all of this. I plan to ask him tonight."

Arnold caught Brenda around the waist and pulled her towards him. He kissed her thoroughly. "Maybe you can stop by my camp this evening, if you are not too busy," he whispered in her ear.

Henry sitting nearby, grinned, but turned his face away to give them privacy.

Back at his campsite, Arnold made a pot of coffee, built a fire and placed the pot in just the right place so it would get hot quickly because he really needed a good cup of hot coffee.

Before he had even one cup, Brenda came walking toward him.

"Can we talk?" Brenda asked. "Father wants to sell the cows on the first week of January and to then advertise his ranch for rent. He agreed to go to Santa Fe the week after or the second week of January."

"I'm really concerned Arnold," Brenda said.

Arnold instantly became concerned too although he had not been before.

"Father is acting very strange, much in the same way he did before his last stroke," Brenda confided.

"Maybe we should take him to the hospital," Arnold suggested. "They will know what to do. Maybe this is an overreaction, but we must be cautious."

Brenda agreed and they walked back to the house and coerced Henry back into the car and took him to an emergency room in Walsenburg, Colorado.

Even though Henry knew the trip was for his own good, he complained "I'm okay," the entire way.

Brenda was very worried, and Arnold easily understood why. She watched her father over the back seat to make sure he was okay. Arnold drove and tried to be a good listener.

"This is a waste of money. I don't have insurance," Henry said.

"How much money do you have in the bank?" Arnold asked.

"$150.00," Henry replied.

"Where is the cattle sale money and the insurance money?" Arnold asked.

"The insurance money and proceeds from the sale of cattle are in a sack in the refrigerator," Henry said.

"Okay then. Tell the emergency room administrator that you are broke and need financial assistance. Make sure I am with you when you tell them this and then let me handle it from there. I will negotiate the final bill to be less than a third of the original charge."

Brenda said, "Okay."

When they got to the emergency room, she did just as Arnold had asked, and it worked.

"Now, you need to take care of another legal issue, Arnold told Brenda. "You should get an attorney to prepare a General Power of Attorney and get Henry to sign it giving you, Brenda J. Gladstone, the authority to conduct all necessary business, medical, and personal transactions normally carried out by Henry J. Gladstone of current address and phone. Have them add, the statement 'This shall be in effect until rescinded by myself, Henry J. Gladstone.'

You need to discuss this with Henry because the authorities, the lawyer who prepared it, will ask for his signature while he is cognizant and rational. The lawyer will prepare his own document, and it will read somewhat different, but similar to what I just told you."

Brenda went to Henry's hospital room and discussed these subjects with Henry. He agreed to sign the papers for Brenda.

Brenda and Arnold left his room to discuss this with the hospital administrator who informed them that a lawyer was on duty each day and is usually very cooperative as they understand the situation and are schooled in the phraseology to be used and the procedure for obtaining the signature.

Arnold and Brenda met with the hospital attorney next, and within one hour, the lawyer had prepared the necessary papers and was prepared to talk with Henry.

"I need a cup of coffee," Brenda said as they finished these tasks.

At almost the same time, the nurse in charge of Henry informed, Brenda that the doctors were going to examine Henry now. He would be busy for about an hour perhaps a little more.

She told Brenda, "It is a good idea to take a break. I will call you or come get you if you keep me informed or your location."

Brenda replied, "We will be in the cafeteria."

As they walked to the cafeteria, Brenda took Arnold's arm in hers. In the cafeteria, Brenda said,

"I am pleased that you thought of the power of attorney and worked out the financial aspects of Father's care. I did not know what you were having us do at the time, but now I understand and remember some of it. Now that it is done, I feel much better. Thank you, Arnold, for all your help."

The hospital administrator found Brenda and gave her five copies of each document and she was told she should put at least one and maybe more copies in a safety deposit box or a place of safe keeping and to avoid distributing copies to anyone other than representatives of health/medical providers who are authorized to administer such documents, such as, the family doctor, a hospital administrator and/or an attorney.

Brenda said to Arnold, "I am getting a crash course in legal matters today."

Arnold replied, "This is just the beginning."

Over an hour later, Brenda was approached by her father's physician and was asked if she had any objections if they transferred Henry to a critical care facility in Colorado Springs. The nearest facility equipped to provide the care her Father needed was in Colorado Springs and the next nearest was Denver.

Brenda authorized the transfer, explained to her father what was happening, and he was loaded into an ambulance accompanied by two medics who would provide medical assistance if Henry required it during the transfer.

"May I go in the ambulance with my father?" Brenda asked.

"No Dear," one of the medics said. "It will be better if you go in a separate vehicle and get there before us."

On the way to Colorado Springs, Arnold brought something up to Brenda that she had not thought of.

"I anticipated you will need to stay with Henry for several days and nights; how many he could not guess. I think I should rent a car for you and get you a hotel room so you can stay near Henry as long as he needs you. I will return to the ranch and care for the cattle and horses. I'll stay there five days and then come back here to stay with you until Henry is well."

Brenda replied, "Arnold I have never stayed in a motel by myself, and I have never rented a car before."

Arnold laughed and said, "Sweetheart, last week you told me you had never had sex before and you did great."

Brenda smiled and then leaned over to kiss Arnold while he drove.

In Colorado Springs, Brenda and Arnold waited impatiently for Henry to be admitted, evaluated and delivered to his room for some needed rest and peace. After 3 hours, Henry's new doctor approached them in the waiting room and briefed them on his condition. He told Brenda, with Arnold listening closely, that Henry was experiencing brief periods of unconsciousness.

The doctor said the greatest concern was his heart beating abnormally, sometimes weak and sometimes strong. The staff had administered medicine to treat the heart situation and expected the heartbeat to stabilize. They thought that this would take care of the on-again off-again unconsciousness.

The doctor said "We will continue to treat and monitor his condition for three or four days and will reevaluate. As for planning ahead, I think it would be wise for you to find temporary housing for at least one perhaps two weeks. Is that possible?"

Brenda looked at Arnold who acknowledged by nodding his head in the affirmative.

"Yes," Brenda said.

"Okay good," the doctor said. "Let the nurse know where you are staying. I advise you to give Henry time to relax and sleep now without disturbing him."

Arnold and Brenda departed to locate and rent a motel for one week with a one- week extension possible. They rented a car on the way to the motel.

Brenda started to say something as they stopped to rent a car and Arnold stopped her.

"Brenda. Let's not worry about the cost until everything was known and then we can discuss it. Take care of your father. He is worth it. I know this because I lost mine and have missed him every day since."

Arnold led as they went to the motel. Brenda followed in the rented Ford. At the motel desk, Arnold took care of everything.

Arnold went to the room with Brenda to make sure everything was in good order. The room was nicely furnished and very comfortable with a nice scenic view from the picture window in the living room. Satisfied, Arnold took Brenda to lunch, returned her to the motel then departed for the ranch.

CHAPTER 12

As he drove Arnold's Fairlane back to the ranch, Arnold went over a list in his head of what he needed to do there.

It was evident as soon as he arrived, that the first thing he needed to do was be available when people responded to Henry's ad about selling the cows and renting the prairie grass because people were already lining up. Four cars and their occupants were waiting when he arrived.

Two ranchers wanted to buy the advertised 200 cows and 50 calves, and one of the ranchers wanted to rent the ranch land.

"What are you all offering?" asked Arnold.

"I can pay $200.00 each for the cows, but I don't want the horses or calves," said a short rancher named Smith.

The second rancher said, "I want to rent the ranch for $3.00 per acre per year. I will pay $250.00 each for the cows, $200.00 each for the calves, $100.00 each for the 4 horses, and I will pay cash by January 15th of each year."

Arnold looked him in the eye and said, "Mister, please tell me your name and address because I think we have a deal."

"Scott Rathmussen," the second rancher clarified.

Arnold nodded.

"Mr. Smith," Arnold said, turning back to the first rancher. "I thank you for coming. I believe I will take Mr. Rathmussen's offer. Good-bye now."

He turned to Rathmussen again, copied his name and address, shook hands on the deal as it was spelled out.

Rathmussen said, "Can we go to the Alamosa Bank now, and I will pay you for the stock? I would like to pro rate the rent for this year and pay the remainder for a year on January 15 of each year. Also, I would ask for a five-year commitment on the ranch rental agreement."

Arnold took the man into the house and made coffee, then he produced a piece of paper and wrote 'total due today, ten thousand and fifty dollars and the balance of ten thousand due January 15.' Scott signed the agreement and they departed for Alamosa. Arnold was pleased.

Arriving at the Alamosa Bank, Mr. Scott Rathmussen made introductions. It was apparent that he was well acquainted with the banker. This also pleased Arnold.

Arnold asked Scott Rathmussen if he could have the banker put the money in a cashier's check made payable to Henry J. Gladstone?

The banker overheard the conversation and said, "Hey, I know Henry. He has banked here for over 50 years. I have not seen him for a while, and I wonder how he is doing."

"I saw Henry and his daughter Brenda yesterday. They are doing okay," Arnold replied.

Mr. Rasmussen said, "Please give him my regards."

Then he said, "Surely we can put that amount in a cashier's check payable to Henry. Do you want it to include Brenda?"

"Yes, that would be fine. Brenda J. Gladstone," Arnold said.

Scott gave authorization to the banker, and it was done.

"Can someone write a promissory note for $12,000.00 due January 15 of each year for five years," Arnold asked the banker.

The banker talked to his secretary and the secretary wrote out the notes. Everyone shook hands.

"When do you want to take possession?" Arnold asked Scott.

"Today," said Scott.

"Are you going to use the house?"

"No."

"Can we use the house for six months? We do not have a place to move to yet. That would be really helpful."

"Of course," Scott said. "It is still yours for six months."

They scribbled this on a piece of paper and both parties signed it. Everybody was happy.

Arnold told the group he would see Henry and Brenda early tomorrow. He noticed a restaurant across the street and headed toward it because he wanted a cup of coffee and some food.

"See you soon," Scott called out to him.

"If you need anything send me a letter or call me on the phone. I will send you my number when I know where I will be," Arnold called back.

At the restaurant, Arnold ate a very nice meal. He noticed the attractive waitress. Out of habit, he thought he should get better acquainted with her. But instead, he got back in the car and went to the ranch house to pick up the clothes Brenda had requested. He filled up the dog's bowl while he was there and wondered what would happen to the dog in the long run. No one had mentioned plans for him. For now, Arnold did not worry about this because he would be back in a few days.

He knew it was going to be late when he got in so he called the motel and asked them to give Brenda a message that he would be arriving between 10:00 and 11:00 PM today. He emphasized to the motel representative that Brenda get his message. He did not want to scare her when he entered her room late at night.

Arnold was happy to arrive in Colorado Springs. He had not slept well the night before and was expecting better sleep tonight. When he got to Brenda's room, she was awake and worried about her father.

Arnold tried to cheer her a bit with information about the sales he had made but, she was too shaken up about Henry to listen and wanted to talk about him.

So, Arnold listened.

"The physician made his diagnosis, and it is not good. We will get a detailed briefing in the morning. Father has a heart condition that does not allow the heart to pump in a rhythm as it should. It seems to alternate but not in the same rhythm, and the medication they gave him last night had no effect or very little effect. They are going to continue the same medicine but increase the dosage this afternoon and watch for a change in his heartbeat. The real problem is they do not understand what is causing this problem in the first place."

Arnold sat silently on the bed to see if there was anything more she wanted to say.

"Did you have some news for me?" she asked after spitting out all the information about Henry's condition.

"Yes, I picked up your clothes. Also, I rented the ranch for five years. I sold the cows, calves and horses. What do you want to do with the dog?"

Brenda said, "I am starved. Can we go eat and talk?"

"Absolutely, if the food is good. Where do you elect to eat?"

"At a restaurant with hot black coffee."

"An excellent choice."

At the restaurant, Arnold said, "I am not a physician, but the news about Henry is not good. I want to volunteer to help you whenever and wherever I can. I must schedule some trips back to Oklahoma, so, tell me what help you expect you will need from me so I can make plans."

Brenda looked at Arnold and said, "Sweetheart I do not know. I would tell you if I did know. I think it is ridiculous for me to plan when

I have no idea what is coming next. Also, even though I do not know anything right now, that could change several times in an hour. I guess the right thing for me to tell you is, 'be flexible and be ready,' if you can."

"Okay, I understand. I will be flexible and ready at the drop of any command that comes from your lips," Arnold said, and they smiled at each other.

A waiter showed up, and they ordered a huge meal. When it arrived, they did not take the time to eat it, but talked instead.

When the waiter noticed what happened, he asked, "Are you newly-weds?"

They said, "No."

"You act like newly-weds," the waiter laughed. "If you do not want the food you ordered, I will take it back."

"Can you fix it to go?" Brenda asked.

"Yes. I would be happy to," the waiter replied.

"Thank you. That would make us happy," said Brenda.

When they picked up their food, the waiter said, "Have a great evening. There is no charge for those who are so fortunate as to be in love. Good night to you both."

On the way back to the motel, Arnold asked, "Brenda, should I plan a trip to Oklahoma soon or wait awhile? I have received three phone calls asking me to make immediate plans to return."

"I think you should go soon because we do not know what is coming next."

"Other than business in Oklahoma, my only plan is to continue traveling around the countryside, camping and working. I will plan to hang loose and periodically visit you and Henry. With that in mind, be thinking about what I need to do to be of assistance to you. I am a free man, and I can help."

"I need to be near my father to be of comfort to him because I do not believe he will be with us for long. This has been discussed at length with the hospital Chaplain who is very understanding and kind. Father is getting weak and frustrated," Brenda said.

"Is Henry a moral man?" Henry asked.

"My father has never been to church," Brenda explained. I've never heard him proclaim a belief in a supreme power, such as, Jesus, or God. He listened to Billy Graham on the radio until Mother died. But he has not listened since she died."

"Do you think he would object, or would you object, if I talked with him about God and his power of redemption that results in a peace unknown to those who do not believe?" asked Arnold.

"I have no idea what he would think," Brenda replied. "I do not mind if you try to discuss this with him. It could do some good."

"Do you want to accompany me when I discuss this with Henry?" Arnold asked.

"Yes, absolutely," Brenda replied.

They drove to the hospital the next morning to visit Henry armed with the happy news of the sale of the cows, horses, and calves; the rental of the ranch; and the Good News of the Gospel.

At his bedside, they told Henry about the sales and asked if Arnold could tell him about God.

"Are you a preacher or something?" Henry asked.

"Henry I am a man who has seen the very bottom of life's barrel. I mean the very bottom with no visible way to stand up. And, now I am here to let you know there is a way out of the bottom. That way is to remember God is the Savior of mankind. When we get into situations like the one you are in and cannot find a way to raise our heads and stand up, the way up is simple. All you need to do is ask Jesus Christ to come into your life and help you. Don't think you have to identify the exact way because it is so simple. Just ask Jesus to come into your life and help you. After you do this, you will see results. Listen to Brenda please, when she says you should talk to the hospital Chaplain. He readily understands the situation."

As we walked out of his room Brenda was crying because she knew Henry was at the bottom of his barrel and needed help. They had left him praying. Arnold knew there was hope because Henry was praying. Arnold could tell something else too; this was not the first time Henry prayed. He felt confident Henry was a believer.

Brenda walked toward the car and waited for Arnold to arrive. When he got there, he gave her a hug and kiss and whispered, "Henry is going to get better."

"How do you know that Arnold?"

"I believe it to be so," Arnold said. "When we believe, it is a powerful force that Jesus uses to touch the lives of people we love. Now, you must know there is another factor in this equation, that being Henry is and has been for a long time, a good man. If he were not, this would not work. Henry has obviously prayed silently for years or he could not have lived this long and been as healthy as he has been. Jesus has intervened before now. Now, if Henry is sincere, and Jesus knows if he is, Henry is in for good treatment from Jesus. Just keep believing."

Brenda and Arnold were due for their evening debrief from the physician about Henry's status. They wanted to know if the medicine was working or not.

They went to the briefing room and the physician came in all smiles and said, "We have great news. The medicine is working, and his heart rhythm has become regular. He does not show symptoms of heart failure. Provided we keep him stabilized this way for 24 hours, we will be able to determine what has been causing the irregular beat and then develop a treatment. For now, he is resting comfortably, his breathing is normal, and his pulse has returned to normal. The next briefing will be in 24 hours. See you then."

Brenda grabbed Arnold by the neck and hugged him and kissed him in her great joy.

Arnold said, "If I couldn't tell, I would think you are a happy lady."

Brenda laughed.

"You might as well go to Oklahoma now. This could go on for a long time," she said.

Arnold made plans to fly to Oklahoma the next morning and planned to return in three days. On the second day in Oklahoma, Arnold received a call from Brenda telling him that Henry had taken a turn for the worse and was being transferred to Denver around noon the next day. Arnold immediately scheduled a return trip to Colorado Springs and departed Oklahoma City at 5:30 AM, arriving in Colorado Springs at 10:30 AM.

When Arnold's plane landed, he called Brenda. "I'm at the airport… taking a taxi to the hospital now."

"We have two hours Arnold. They are taking Henry by ambulance to Denver and leaving at 12:30. Henry was doing okay, but they could not determine why his heart was behaving as it was, so they are transferring him to Denver. I want to go to Denver too, Arnold."

Arnold arrived at the motel and they informed the manager that they were leaving, and he cancelled their reservations. Within an hour, they had turned in the rental car and were on their way to Denver.

Although they left Colorado Springs thirty minutes after Henry, they made it to the hospital before him and were there when Henry arrived.

Henry was relieved to see them. Brenda informed him of the cattle sale and ranch rental. They showed him the check.

"If I'd seen this check earlier, I would not have agreed to come to Denver," Henry joked weakly, giving Brenda a wink.

Brenda and Arnold found another motel that was fully equipped with a kitchen and more moderate rates for extended stays. After checking in, they shopped for groceries and stocked the refrigerator.

Henry was restless all night, and they stayed up late with him at the hospital. Brenda was deeply concerned. While they were sitting in the waiting room, the Chaplain that had attended Henry showed up in Denver offering a friendly shoulder to lean on. The Chaplain was a tall slender man with brown hair and a trim mustache over his top lip. His appearance in Denver was not a pleasant surprise for Arnold.

He eyed the Chaplain with suspicion. Although the Chaplain claimed he had transferred hospitals to be near Henry, Arnold suspected he really meant he wanted to be near Brenda. Brenda was a desirable woman and even a Chaplain could see that and be tempted. Arnold felt his budding jealousy with unhappiness. The feeling reminded him too much of the divorce he had recently survived.

Brenda spoke quietly in the waiting room about her plans if her father died. She was planning to return to Las Mesitas and find a cemetery in which to bury her father and then have someone relocate her mother to the same location. When her mother had died, she and Henry had not had the money to bury her mother in a cemetery.

Arnold knew quite a lot about what Brenda was going to have to face in the near future if her father died, and it seemed likely that he would. In the past, Arnold had been the one left to tie up the family affairs when his own father and mother died. It was a lonely task. Brenda did not know about his experience though and was sometimes impatient with his offering of advice, so he hushed and let Brenda consult with the Chaplain and relieve her stress by fretting about details.

Arnold knew that Brenda was not playing a game with him. She did not realize that he had come to love her as much as he did.

"Arnold, I know it is an imposition, but would you return to the ranch and try to arrange these details for me? Brenda asked. "I do not have any living relatives or close friends that I can ask to do this. I don't even know a minister to hold the service."

Despite his misgivings over the closeness developing between the Chaplain serving Henry and Brenda, Arnold agreed to undertake the task because he knew she really needed his help and trusted him.

Brenda and Arnold agreed to use the motel telephone as a message center so they could stay in contact while he was gone. After breakfast the next morning, Arnold departed for Las Mesitas. From there, he went on to Oklahoma.

For now, Arnold dismissed his concern that Brenda enjoyed the companionship of the Chaplain as much as she seemed to and he tried to ignore what he considered breaches in the Chaplain's professional demeanor that he noticed from time to time when Brenda was around.

CHAPTER 13

Arnold finished his business in Oklahoma and returned to Denver in one week.

He went directly to the hospital to check on Henry.

Brenda told Arnold that Henry was holding his own, but nothing else.

After greeting Henry, who was laying in his hospital bed looking pale and tired, Arnold asked Brenda if she wanted to take a walk around the hospital grounds.

"Yes. I do," she said. "And, I want to know where you have been and what you have been doing?"

"Do you want the whole story?" Arnold teased.

"Only tell me the parts you want to tell me," Brenda answered seriously. "Arnold, I want the two of us to get married someday. Until then, I want to be with you, around you, and to love you every day and night. Whatever you do is fine, just keep me posted and live a happy life. Tell me what you expect of me, and I will be there for you day or night, except for the times Father needs me. He comes first."

She took a breath and continued. "I know you expect me to care for Father as you have said you would for your father if he were here. Am I correct?"

"You are correct in everything." He grinned wrapped his arms around her, stopping their progress and kissed the top of her head. He relaxed for the first time in weeks with Brenda so close.

Brenda and Arnold visited Henry again before they went to find something to eat. This time he was napping.

They returned to the truck, drove to a nearby restaurant and ate a nice dinner.

Brenda ate more than Arnold had seen her eat since Santa Fe.

"I'd like to go to Oklahoma with you Arnold," Beth said as she dug into a steak.

"Of course, you can go. Let's go today."

"Do you have a picture of your place in Oklahoma?" Brenda asked.

"I don't. I'm sorry." Arnold apologized.

"Excuse me Miss," the waiter said. "You have a call and they say it is urgent."

Brenda paled and went up to the restaurant office to take the call. When she rejoined Arnold, she was shaken.

"Father is experiencing a heart attack. We must go to him now."

At the door to Henry's room, they were allowed in immediately. Henry was sweating profusely and trying to breathe.

Brenda whispered his name and asked how he was doing. He smiled crookedly at Brenda through his pain. Then he grimaced. His eyes closed, and he choked out a long, ragged breath, and it was all over.

Henry's heart stopped beating. He was 93 and one-half years of age.

The hospital room was very quiet now. The hospital staff left Brenda and Arnold to sit by Henry. Brenda held Henry's hand while Arnold held hers, and they prayed.

"I'm glad he is out of pain and not living cooped up in a hospital room any longer. I know he hated that," Brenda said to Arnold and to herself as they went to the nurses' station to ask the nurse to prepare the body.

"Are all the arrangements made in Las Mesitas?" Brenda asked Arnold.

"Yes. Everything is arranged. All we need to do is notify the funeral home in Las Mesitas. I'll do that as soon as we know when the hospital and funeral home here release the body for transport."

Later that day Arnold conferred with the hospital administrator and the local funeral home regarding the process, the scheduling and the cost. The hospital administrator informed him the hospital in Colorado Springs and the one in Denver were waiving all costs because of Henry's age, his lack of insurance and his subsequent death. The local funeral home was also waiving their costs. The only cost for which Brenda would be responsible were those in Las Mesitas.

She thanked the administrators and the Chaplain and began to cry. Arnold watched from the hallway as the Chaplain held Brenda as she cried. He wondered what she was thinking as she clung to the other man.

Arnold informed the funeral home in Mesitas of Henry's death. They told him that they had already exhumed the body of Brenda's mother and had it in storage until he wanted to schedule her reburial. He and asked that both burials be scheduled to occur at the same time in the same cemetery.

"I will pay the entire cost," Arnold told them.

Within an hour both the funeral home in Mesitas and the one in Denver had called Arnold and confirmed that both funerals were scheduled two days from today at 1:00 PM at the funeral home in Las Mesitas. Burial would follow in the local cemetery immediately. Arnold asked if the flowers had been ordered and was informed that they had.

Beth and Arnold traveled to Las Mesitas the next day and stayed overnight at the ranch house that used to belong to Henry and Brenda at the new owner's insistence.

Following the funeral, Brenda and Arnold departed feeling the relocation of Brenda's mother to a grave next to her father was completed perfectly. They were both happy with the placement of flowers on the casket of each.

When they returned to the ranch, Arnold confronted Brenda about the Chaplain?

"I'd like to know what you feel for the Chaplain?" Arnold asked abruptly as he drank coffee at the ranch house table.

"Nothing happened worth discussing," Brenda answered. "The crisis has passed, and the Chaplain must return to his own obligations and responsibilities and so must I."

Arnold reddened. He wanted her to say that nothing had happened. He wanted reassurance. He was hurt by her inadequate answer. He felt shut out or that she was hiding something from him. He was still very haunted by the betrayal of Charlene.

I should let the subject drop, he thought. The death of her father was one of the most emotional experiences of her life.

"I want to spend more time with the Chaplain under less stressful and sorrowful conditions," Brenda said. Her chin rose and her cheeks flushed.

"Why would you want to do that," Arnold shouted, his anger rising.

Suddenly, the thought of her eager participation in sexual activities hit him. He wondered if now that she knew about sex, she was just as eager to experience it with other men.

"Does your plan include any form of love making including kissing, touching breasts and other parts of the body? Does it include sexual intercourse?"

"I don't know," Brenda said.

"Do you want to take a vacation with me, maybe take a trip to Oklahoma to see my farm?" Arnold asked.

"No," Brenda said. "I want to understand the Chaplain better than I currently understand him."

"So even though you said you want to marry me, you don't plan to be true to me alone," accused Arnold.

"Arnold. I must clear my mind before we proceed further. The Chaplain is currently important to me, and I want to get some information from him."

Arnold felt confused, depressed, and angry.

She is obviously confused and needs time, he thought. But I need the answer to the question about sexual intercourse with the Chaplain. I have already experienced the betrayal of one love when Charlene had sexual intercourse while she was married to me. What are Brenda's intentions? Her answer is extremely important to our relationship.

Despite their disagreement and stilted relationship, Arnold continued to assist Brenda with the legal and financial aftermath of Henry's death. He helped her sign all the required papers and handed over to her the check for the sale of the cattle and horses and rent for the ranch. Now she could legally sign the check and do as she pleased. She could receive her money without worry.

Brenda's only concern was the tax consequences of receiving the money. Arnold took Brenda to Alamosa so she could talk to an old friend of his about her tax obligations, including payment of any past due taxes. Linda Ivory was a tax expert and she happily helped Brenda.

After everything, all his help with finances and legal matters, all his free advice and friendship, Brenda asked Arnold to take her back to Denver and to allow her time to converse with the Chaplain.

He complied but unhappily. He drove Brenda back to the motel in Denver. They travelled in silence. She would not answer his intimate questions about sex. She was completely silent on the subject.

This angered Arnold, but he hid it. As they parted, Arnold gave Brenda a tight hug and a warm kiss.

He drove off without indicating where he was going.

Brenda had not asked where he was going, he thought as he adjusted the rearview mirror and turned out of the motel parking lot.

CHAPTER 14

Ever since Arnold, had left Oklahoma, his travels had been purposely directionless. This had been even more true since he left Brenda in Denver. He just drove. The scenery had become mountainous. It was rural, with plenty of cattle and barbed wire fences, but few people.

Several hours out of Denver, Arnold began to think about food and water. He had very little of either with him. Planning ahead for the simple necessities of life, beyond hot coffee and lucrative investments, had never been one of his strong suits. Food and water were sometimes neglected.

Before long, a road sign appeared indicating the presence of a small town. The town was a two-store situation with one small restaurant and a filling station that offered assorted supplies besides gas.

Arnold wondered to himself, what could possibly provide enough business for a town of this size to survive?

The outskirts of town on the far side quickly passed by his window and he realized he had passed the town completely. Turning around was not a problem. There was no vehicular traffic, only a cowboy on a horse. Finding food became his focus.

There were no cars parked in front of the town's restaurant. As he entered the restaurant, he noticed it was clean, small and occupied by two women, both appeared to be waitresses.

One waitress greeted him immediately. Her name plate indicated her name was Janice, but when she greeted him, she called herself Nancy.

"Why is your name tag wrong," Arnold enquired.

She corrected him quickly.

"My name tag is correct," she said, "the wrong person is wearing it, but she is smart enough to know who she was."

Well that answer satisfied Arnold. He thought she was interesting. He sat down at a table in the center of the small room.

The other waitress was thin and past middle age. She came up to the table and asked him if he wanted to eat and presented him with a small menu. She was an attractive woman. Her dark hair was turning gray in streaks. She wore a wrinkled white apron over a turquoise cotton dress that did not have a name tag pinned to it. Arnold thought she was a waitress, but perhaps she was the cook, or the manager.

"I can make anything you want as long as it is listed up there." She pointed to the wall.

"What is the most popular dish you serve?" Arnold asked.

The waitress or cook pointed to a flat iron steak and a baked potato with a salad that was listed on the menu.

"That, then, will be my order," Arnold said.

The older waitress disappeared into the back of the restaurant and for several minutes the room was quiet. When she returned to his table, she brought a salad, a large cup of coffee and a local paper, which she said was printed monthly.

The paper contained ads for services, items for sale and a real-estate section offering one ranch that included cattle, horses and roving mountain lions at no additional cost to the buyer.

Arnold noticed an ad in the paper that indicated possible employment as a handy man.

Raising his voice slightly, he asked the woman who had brought him his coffee,

"Do you know anything about this ad for a handy man?"

"That is my ad." The woman informed Arnold. "I am interested in hiring someone to do odd jobs around the restaurant and the small motel located behind the restaurant."

She returned to the back of the restaurant, out of sight.

Arnold sipped his coffee and thought about this job. So, she was more than a waitress. She was waitress, cook and manager.

It was still relatively early in the day, and he had planned to drive further before sleeping, but the job sounded like a good opportunity for him to get food and a place to sleep at a low cost.

"I might be interested in the job," Arnold said as she returned with his steak and potato on a steaming platter.

"My name is Maggie," the waitress-cook-manager said as she placed his food in front of him. "I run the restaurant and motel. How much do you charge for your work?"

"What is the going rate?" Arnold asked.

"$5.00 per hour."

"How much does a room cost at your motel?"

"$10.00 a day or $7.50 for a half day."

Arnold pretended ignorance. "Why would someone want a half-day rate?" he asked looking curious.

Maggie looked at him with a suspicious expression.

"Since you are so slow to think, you will probably need a full day," she retorted. "Do you want the job? Do you need a room?"

With a grin, Arnold accepted Maggie's job, "Can I take the job and the room and be gone to Oklahoma for a few days?"

"That is not a problem," Maggie said. "I just want to know when you can start working?"

"I can start tomorrow," Arnold replied, "assuming I can return to Oklahoma later and stay for a longer period of time."

"I have some work that needs to be done now," Maggie stated. "Just so you know, out here, where God can see everything you do, we do not work on Sunday."

"Monday, Tuesday or Wednesday will be fine," Arnold quickly replied.

"Is the restaurant open on Sunday?" Arnold asked.

"Only for people occupying the motel," Maggie replied. "I'll get a room key for you."

Maggie came back with a key to room 14.

Early the next morning, Arnold was awake and ready to see the countryside. He went to the restaurant he had eaten at before and ordered breakfast. He sat at the same table in the middle of the small room. He was greeted by a woman who was not Maggie. She was younger than Maggie, very attractive and friendly. She took his order and retreated to the back where Arnold assumed the kitchen was located.

She brought Arnold coffee while he waited for his breakfast. Her hands as they set the cup in front of him were small, tanned, a little rough, strong and capable. Her long and thick brown hair was held back by a plain rubber band at the nape of her neck. Overall, she was a petite woman with an oval face, blue eyes, and a determined chin. She wore cowboy boots and jeans that fit perfectly, as if made for the man who might be looking.

The waitress returned to Arnold's table when his food was ready and set it down. She smiled at him, then left him alone to eat without saying anything. But, as she walked away, the swing of her hips and the swish of her long ponytail seemed to Arnold to be an advertisement of her charms, perhaps even an invitation.

After he was done eating, the waitress appeared again. As she cleaned up the table, she informed Arnold that today, they were going to do ranch work and feed the cattle and horses.

"This is news to me," Arnold said, "but okay."

"You can call me Little Maggie," she said.

They left the restaurant, walked to a white pick-up truck in the parking lot and drove through town a short distance then turned off on a ranch road that ended in a circular turn around flanked on one side by a large dusty yard and a small ranch house and on the other side by a large weathered barn and tired-looking corrals. At the barn, Arnold helped Little Maggie, load several bales of hay into the bed of the truck. They drove to a pasture gate on the same road and spread the hay out for the cattle and horses that gathered there to be fed.

Arnold had dreamed of working on a ranch with cattle and horses again since he left the farm of his youth and went into investment finance. The hard work came natural for him. He loved the fresh air and the animals. He decided to make the most of it. The morning passed quickly.

"Hey Boss, 'Little Maggie,' is that really your name?" Arnold asked as they worked side by side.

She gave him a sidewise glance and said, "for now."

Arnold decided to give Little Maggie a nickname of his own. He decided to call her double AA for Ambitious Andrea.

Yes, she seemed ambitious since she was involved in the ranch, the motel and the restaurant, thought Arnold. What else is she involved in?

The sun started to settle behind the mountains and AA said they would spend the night at the ranch house. This was okay with Arnold. He had not told her yet that he had named her AA.

They drove to the ranch house, parked near the barn and walked across the large barnyard to the house. When they entered the house,

Arnold saw that it was sparsely furnished and western in its decoration. AA offered a tour which he appreciated.

AA informed him that she owned the ranch, which encompassed 2,500 acres, on which she had in the neighborhood of 500 head of cattle and 20 horses.

"Are you interested in ranching, Arnold?" she asked.

"Yep. I always have been," Arnold answered.

"Are you hungry?" she asked.

"Yep. I always am," Arnold answered.

AA looked at him with a laugh and he returned her smile.

Together they rummaged around in the kitchen and freezer and found steaks and materials to make a salad. AA baked biscuits while Arnold lit the fireplace.

Sitting by the fireplace following dinner, the two conversed about many things. Arnold felt at ease and relaxed. The location of the ranch came up and AA dug out an old map that had been stuffed into a magazine rack.

The ranch was located in northeast of Colorado off route 285 on an unmarked county road. Arnold was pleased.

The more remote the better, he thought.

So, 'Little Maggie,' I'm going to call you Andrea because I know 'Little Maggie' is not your name," said Arnold. "I've been calling you Andrea, or AA in my head all day."

"Okay. I'll be Andrea. Andrea is a nice name," Little Maggie answered.

After that they sat in silence for a while watching the fire. Arnold was a little disappointed that she had not told him her real name, but he understood wanting privacy.

"What are your plans, Arnold?" asked Andrea.

"I'm in no real hurry to get anywhere in particular," he answered vaguely, but truthfully.

"Will you stay a while and work on the ranch while I wait tables at the restaurant and tend the motel?" she asked.

"Sure. I can do that, at least for the near future," Arnold replied without hesitation.

"How much do you want to be paid and how often, weekly, monthly, daily?" Andrea asked.

"Pay me what you and Maggie think I'm worth and weekly is okay," Arnold responded.

"Where are you from Arnold and where were you going and how long were you planning to travel?" Andrea inquired.

These were too many questions for Arnold, so he ignored them.

"Can you tell me an address to give to a real estate contact that is watching my possessions while I'm gone?" Arnold asked instead of answering her questions.

Andrea's answer seemed just as vague as Arnold's had been.

"About ten miles east of Highway 285, south of Alamosa, Colorado on County Road B. It is the only residence on this stretch of road and the mailman knows how to find it."

Arnold wondered if a letter would get to him using that address. He would be sure to give it a try.

"What exactly will my duties be?" asked Arnold.

"Take care of the cattle and horses just as you and I did today. And, keep me informed about any problems or needs and ask any questions and do not be shy."

"Don't be shy," Arnold repeated after her his eyes twinkling, "Okay, do you have a male friend I might need to be concerned about?" Arnold asked boldly, leaning forward in the chair he was sitting in by the fire.

Arnold didn't know what to expect when Andrea stood up from her chair and faced him. He sat back in his chair as she began to undress. She started with her jeans. Arnold was startled into silence when she pushed her jeans and panties down. A male penis appeared, emerging out of a plush growth of dark brown pubic hair.

With a raised eyebrow and a wary expression that Arnold took as acknowledgment of his surprise, Andreas proceeded to remove her shirt and unclasp her bra. Her bra fell to the floor and large beautiful breasts above a narrow waist completed the confusing picture. Arnold did not look away.

"I am a hermaphrodite. I possess both a penis and a vagina. You could say that I am sexually confused, but I am not. I am a woman inside with a penis on the outside. Sometime, when we know each other better, perhaps we can explore this further."

She pulled up her jeans and picked her shirt and bra up off the floor. She slowly redressed.

"Is there any whiskey in the house?" Arnold asked with a grin.

Andrea looked straight into his eyes for a very long moment than mirrored his grin.

"I'll see if I can find some," she laughed.

CHAPTER 15

Early the next day, Arnold saddled a bay mare that was in the barn and turned the mare's head to the east.

As he rode, he became lost in thought, thinking over the experiences of the night before instead of studying the terrain. He had not realized how large the ranch was. He had ridden longer and farther east than he intended and soon became concerned that he might get lost. The sun was in the middle of the sky by the time he turned the mare around and set about returning to the ranch house.

As the sun disappeared behind the mountains, he was mighty pleased to see the ranch house come into view because he was hungry.

When he arrived at the barn, Andrea stepped out and greeted him.

"Do you have a new nick name for me?" she wondered.

"No, the one stated earlier is fine. I still like Ambitious Andrea, AA," he answered as he unsaddled the bay mare.

"What do you think?" he asked.

"About what?"

"About the name."

"I really don't like it," Andrea said. "When I have my next operation, it may become inappropriate."

Arnold remained silent.

"Don't do that," Andrea said with a hint of pleading.

"Do what? Remain silent?" Arnold asked.

"Yes. I don't want you to shut me out or become overly conscious of my differences."

Arnold noticed tears in Andrea's eyes.

"Tell you what," he said, "let's go over to the motel and while we are there, we can get my truck and dinner, then come back here to our fireplace and whiskey. How does that sound?"

"Good," Andrea murmured, blinking quickly to get rid of the tears.

He clasped one arm around her and gave her a squeeze. They climbed in her truck.

Maggie was serving at the restaurant and greeted them before she disappeared into the kitchen with an order.

Andrea, knowing the setup intimately from years of waitressing, retrieved a menu and plates, silverware and cups of coffee. She set them down on Arnold's favorite table in the middle of the restaurant before she settled into the chair across from him.

They ordered the steak and salad and talked about the ranch while they ate. Then, they headed back to the ranch, Arnold following Andrea in his truck.

Once in the ranch house, Andrea rekindled the fire and she and Arnold settled on the couch in front of the fireplace as the flames began to catch and warm up the room.

Arnold scooted over next to her and wrapped his arm around her shoulders, acutely aware of how quiet she had been all evening.

"When you disappeared today for the whole day, I thought you were gone for good," Andrea confessed. "I thought my sexual situation scared you off."

"Andrea, tell me about you, starting with your real name," Arnold pressed.

"You want to know?" Andrea burst out in a voice just below a shout. "It is not a pretty little tale you know."

Arnold stayed quiet.

Andrea got up from the couch and sat straight across from him on a footstool. Her face was red and contorted into a pain-filled grimace. A couple of small tears meandered down one of her cheeks as she spoke.

"Andrea's real name is Beth," she said loudly. "Beth Howser."

"Maggie is my aunt. She is not my mother. I inherited the ranch, motel and restaurant from my late father. I owe no money, have never dated anyone, and have worked the ranch, restaurant and motel since I was 12 years old. My father died five years ago. I am now 38 years old with an appointment to have surgery in two months. I am both worried and excited about that. I'm worried about the procedure and how I will run the ranch while I am recovering."

Arnold pulled Beth off the footstool and back onto the couch beside him. He replaced his arm around her shoulders and pulled her into his side.

"I'll help you Andre…Beth," he said.

They say for a while in companionable silence.

"Beth are you a believer in God?" Arnold asked.

"Yes," she replied. "I was saved when I was 10 years old, and I have practiced reading the Bible ever since. I have not attended a church as there are none around here, but I know God hears me pray, and I believe I am a Christian."

"I think God hears your prayers too," said Arnold.

Arnold kissed her on the forehead and said good night. She got up and went into her bedroom. He slept on the couch that night.

The next morning, the two met over coffee and biscuits at the dining room table, and then both went outside to start through their list of daily chores.

Beth headed to the restaurant for her morning shift.

Arnold told her he would be repairing fences east of the ranch house.

"I'll be back for dinner," he said.

As she drove her truck down the dirt road to the highway, Arnold thought,

Beth is something special. She is so beautifully a woman on the outside, petite, but strong; gentle, but wounded by a biology she had no say in. By choosing, she will have to undergo a radical surgery and take hormones that will take her into an unknown future.

In contrast, I am a hulk of a man with long legs, who walks without hesitation like I am crossing wind rows. I am strong, but not particularly gentle; big with broad shoulders and muscled arms that sometimes make me look like I have no neck. And God has thrown Beth and I together for a reason.

Arnold tried to focus on the task at hand. He saddled the bay mare he had ridden the day before and proceeded along the fence line in search of stretches that needed repair.

After following the fence to the eastern corner post, he had a better idea of what supplies he would need to make repairs. He returned to the barn and rummaged around until he found what he needed, new wire, u-nails, and fence posts along with a post-hole digger, pliers, and hammer. He found food for lunch in the house.

He returned to the broken fence and dug post holes for posts that needed to be replaced, repaired broken barbed wire, and tightened the fence as much as he could. The fresh air and hard work gave his mind something to focus on and it cleared.

After a couple more hours of work, he thought of a strategy that might bring comfort to Beth. He decided to return to the ranch house, eager to share his idea with Beth and plot a course of action. As he approached the ranch house for the second time that day, second thoughts assailed him. He was reminded of his objective when he left home in Oklahoma; the one that said he was only responsible in the end for himself. Other responsibilities were manufactured, not real.

Beth is not my responsibility unless I make her so, he thought.

'What are you doing with Beth?' he asked himself.

'What causes this responsibility to be yours?'

'Why am I thinking about helping her?'

'Why did I promise I would help when I have responsibilities in Denver with Brenda?'

Arnold did not want more responsibilities now, but he realized he had to keep an open mind.

I am not replacing Brenda with Beth in my heart, he thought. I must respond to Brenda whenever she calls, that is if the Chaplain has not changed Brenda's mind about marrying…me.

Arnold decided to go back to work on the fences and not return to the house. He needed to let the physical exertion and fresh air clear his mind again. He turned the bay mare around and headed back out into the pasture.

Beth was back from the restaurant and had saddled her horse while he was working. She spotted him as he was riding away and cantered to catch him and suggested she ride along with him.

When he realized someone was beside him by the reactions of his mare's ears, he turned and welcomed her. As they rode across the ranch, Beth asked if he knew anything about artificial insemination for cows.

Arnold told her that he knew of the process, that it required the use of a veterinarian, and that the cows had to be scheduled for a vaccination prior to the actual insemination. He also said the process helped control the choice of the breed of calf wanted and eliminated the need to have a bull among the herd.

Brenda said she had been thinking of talking to the veterinarian about undertaking that process, and she was interested in Arnold's point of view.

He thought for a while, then said that the procedure had many advantages. The only drawback he could think of was the cost and the need to have a large area in which to keep the cows together during the process. The large fenced area must also provide a way to isolate each cow for the injection and then the insemination.

She said the veterinarian quoted her a price of $35.00 per Herford cow.

As they continued to ride and discuss the artificial insemination process, Arnold periodically thought about his previous debate with himself about why he was becoming involved with Beth.

She is a looker all right. There is no question there. Her smile is radiant. Her blue eyes are warm and friendly. When she looks into my eyes, I lose track and control of my thoughts.

Arnold and Brenda approached a clump of trees where a spring came to the surface, the spring water running through the middle of a secluded circle of trees. The grass surrounding the trees was tall and green. The entire scene was serene. Flowers of lavender poked out from the tall grass that was still green even though it was September. The air was fragrant with their scent.

"Maybe we should stop here," Beth suggested. "It is so beautiful and peaceful. Let's take a minute to enjoy it."

She dismounted from her horse and beckoned Arnold to do the same. Having ridden for most of the day already, this seemed like a good idea to Arnold. Beth pulled a blanket out of one of her saddle bags.

They walked a short distance, to where water from the spring ran over some rocks.

Beth spread a blanket in the deep green grass, squashing some of the flowers. More of their fragrance released into the air. She retrieved sandwiches from her saddle bags and a thermos bottle of coffee. She laid these on the blanket.

Arnold followed Beth and they both sat down cross legged on the blanket.

Beth said, "I have been wondering why you seem to care about my situation?"

"I've been asking myself the same question for hours," Arnold admitted. "You must have read my mind. It is a question I've been asking myself since I left Oklahoma."

"What is your answer to this question that you have asked yourself even before you met me?"

"It is a long explanation," Arnold warned.

"I have all afternoon," said Beth.

Arnold told Beth how fortunate he had been to have a large caring family, a great job with good pay and benefits, a knack for investments, and a few friends. He told her about how disappointed he was in marriage and relationships and how his divorce had seemed to leave him with no future. He told her how he distrusted people because of all the complex and endless responsibilities they embroiled him in.

"I'm searching," said Arnold, "for experiences that might help me decide where my future lies. My plan is to travel and explore the entire United States for as long as it takes for me to decide what my future direction should be."

"You did not mention your religion. That usually helps a person decide their direction."

Arnold waited before answering. He ate part of a sandwich and drank some coffee. He surveyed the beautiful scenery and listened to the water flow over the rocks. He let the fragrance of the flowers reach his senses.

Beth sat patiently.

"My religion is my foundation and very important," Arnold admitted. "It provides me with inner guidance and a strength that works all the time not just when my thoughts turn to God. Before I even knew of your sexual dilemma, before you had shown yourself to me, I felt a commitment to helping you that I cannot explain. After you showed yourself to me, that commitment became stronger. You are someone special, and I decided to help you because it is the right thing to do. I believe, this feeling of rightness is really my father's faith working through me."

He paused a moment, and Beth did not say a word.

"When I recall my past, there is no doubt where my faith comes from, from my father. My father always said, 'always do the right thing regardless of the consequences.' Helping you is doing the right thing regardless of the consequences."

Beth turned to Arnold and hugged him. Tears formed in her eyes. Together they laid down on the blanket and held hands.

Arnold was still thinking about the teachings of his father, and the pain of his father's passing assailed him again from the past. He wished he could talk to him now. He knew he must make a trip back to Oklahoma soon to visit the graves of his parents.

While they lay holding hands on the blanket under the blue sky, smelling lavender and listening to the splashing of the spring water, Arnold tried to explain his turmoil. The thoughts poured out of his mouth where they were diluted and washed by the fresh mountain air. Beth listened without interruption.

"I experienced significant success in the business world along with compensation sufficient to take care of my current needs and my future retirement expenses. Then, there was a downturn in the economy. I experienced losses for the first time and lost my confidence. Everyone had losses, and everyone felt the loss of confidence in business. I worked diligently for two years to recover my losses and to find new opportunities. I did not find any, and I became despondent. Thinking back, I see that I had decided it was too risky to start over. The lack of opportunity on the horizon caused me to lose the will to try again.

My wife's disloyalty and deceit also left me struggling to regain my confidence. Everything seemed so temporary. I thought I would be a fool to count on anything ever again. That is when I decided I needed a rest from it all and drove off to the west on Route 66 looking for experience without responsibility. So far, I have found little experience that comes without responsibility."

"Do you think ranching is the answer?" Beth asked, breaking the silence.

"Only for now," he said.

"I don't know where my choices will take me or what your choices will have to do with mine," admitted Beth.

"Tell me, Beth, about the options the doctors have given you," Arnold said.

"It is kind of late Arnold," Beth pointed out. "I suggest we return to the house before I start that discussion."

"I have forgotten the time. There is work that needs to be done," Arnold noted.

"Yes, there is work to be done," Beth agreed. "But not today. It will soon be dark."

They saddled up and began the ride to the house.

CHAPTER 16

As they returned to the ranch house, they talked quietly about the work that needed to be done.

Beth brought up the cows' birthing time and the need to determine which cow should be taken to auction or shipped to a slaughterhouse.

"How do you normally make that decision?" Arnold asked.

"I contact the people who run the auction, and they will determine which ones are ready or should be ready due to their age and health."

Arnold asked if this was less expensive than hiring cowboys to do it.

"I really don't know because this was the way my father did it."

"It works, so let's call the auction representative and see what happens. Do you have a holding pen to round up the cows in?" Arnold asked.

"The people from the auction house do not seem to need a fence or holding pen. They do it all with the horses they ride," Beth said.

"If you are going to do the artificial insemination, it will be different than loading," Arnold observed.

"Yes. I understand. We need a holding pen. I wonder what my father would do in this situation?" Beth wondered.

Dismounting, they removed their saddles and brushed down the horses. Arnold discovered the feed troughs were bare. He filled them with ample amounts of grain and hay and insured water was available in the watering tanks.

Recalling Beth's wondering about her father and what he would do in a similar situation, Arnold again thought of his father and his frequent reminder, 'Arnold, do the right thing.'

In view of the lateness of the day, Arnold suggested they eat at the restaurant and he would pay for the meal. Beth agreed readily, and they drove to the restaurant, ate a hearty dinner of roast beef and apple pie along with hot coffee. Business at the restaurant was bustling. All five tables were occupied and three take-out orders filled while they were eating.

Maggie sat down at their table and joined them for a cup of coffee.

"I am thinking of taking a vacation," Maggie said, "something I have never done before now."

Before anyone else could comment, Maggie said as if reassuring herself, "Yes. I surely think I will. Can you tend to the restaurant and motel for a month, Beth?" she asked.

"I'll have to think about that, Maggie. I've a lot planned for the ranch. Where do you want to go on vacation?" Beth asked.

Maggie replied, "I want to go as far away from here as my money will pay for."

"I will pay for your travel expenses if you will give me an estimate of how much it will cost," Beth offered.

Arnold stayed silent but followed the conversation with interest.

Following dinner, which was extended due to the lengthy conversation with Maggie, Beth asked Arnold if he was going to stay at the ranch house instead of in the room he had booked at the motel. Affirming that he would, he and Beth stopped by his room to retrieve his clothes and other personal items then returned the room key to Maggie before they returned to the ranch house.

On the way, Arnold asked Beth how she was going to deal with trying to work the motel and restaurant, plus take care of the ranch.

"We've discussed culling cows, repairing fences, building a holding pen for the artificial insemination process," Arnold reminded her.

"Yes. And, I need to converse with the doctor and schedule my surgery," she added solemnly. "I really must think seriously about organizing my life."

As they walked from the truck to the house, the coolness of the evening underlined the changing seasons. Arnold looked at a calendar hanging on the wall as they came into the kitchen. It was the middle of September. In Colorado, that often means snow any day.

Taking care of his business in Oklahoma also crossed his thoughts. He had been gone two months now. Brenda crossed his thoughts. Brenda was not something he could discuss with Beth. As Beth changed clothes, he made a phone call to Brenda and was surprised that she answered.

Once again, Arnold asked Brenda to answer the question he had asked about her and the Chaplain.

Brenda responded in a vague manner that irritated Arnold all over again, and he said, "I will call you after you have had time to decide the answer. In the meantime, here is the number where you can reach me when you decide."

Brenda replied, "Please give me time and it will be okay."

"Why do you want more time?" Arnold asked.

"I am not sure," Brenda replied.

"I hear you, and I am troubled by your answer," Arnold grumbled. He ended the call with a brief, "Goodbye."

Beth returned to living room in clean jeans and a sweater.

"I am trying to decide when to go to Oklahoma," said Arnold. "I've got business to tend to, and I have been away for over two months. What do you expect from me? What do you want me to do?" Arnold asked.

"I need you to stay on the ranch until Spring, help with the insemination process, help with culling the cows to go to the auction, repair fences, and then tend to the spring birthing process," she responded. "That will give me time to have my surgery and recover, and Maggie can go on vacation and return. Hopefully, then we can all live happily ever after."

Before he committed, Arnold asked to see the latest newspaper. Scrutinizing the market page for the current price of cattle, mainly older cows, he realized it had been a while since he had watched the stock market or the price of beef on the farm market.

Beth joined Arnold as he looked at the prices. They discussed the sale of 200 cows weighing 900 pounds each and of 400 calves weighing approximately 300 pounds each. They estimated the sale of the calves would bring .60 per pound and the cows would bring $40.00 each. Together they would net approximately $144,000.00 dollars.

"Do you think I can hire someone to work for Maggie while you work for me while I have surgery?" Beth asked Arnold.

Arnold asked humorously, "Since you are paying me for what I am worth to you and that has been very little, what do you plan to pay me in the future, knowing you will have money?"

"To describe my financial situation now based on the future money I will have would be unfair because I do not yet have the money to which you refer." Beth shot back. "As a matter of fact, I still owe last year's income taxes, which I plan to pay as soon as we sell the cows. Starting with the date of the sale, we will discuss your compensation, which I assure you, will be generous. You will be pleased."

Arnold went to bed completely exhausted. He lay in bed with his eyes wide open, his brain working overtime. Conflict surfaced each time he tried to apply his 'no responsibility' rationale to the situation.

He had no money, his resources were tied up in investments, and time marched on.

One thing became clear. Staying at the ranch until spring would be a good thing for everyone.

If he went back on the road, he would not know where he would sleep at night, where and what he would do during the day, or how much it was going to cost him for all of his travels. The decision to stay at the ranch made all his issues dissolve. He was about to close his eyes in sleep when Beth cracked the door to the bedroom sometime late in the night.

"Are you sleeping Arnold?" she whispered.

"No. Thinking. Is everything okay?" Arnold asked her.

"I can't sleep either," she admitted.

"Would you like to join me?" asks Arnold moving over in the bed.

"Yes," she whispered crawling under the covers next to him. She wore a chamise and panties only. He wore briefs. Their skin warmed where it touched.

"I have never been penetrated sexually, Arnold. My condition has made it uncomfortable to even try, and I'm uncertain about my physical ability to accept penetration by a penis. I'd like to sleep with you though. It would be comforting. Will it be okay with you if we only touch the surface?" she asked.

As she looked into his eyes, she clarified with a smile, "All the surfaces."

Arnold stared into her beautiful eyes and wondered if he would survive such pleasure. She was soft and warm and smooth next to him. He placed his hands on her shoulders and turned her into him.

"I think I can handle it," he whispered against her hair. His hands traveled over her back and then slipped under her panties and over her buttock, continuing down the back of her thighs and pulling her knees up and apart so she straddled his hips. "I hope it is not too much like high school though."

Beth slid her hands down his chest, exploring his chest and stomach. Her hands brushed his arms, following them down to his hands that grasped her behind her drawn up knees.

Releasing her knees, Arnold allowed Beth's legs to straighten and entwine with his. He tipped her over onto her side and explored the front of her body with one large hand while he balanced on an elbow and his other hand spread over her back. His hand skimmed in circles around her breasts and teased her nipples into points before he lowered it to her belly where his one hand almost covered her width from side to side.

His roving hand moved lower to that part of her that seemed male. His palm slid over the penis rising against her silky panties. He paused and pressed. Then he explored beyond to the warmth of her inner thighs. The hardening of her penis against his wrist as his fingers probed the opening to her vagina brought him a confusing fantasy that there were two bodies with him in the bed, a man and a woman. She became wet between her legs like a woman would who was ready for the penetration of a man.

Beth touched Arnold's penis at the same time he touched hers. They both stopped breathing for a heartbeat and stared into each other's eyes, seeing acceptance there at close quarters. Arnold wrapped his arms around Beth. They rolled together. Beth's hands were trapped between their pressing bodies. They undulated, chests rising, hips falling, legs following, pressed together as one body, mimicking penetration and acceptance, like the rise and fall of a porpoise in gentle waves through the sheets. That was as close to matting as they came. Neither felt compelled to go further. They lay entwined and warm under the covers as first Beth then Arnold drifted off to sleep.

CHAPTER 17

Arnold woke early. As soon as he opened his eyes, he knew he was committed to staying until spring, making periodic trips to Oklahoma to take care of his business.

He left Beth sleeping and started a pot of coffee in the kitchen, went to the barn and fed the bay mare he had been riding and Beth's gelding. When he returned to the house, Beth greeted him with a smile and a fresh, hot cup of coffee. They took their coffee out onto the porch.

Arnold informed Beth he had decided to stay until spring.

She hugged him and began to cry.

"I wish you would smile instead of cry," Arnold chuckled balancing the coffee cup through the hug.

"I'm doing both," she said. She smiled, a little of her coffee spilling out of the cup.

"Arnold. I've been thinking. The mare you are riding is getting a bit old for handling cows. Would you like to have a trained quarter horse that is much younger?" Beth asked.

"I would like to do something for you since you do so much for me, and I heard you say last week that you like horses as well as cattle.

Perhaps, you would like to own your own saddle pony, a quarter horse of your own."

"I would love a horse of my own," Arnold replied, "and I agree, it is time for that little mare to retire."

Beth jumped up and went into the house to make a phone call.

Arnold spent the morning fixing more of the fence line. Beth went to the restaurant for her morning shift. When Arnold was in the house eating lunch, Beth's house phone rang. It was a rancher with quarter horses to sell. Arnold made arrangements to meet at the rancher's place late in the afternoon and got directions.

When Arnold arrived at the Rocking R ranch with a horse trailer, the rancher, Edward Richards, led him out to a corral where 10 quarter horses of various ages were milling around.

Arnold studied each one and asked questions of Richards about each one. He finally narrowed it down to two horses he liked. He patiently looked the horses over, lifting their feet, touching their ears, and looking in their mouths. With Richard's permission, Arnold bridled and saddled each one and rode them around the pasture in turns. Both horses were attentive to direction, had smooth gaits, and calm dispositions. Both horses were excellent animals.

"What is the price of the black stallion?" Arnold asked.

"I was instructed to not reveal the cost to you because the horse is a gift," Richards shrugged apologetically.

"What is the price of the dun then?" Arnold asked.

"I would normally charge $700.00 for it because it is trained, but for you it will be $300 because I think I know what you are going to do. You are going to purchase both horses and give the second horse as a gift. Am I right?" laughed Richards.

"You are very perceptive. I will take both horses."

Beth was home from the restaurant by the time he drove in with the two horses in the horse trailer. Beth came out of the house to look in the trailer.

"What are you doing with two quarter horses?" Beth asked.

I'm giving one to you. That is the right thing to do."

Beth clapped her hands and beamed. They hugged and proceeded to unload the horses. At the barn, they saddled the two horses that did not have names yet and rode aimlessly testing their new horses' skills and temperaments.

Arnold was in deep thought. This is a big commitment, he thought. He began to feel queasy and trapped. His return gift of a quarter horse to her on top of Beth's gift of a quarter horse for him increased the commitment between Beth and himself beyond his expectation.

Arnold was really starting to feel poorly then he noticed how good Beth looked on her horse, how happy she looked, how at home she looked. Looking at her, life brightened for him suddenly. He began to dream of possibilities, of challenges and of opportunities for the future.

Even though the wind was cool, hinting at the arrival of winter and the snow that would come with it, Beth brought her horse close to Arnold's and suggested they ride their latest purchases to Maggie's restaurant and have dinner.

"I'll buy this time," she said.

Arnold agreed, and they cantered off in the direction of great food. Once at the restaurant, they tied the ponies to the fence. As soon as they sat down at their table, it became evident that Maggie had heard of his decision to stay and help on the ranch. She had scheduled interviews to find someone to replace her for a month.

Maggie was chattering with the customers as they asked questions about her plans. She spoke excitedly about where she might go, mentioning Washington DC, the Kentucky Derby to see the horse races, and to Israel to visit the birthplace of Jesus. Everyone was stunned by the suggestion of Israel.

"Ah, Israel is my dream," Maggie sighed with tears building in her eyes, "but a trip that far is too expensive."

"Remember my promise Maggie," Beth said. "If you will let me sell my cows and steers, I will pay the price of a round trip to Israel. It is the right thing to do."

Maggie jumped from her chair and hugged Beth, Arnold and three customers who didn't know why Maggie was hugging them. They looked around the room in wonder at what a happy place this was to eat in.

Returning to the ranch house, Beth and Arnold hardly said a word to each other. They were content, enjoying the ride and the easy gait of their new quarter horses. At the barn, Arnold took charge of the mounts, removed their saddles, made sure they were fed and watered and closed the big barn door.

He stood outside the barn thinking of the farm where he had been reared. The work on the farm was similar to that required on the ranch. He felt the need to return to Oklahoma tug at him again. He really should return. It was his responsibility, but he had let life complicate and confuse his priorities once again.

"I will return to Oklahoma soon," he promised himself.

Beth called out to him and wanted to know if he wanted a cup of coffee.

Arnold knew he had a reason to be in Colorado, but one question loomed large: Is Beth really my responsibility, or am I making her my responsibility?

He kept turning it over in his mind. The same issue all over again and Arnold seemed to be powerless to resolve it.

When he reached the porch, Beth met Arnold with a cup of hot coffee. They sat outside and discussed the events of the day. She told him she had scheduled the auction representatives to cull the cows and determine the calves that should be sold.

"This is only the second sale we have had since my father passed on," she informed him.

"The first sale was not successful because the dry weather and withering grass had left most of the cattle in poor condition. This one is going to be great," she said smiling and holding up a pad of paper upon which her calculations were penciled in.

She gave Arnold another hug and reminded him how good it was that he was staying until spring.

"This cool wind tells me that spring is far off and winter just arriving," Arnold said.

"Yes, I noticed," Beth replied, "and I think I will soon need a regular bed partner to help keep me as warm every night as I was last night. Do I have a volunteer?"

"I believe you do," laughed Arnold.

Beth smiled and motioned for him to come indoors.

Because of Beth's sexual condition, she and Arnold touched and cuddled and petted, but did not have intercourse. Both were people alone in the world and the mere presence of another person nearby comforted them even without intercourse.

Morning found Arnold thirsty for coffee and grateful to be alive. He stepped outside to see the sun appear over the mountains in the east. The clear sky lightened with dawn and only a light breeze stirred the changing tree leaves. Oranges, browns, yellows, and bright pinks added color to the hills. Arnold's nostrils flared to catch the aromas of a new day.

As he drank his coffee and wandered aimlessly toward the barn, Arnold could not imagine a more perfect picture. Two beautiful quarter horses stood looking at him from the pasture. They seemed to be begging to be ridden, as if they knew there were miles of ranch land to roam.

'What did I do to deserve this blessed situation I am living in?' He asked himself.

Last night he had spent several hours caressing Beth, a beautiful person who had been born with a condition beyond her control, one she did not choose. His resolve to sign on for the responsibilities involved in running the ranch would allow Beth to grasp at the chance for happiness and normality that surgery presented. He knew he was facing responsibilities beyond his comprehension and levels of commitment beyond anything he had previously attained.

Arnold felt more whole than he had in a while. Instead of repelling him, the responsibilities that went with helping Beth manage the ranch beckoned, even though, he knew they would likely demand from him sacrifice, commitment and resolve.

He returned to the ranch house and ate a large and filling breakfast and asked Beth to schedule her surgery. Following breakfast, Arnold and Beth held each other while Beth drummed up the courage to contact her doctor.

"This is the most difficult decision I have ever had to make. I want so much for everything to go well. I want my life to turn out right, but I dread that the end result will not be a good one. Once, done, I cannot take it back," she worried.

Beth called her doctor and set up an appointment to meet with him in Alamosa that very afternoon. Beth drove herself to her doctor's appointment, and when she returned, Arnold thought she looked distraught, but she stood tall and straight and appeared to be facing the world by herself.

She walked up to him where he stood on the ranch porch and took a deep breath.

"Arnold can we go to our favorite place where the spring is running, the grass is tall and green, and the fragrance is heavenly?"

Arnold saddled the horses up right away, and they reached their spot within an hour. The scene was even more beautiful than it had been the last time they came. It seemed as if the trees deepened their fall colors every hour. They dismounted and lay on the grass. They laid down directly on the grass and felt no need for a blanket. They smelled the fragrance of the grass around them and the nearby lavender. They gazed upwards into the trees.

After a minute, Beth stood up. A light breeze tugged at her hair

"My conversation with the physician has made me very afraid. I might have to stay in the hospital for 2 weeks and recover at home for 3 or 4 months. I have asked the surgeon to remove the penis and the underdeveloped testicles. I will be sterile and would have to take medication for life. There will be significant changes in my voice, my attitude, and my demeanor."

Arnold sat quietly then asked, "In what way will your attitude and demeaner be changed?"

"I really don't want to discuss it now. Just let it be Arnold," Beth replied.

They lay back on the grass and held each other and prayed for guidance from their Lord and Savior, Jesus Christ. Prayer calmed them both.

Beth smiled and asked, "If I schedule the surgery for January or February, will you stay until I'm through the recovery period? That could be well beyond spring."

With a smile, Arnold replied, "Whatever you may need, I will provide, if it is at all possible. I feel better helping you than I would leaving you. It is the right thing to do." Beth smiled at the familiar phrase.

Later that day, after they had returned to the barn, Beth approached Arnold while he was filling feed bins in the barn. Sitting on a bale of hay, she said, "Arnold the doctor is sending written information that describes, in detail, the procedures to be followed, based on my choice of which organ was to be removed, and the projected timeline for the reconstructive surgery if it was required."

"When we see the materials, I can learn more about this procedure. I imagine you already know quite a lot about it, but I am not familiar with any of this," Arnold said.

"I've visited hospitals where this type of surgery is performed several times over the years. I have to choose whether I want to keep the male or the female organs," Beth explained. "I've decided to have the penis and the undeveloped testicles removed. Neither organ will ever be fully developed."

"Is the surgery complicated? How life threatening is it?" asked Arnold.

"The issue is not the danger to my physical wellbeing, it is my inability to accept my situation,' Beth replied.

"I understand," Arnold said, to give her ease, even though he did not really understand.

That night, he sat down at the kitchen table and reviewed all the printed material she had dealing with her condition. After several hours, he decided he needed to talk to an expert so he could ask questions. He returned to the living room and the fireplace.

He wanted to talk about it, but she declined and went to bed. He knew she was worried and confused.

Arnold walked to the barn and tried to clear his head. When he sat on a bale of hay and looked out over the barnyard, he could not focus on any one subject. His mind jumped around from one worry to another. Soon he felt Beth beside him in the barn. She sat down on the hay with him.

"I'm sorry that I shut you out Arnold. The subject is extremely uncomfortable for me to discuss, but I realize you and I have a bond that is too important to carelessly mess up. Come back in the house where it is warm." Beth said.

For a while they sat in silence by the fireplace and then they went to bed. Beth tossed and turned beside him unable to get to sleep. He knew she was seriously worried.

CHAPTER 18

Arnold could think of no way to help Beth through her decision or out of her worry except by his tried and true method of focusing on his faith in God and the business of the day. He decided to get busy, schedule a sale date with representatives of the auction company, contact the veterinarian to discuss the artificial insemination process, and if necessary, construct a temporary corral that would provide facilities for the veterinarian to use.

During breakfast, Arnold asked Beth if she wanted him to handle the scheduling with the auction representatives or leave it for her to do? Beth asked Arnold to do it, and they discussed the process with the veterinarian. Assuming they sold 300 cows and 200 calves, 200 cows will be left needing artificial insemination.

"I will not have money to pay the veterinarian until the cows are sold," Beth reminded Arnold.

"That sets the priority then. I will schedule the sale with the auction representatives today," Arnold replied.

Arnold listened to the latest market report on the radio to refresh his knowledge about current market conditions for cattle. The market was active, so Arnold placed a phone call to the auction representatives and discussed the sales process.

The auction company was eager to have such a large herd of cows to sell and set up an appointment for that day at noon for Arnold with the General Manager, Marc Evans. The meeting would be held at the local restaurant, and Beth agreed to attend. Marc, Arnold, and Beth got along well. The food was delicious and the conversation stimulating and positive. Given these conditions, it was not hard to reach a decision even during a short dinner.

Marc calculated that they would need 10 large trucks to haul the cows to the sale barn and a temporary corral. He would take care of hiring additional cowboys to round up the cows, cull those to be kept and assess the per pound value of the remaining ones.

This information lifted Beth's spirits and she was happy over the news that she would soon have lots of available money, more than she had ever had before. She began talking about the many things she wanted to do to her house. Just seeing her happy made it a good day for Arnold.

Marc asked how they were planning to control the cows during the breeding process.

"We were planning to use the temporary corrals you use during the sale roundup," Arnold said.

Marc readily agreed that they could use them.

"How much will it cost us to rent the corral?" Beth asked

"No cost, for you," Marc said. "We should schedule to have the sale soon, in the next two weeks.

Marc made a call from the restaurant's business phone and confirmed a sale date of November 6.

As they left the restaurant, Arnold asked Beth if she wanted to talk to the banker about the large amount of money that would be transferred by mail. He thought they might need to know if the amount would need special handling due to insurance limitations for protection on deposits.

Beth looked Arnold square in the eyes.

"I have no idea if I want to talk to the banker about 'insurance limitations for protection of deposits.' I don't even know what that is. How do you know anything about such a thing?" Beth asked with a laugh.

"Well then," Arnold said. "Let us proceed to the bank and ask questions."

Upon their arrival, they were introduced to the Vice President of the First National Bank of Commerce, Mr. Newville. He was very helpful and provided important information and suggested ways to handle the nearly $200,000.00 they would be depositing.

They left the bank and returned to the ranch.

It seemed to Arnold that Beth was much happier and not so worried.

"I am extremely pleased with our accomplishments today," she said.

Then she asked, "Since the bank does not insure deposits exceeding a half million dollars, what do you plan to do after I pay you?"

Arnold gave her a questioning look. "I hardly have half a hundred to deposit, how much do you intend to pay me that would cause me concern?" he asked a bit muddled.

"Two hundred dollars," Beth stated.

Two hundred uncommitted dollars, Arnold thought, this was more than he ever dreamed to see again.

Without saying a word, he looked seriously into Beth's eyes, smiled broadly, then gave her a big hug.

Beth asked, "Does this cause you to change your mind about staying until Spring?"

Arnold replied, "No there is too much work to do."

Nightfall was approaching as they pulled into the ranch. Arnold needed to take a ride on his new quarter horse. He also decided to give the stallion and the horse owned by Beth names.

"Have you named your pony?" Arnold asked Beth.

"No, but I have thought about it. Perhaps, 'Autumn time.' That has a nice ring to it. I would name her that because she became mine in the autumn," Beth said.

"Maybe you should name your horse, 'Forever,' Beth suggested, "like a promise."

Arnold didn't think he liked that name, but he didn't say anything. At the moment, he could not suggest another one. The name 'Forever' seemed kind of tame, or too philosophical, for his large, black quarter-horse stallion that exuded life and spirit from the top of its flowing mane to the tip of its long full tail.

He saddled his stallion and went for a ride. It was almost dark as he rode across the ranch.

Arnold became aware of the stallion's smooth gait. He relaxed and let the horse run, enjoying the wind as it caressed his face. He unbuttoned his shirt and let it flap at his sides. The cool wind lashed his chest. He marveled at the feeling of freedom and exhilaration he got from riding on the open prairie.

He decided to give his mount a name that captured the feeling of galloping free and smooth in the wind.

'Shadows' would be an appropriate name, he thought, because the horse slipped swiftly and smoothly through the air, much like shadows do when they slip through the darkness. I'll let that idea rest for a while and see if something better surfaces, thought Arnold.

For some reason riding the stallion allowed his thoughts to drift to Wyoming and his frequent fantasy of camping along the Snake River within view of the snow-capped Tetons. With Beth's surgery date uncertain, he would not likely be able to schedule any camping dates soon.

He could see how the uncertain schedule for the surgery could cause him some depression. He reminded himself, It is Beth's body, Beth's surgery, Beth's future. He wondered if she had progressed yet beyond the worrying stage.

Arnold returned to the ranch house intent on encouraging Beth to make more definite plans for the surgery. He unsaddled the still unnamed stallion and brushed him down before turning him out into the small home pasture.

Inside the house, he found Beth reading information she had received from the doctor.

"Where are you planning to have the surgery?" He asked.

"Pueblo, Colorado," she replied. "The doctor is in Alamosa, Colorado; however, the surgeon who performs the surgeries that are similar to the one I am having is in Pueblo."

"What should we do about taking care of the ranch when we are both gone?" Arnold asked.

"What do you mean?" Beth looked at Arnold questioningly. "Are you going to go to the hospital with me?"

"Do you want me to?" Arnold asked.

"Yes! That would make me happy. I have been concerned about going alone," Beth acknowledged.

"Why have you not raised the subject then?" Arnold asked.

Beth got up and joined Arnold in front of the fireplace and gave him a hug. They sat in silence for a long time, enjoying the peace of the moment that surrounded them.

"I did not know you well enough to pry into your plans," Beth replied after a while.

"Let us get over this kind of thinking and be more open to each other," Arnold suggested.

Beth looked at Arnold.

"I do not even know your last name, or anything else about you. I learn something new every day. So, what is your last name?

"My first name is Arnold and my last name is Barkley. What is your last name?"

"Howser," Beth said. "My full name is Beth Howser."

"Now we are ready for business," Arnold commented.

They let silence fall comfortably between them again.

"Speaking of business, we should discuss my health insurance plan, which should cover both hospital and surgery expenses," Beth said getting up and pulling two sets of paper out of a drawer.

"I purchased the policies several years ago thinking they would be used within a year. The premiums were difficult to pay, but now I am happy that I did."

Arnold and Beth examined the coverage, and Beth showed Arnold an analysis of the plan which had been prepared during discussions with the surgeon and the hospital several years ago.

"I wonder if there have been any changes to this plan?" she wondered aloud.

They agreed it would be smart to contact the hospital, the physician and the surgeon, just to be certain all expenses were going to be covered.

Beth made the call first thing the next morning.

"Arnold, the date of surgery is December 14. The hospital accountant told me that procedures like the one I'm looking at normally cost $50,000.00 to $65,000.00 provided there are no complications. If complications surface, the cost can easily exceed $100,000. The accountant told me that the insurance will cover complications.

Thinking Beth and he had done their best to prepare for Beth's pending surgery, Arnold suggested they take a trip and camp out along the Snake River in Wyoming. After checking the weather, they decided the nights may be too cold for sleeping in a tent, so they prepared to stay in a motel if necessary. Beth had not been too enamored with the idea of camping in a tent anyway.

CHAPTER 19

The closer the date came for Maggie to fly to Israel, the more reality she had to look at. She discussed her misgivings with Beth and Arnold, and she began to question her wisdom in going.

"Sitting aboard a Lockheed Constellation airplane for more than 32 hours with periodic stops to refuel does not seem like such an enjoyable way for a 72-year-old woman to spend her time," she worried out loud.

"I am going to need new clothes and a comfortable pair of shoes to wear when I am touring important sites in Israel. I can't stand shopping at the local store, so I tried to order from a catalog only to find it will take too long for delivery."

Arnold suggested they take a car, drive to Alamosa, purchase her clothing and have lunch and return home, all in one day.

Maggie thought that was a splendid idea.

Shopping with women had never been his favorite task but to do so with two attractive ladies could not be all that bad, thought Arnold.

On the drive to Alamosa, Maggie told Arnold that she had interviewed a new prospect to help in the restaurant.

"I think I like her. Her name is Shoo Ann Audrey," Maggie said.

"Is the lady old enough to know how to act around a bunch of cowboys?" Arnold asked.

"That is not going to be a problem. She is Asian and has seven sisters and four brothers," Maggie said.

"I'm not sure how that is going to be any protection against a horny cowboy who only cares about what she looks like without her clothes and whether or not she indicates she is willing," Arnold said.

"Are you speaking from experience," Beth quipped.

Maggie giggled.

Arriving in Alamosa Arnold suggested he shoot pool while they shopped. This suggestion did not generate a comment from the ladies, but he soon found himself dropped off at a well-lighted building that did not look like an Oklahoma pool hall, but it did contain pool tables, and an attractive female attendant was available for stacking the balls.

"How much does it cost to play pool?" Arnold asked the attendant.

"$3.00 per hour and whatever beer you drink plus whatever beer I drink," came the answer.

Two hours later Maggie and Beth arrived wanting to play pool too. Although the original plan was to return the same day, the afternoon passed quickly with everyone having a good time playing pool. Before they knew it, it was getting dark.

"We need to get a motel room or two," said Arnold. "How many rooms do we need?"

"Two rooms, each with two beds or three rooms," said Maggie.

Three rooms were available, so they took them.

Arnold had not slept with two women before, but he was thinking it might be a good time. Before they went to their separate rooms, Maggie warned Arnold that she sometimes walked in her sleep.

"That is okay with me as long as you can handle whatever you encounter in your walking journey," Arnold chuckled.

"I can dream," Maggie said with a smile.

In the morning, Arnold thought, how am I going to explain to all my friends how frustrating that night was? Sleeping in the same motel with two attractive ladies, but they in separate adjacent rooms. How good life is.

He went down to the motel restaurant for a large breakfast and several cups of coffee. The ladies joined him later, and afterwards, they headed back to the ranch.

They dropped Maggie off at the restaurant and returned to the ranch house.

Arnold ate lunch at the restaurant the next day while Beth was working, and she introduced him to the new waitress Maggie had hired.

"Arnold please meet Shoo Ann Audrey. She will wait on you today."

Arnold saw that she was a beautiful young lady with a great smile.

"Nice to meet you," Shoo Ann said.

"What is your last name?" Arnold asked.

With a friendly smile she said again, "My name is Shoo Ann Audrey. Audrey is my last name."

"Ah. I am a little slow," Arnold told her, "I thought you had three first names. Now I've got it."

Shoo Ann's service was terrific, and Arnold left her a nice tip. Shoo Ann asked him to come back again soon.

When Arnold returned in the mid-afternoon, he received a call from Marc telling him that the auction sale schedule had been moved up to get better rates on the truck rental. Arnold quickly checked the market to determine if there was a disadvantage to selling sooner, and there was none.

He and Marc began to prepare for the roundup and sale. The auction personnel began arriving by 4:00 PM. They installed a temporary corral but made it strong enough to last awhile. They surveyed the barn and loading chute and made the decision to install a new chute along with the corral. A water truck arrived along with a portable tank. Soon the tank was full of water, ready for the cows. In the next day or so, Arnold expected that Marc would let him know when the auction house would be ready to roundup the cows.

Maggie came by and asked Beth if she or Arnold could drive her to the plane in Denver. Beth said she had a conflict, but she thought Arnold would be free to drive her.

Arnold agreed that he had the time.

"We will have to leave early tomorrow because the flight is scheduled to leave at 4:30 PM," Arnold said.

Maggie's flight would arrive in New York around ll:00 PM and leave for Israel at 9:30 AM the next day.

The drive to Denver was enjoyable, but it was mountainous, and many roads were being repaired. When they got to the airport, Maggie's flight was delayed due to mechanical problems and not scheduled to depart until the next day.

Maggie and Arnold decided to stay at a nearby motel because the airline was paying for the expense of the room. The motel room contained two single beds and a radio. As they unloaded their luggage, Maggie indicated she was ready to go to bed. Arnold went to get ice for some drinks and went to the restaurant to purchase wine. Upon his return, Maggie was in her night dress. He looked her over discreetly while he poured wine for both of them.

Maggie's thin arms and legs were still shapely for a woman of her age. Her work at the restaurant kept her in good shape. Her skin gave her age away though; it was slightly wrinkly, thin, and dotted with patches of color. It looked very soft. She helped herself to two glasses of wine and instead of sleeping, she invited Arnold to share her bed.

Arnold did not hesitate. He lifted her face to his and smoothed her skin out against her cheekbones with his thumbs. He then reached down and slipped the flimsy night dress over her head. Without undressing himself, he set her on his lap and kissed her while he explored the lush softness of her breasts and the slenderness of her ribs, waist, and thighs. She was a thin woman. Her skin was slightly loose on her bones, but soft as velvet under his rough hands.

Maggie wrapped her arms around his neck and straddled his knees. She shakily unbuttoned his shirt as his hands roamed over her. Pushing his shirt off his wide shoulders, she happily explored his muscular chest and arms, entwined her hands in his hair and kissed him with her eyes closed.

Arnold stroked her womanhood gently until she squirmed and ripped her lips away from his so she could breathe. She tried to press him back into the bed, but he was too heavy for her. He picked her up and laid her down gently. He unbuckled his pants and shed his underwear in one move. With his shirt unbuttoned, but still over his arms, he pressed down into her and penetrated her swiftly. Their bodies carried them away from there moving them to completion in an age-old rhythm that both were well familiar with.

The night was a busy one for them both.

The following morning, the phone rang, and they were informed by the airline that Maggie's plane would be leaving early. Together they went to the terminal area, and he wished her well as she boarded the flight that would eventually take her to Israel. Arnold reminded her to let them know when she intended to return to Denver. She waved in acknowledgement.

Back on the highway, but barely out of Denver, Arnold saw a large gas station on the corner. Whether it was from being in Denver or from the memory of being satiated after a night of loving, he didn't know, but he thought of calling Brenda. Finding a pay phone in the gas station, he called Brenda and they chatted for a long time. Arnold ran out of coins and they had to pause while he obtained additional coins.

Not long after that, Brenda said they should terminate the conversation because the Chaplain would be coming in soon.

The Chaplain again! Arnold thought.

"What is the Chaplain doing for you now?" Arnold coldly.

Arnold's imagination made him feel sick as he visualized Brenda and the Chaplain in an intimate situation. Brenda insisted she hang up. She did and did not answer his question. Her deceit seemed apparent to Arnold.

His loss here in Denver and his loss in Oklahoma made him feel depressed and slightly lost.

As often was the case, Arnold found comfort driving on the highway. He relaxed and longed for a cup of coffee. Noticing that he had been driving for two hours, Arnold decided breakfast was next on his agenda. He began watching road signs for the next available restaurant, but the stretch of road was sparsely populated.

When a restaurant finally came into view, he also needed to refuel his truck. He filled up at a nearby gas station and made his way to the attached restaurant and took a seat where he could watch people come and go. During his lunch, he wondered if any of the people around him actually knew what they were doing. When he concluded that none did, he knew his thoughts were reflecting his own confusion.

He resumed driving, anxious to get to his new home. After four months, he was starting to think of Beth's ranch house as home. He felt a longing to hold Beth and feel comfortable; something he felt whenever he was close to Beth. He thought about this feeling for a long time. He began to identify what he longed for: genuine affection most of all, the experience of touching and the excitement of chills in his stomach. He thought he had had that with Brenda, but now he was unsure because of the presence of the Chaplain in Brenda's life.

Arriving at the ranch, Arnold retrieved his suitcase from the trunk and proceeded to the house. Beth raced out to meet him.

Seeing Beth running to him, he experienced a flashback of his thoughts in the car. As he and Beth hugged, he decided that he wanted to avoid thinking of the past and wanted to end his depressing and continuous self-analysis of his every feeling and motivation. He vowed to accept things as they came from now on. He held Beth tightly, as though he might lose her.

Enjoy and believe in true love, true acceptance, trust; absence of anger, worry and doubt; just true love and true acceptance, he thought.

He and Beth walked to the house, oblivious to the world beyond themselves. They relaxed by the fireplace and went to bed early.

CHAPTER 20

The next day was Friday, and Arnold awakened early, poured a large cup of coffee and walked to the barn. He put a bridle on his mount and proclaimed that he would name the horse Black Shadow because of the vision he'd had of the horse slipping like a shadow through the darkness.

Black Shadow, much like his master, was large and muscular. He exuded a spirit of strength and freedom. Arnold decided to ride him without a saddle to experience the play of the horse's powerful muscles as he seemed to glide through the space above the ground. He brushed Black Shadow thoroughly, repeating his name several times so it would come to his lips naturally and he would remember it.

Black Shadow was his and he was beautiful. The horse seemed to sense the beginning of a new relationship. He nuzzled Arnold repeatedly and was on his best behavior, standing perfectly still while Arnold brushed his legs, tail and mane.

I feel like a 10-year-old boy with my first horse, Arnold thought.

Arnold mounted Black Shadow and was walking away from the barn when Beth called to him from the yard.

"Can I ride with you?"

"Sure!" Arnold called back.

Arnold dismounted intent on saddling Beth's mount, Autumn Time, for her.

"May I ride bareback like you?" Beth asked.

"Get aboard." Arnold replied. "I'll hold Autumn Time for you."

The early morning sunrise was beautiful. The air was crisp, just cool enough to remind them of the upcoming winter. The quarter horses were frisky, their nostrils wide, and their muscles responding quickly to any command to run.

Beth smiled with excitement and encouraged her mount to go faster and faster. Arnold asked Black Shadow to stay abreast of Autumn Time, and the horse responded as though he understood. Arnold remembered that Autumn Time was a mare. He wondered if Black Shadow had been stripped of his stallion instincts. Then thought that Autumn Time was probably not in season or his horse would not be so well behaved.

Watching Beth and the manner in which she rode her mount, Arnold marveled at her expertise. Their relationship was really pretty new. There were many things they did not know about each other.

They didn't talk as they rode and soon arrived at their favorite place on the ranch, the site of the spring. They each enjoyed a handful of water from the spring. The water was cold, just right for drinking, but too cold for bathing.

Arnold found that he wanted to talk about relationships, relationships between two people, not between people and horses. Arnold approached the subject and asked Beth how she would describe their relationship with each other.

She looked straight at Arnold searching his expression. She took his hand and gave it a tug.

"Let's lay down on the grass," she suggested. "Lay right beside me."

Arnold was more than eager to do this, and they lay close to each other, face to face in the grass.

"Arnold tell me about your childhood. Tell me about where you have been, where you attended college. Were you in the military? Where have you been employed? How are you able to travel and not worry about incurring expenses? Did you ever belong to a church? Did you and do you have brothers or sisters? Who are your friends? Do you have friends? What are your plans for the future? Do you plan to get married? Do you plan to have children? Will you stay on the ranch beyond spring? Where will you go after you leave in the spring? Do you think we will see each other again after you leave in the spring?"

Arnold laughed. "How can anyone respond to you with all that information before breakfast and another cup of your coffee?"

Beth replied, "We must return immediately then for breakfast at the restaurant and settle in front of the fireplace. Then both of us must talk and exchange information like the type I asked for."

"You are right. My brain has been thinking these same questions for days and I'd like answers to them all."

"I agree as long as you are truthful with me about everything."

They jumped up from the grass, remounted their horses, and raced each other to the restaurant. The two horses rested as Arnold and Beth ate.

Shoo Ann Audrey presented them with a menu and asked what they wanted to drink.

Arnold replied, joking with the new waitress, "A Jack Daniels and seven up, and Beth would like some kind of wine."

"I wish I could get that for you, but I am not 21 and cannot serve alcoholic beverages." Shoo Ann said.

"That is okay, I will have coffee and Beth can tell you what she wants."

Beth said, "Water."

They enjoyed their breakfast and returned to the ranch house intending to have a long conversation. Arnold put additional wood on the fire, and they sat back in the armchairs in front of the stove.

Trying to remember each item Beth had asked him to talk about concerning his childhood, Arnold began at the beginning, intending to tell everything.

"I was born in a farmhouse on 160 acres of Oklahoma soil; graduated from Calumet high school; attended the University of Oklahoma until I ran out of money; then, I joined the U. S. Air Force, went to Morocco, was reassigned to the States, refused to reenlist, and returned to civilian life.

I worked at several jobs until I got lucky and met a contractor who wanted my services. After I worked hard for a long time, the economy went sour. I resigned and planned to invest my money and live like a king.

I was lucky enough to have earned enough money to pay for years of enjoyment if I closely monitored my pennies. My relatives died leaving me as the only survivor. While I was in the business of investing, I lost my friends, my relatives and one wife who refused to be happy with one man. I found her in bed with another man. I ultimately disowned her. Later, her lover was killed in a car accident. We had no children.

I have a few friends. I am currently traveling to experience new and exciting adventures.

Ultimately, I want to find out about myself, who I really am and/or what I want to become. I do not want to hurt anyone, but instead I want to help people where help is needed and appreciated. I do not want grief. I do not want to cause grief."

He paused and took a long breath.

"Beth, now it is your turn. But first, did I answer your questions?"

"Almost." "Did you become a Christian? What church did you belong to? Are you planning to marry again and have children?"

"You will need to ask Jesus what church I may belong to, whether I will marry again, or have children. This is all in the future. As He is my Lord and Savior, He will determine my future. Before I can answer these questions, I must figure out who I am and what I want to do and why. These things remain unclear and uncertain to me.

During my business career, I earned a lot of money, invested it wisely and now I am enjoying the fruits of my labor. However, I have become perplexed with corporate America because it has become rotten to its core with dishonesty, corruption, selfishness and greed at every level. I choose not to participate any more except in the investments I have already made. Hopefully, I will continue to succeed and be happy," Arnold answered. Then he added, "Right now, I am interested in you and your pursuits and that is my only focus for the immediate future. Beth—it is your turn."

Beth smiled and began, "First, let me be candid. There is a part of me I cannot explain because I do not understand it, my condition, myself. Having said that, I am technically a hermaphrodite, meaning I have sex organs of both male and female, a penis and a vagina, both of which are only partially developed.

I am 38 years old. My mother died the same month my father died, six years ago. I had a great relationship with my father until I was 15 when he tried to have sex with me and found I had a penis instead of a vagina. As it turned out, he was mistaken because he did not explore me long enough to find out I had a vagina too. We did not have a loving relationship after that, but he never tried to have sex with me again. Instead, he disowned me and refused all affection. My mother continued to love me until she died 21 days before my father died.

I have no living relatives except Maggie. I refer to her as my aunt, but she is not a real aunt. She needed a home. I needed someone to help me. So, we agreed to the relationship we have now. She manages the restaurant and motel. She lives in a part of the motel that was converted to a suite for her. We have only a verbal contract that either of us can terminate at will.

I have never dated a man or had sex with anybody. I have not traveled outside of Colorado. I plan to have surgery in about three weeks. I am eager to develop a sound relationship with one Arnold Barkley, and I await my future eagerly."

After her disclosure, Beth sat, rigid and uncomfortable. Arnold felt helpless to reassure this woman he was becoming very fond of. All he could think to do was hold her and assure her everything was going to be okay. The term "sound relationship" sounded like such a good thing to him that it stuck in his head like a song that sticks in your brain and is sung over and over.

Arnold knew he was so much more experienced than Beth. He had years of experiences crammed into deep crannies in his head. His recent experience with Maggie loomed as an issue, but he knew it would not hang around in his conscience for long. He and Maggie were not married. They were both experienced adults. They had sex for the momentary pleasure of it and had moved on.

Beth moved closer. "Can I be specific about my worries?" she asked.

Arnold said, "Sure, that is what this is all about."

"I have started falling in love with you, Arnold, and I have never experienced such deep feelings before. I am afraid this is a one-way trip, for me, but not for you. Just think of it," she continued. "One day you appeared in the restaurant and I waited on you. Next thing I know you are working for me at the ranch and living in my house. I cannot believe how good you are to do what needs to be done without my asking. I do not know how you know what to do and when, but you do. The next thing I realize, I want you in my bed. I enjoy everything you do. I want more.

You comfort me when I cry. You handle my business dealings as though they were your own. You make decisions that are sound and that

I totally approve of. I worry it is all going to end. So far, the dream continues, but and I am afraid of its end. Do you understand?"

Arnold was mesmerized. The words he needed would not come. He said the only thing that he could think of to say. "I need to think about your comments, and I promise I will. When I have thought through each word, I will respond to you in a loving and understanding way. For now, do not be afraid."

As he rose from the couch and started to walk to the barn, the thought that always came to him whenever he was stressed entered his mind: He thought of camping along the Snake River where he could see the snow atop the Teton mountains and listen to the flow of the water rushing down the Snake River. For the most part, it was just a dream, unrealistic; but he keeps thinking of it. Perhaps someday it will come true, and he will truly enjoy his visit.

Wyoming and the Snake River, here I come. My brain and emotions need a rest.

CHAPTER 21

When Arnold approached the barn, Black Shadow trotted over to the open door and nuzzled his shoulder. It made Arnold smile to think the horse recognized him and liked having him around.

As he stroked Black Shadow's neck, the conversation with Beth continued to swirl in his brain. He needed to think about it and decide how to respond to Beth. She truly needs someone to comfort her and to be true to her.

I am beginning to think that I am that person, the one who will be good to her and be true, thought Arnold.

Conversations with his late father and mother resurfaced in his mind and mixed with recollections of his experience with his ex-wife. It has been several years since he last spoke with Charlene, and he intended to keep it that way. While memories of his ex-wife were sufficient to stifle his confidence and send his emotions into a tumult, the words of his father and mother continued to inspire him and keep him on an even keel, even when the situation seemed complicated.

In situations like the one he was encountering with Beth, his father's and mother's saying, "always do the right thing" could provide guidance if he could determine what the 'right thing' was. The saying originated with the Bible. His father and mother would spend hours and hours reading and discussing the words of the Bible and say to him in loving terms, "these messages originated with Jesus Christ, have been passed to us through the Bible and other books and we emphasize them to you because we are people who love you for who you are." His parents had made sure that the words of the Bible would always mean more to Arnold than any other guidance he received.

As Arnold thought about what the right thing might be to do, the subjects Beth had talked to him about came to mind. He decided that he needed to write the problem and options available to him down on paper to help him decide what "was the right thing." Writing would help him capture the many thoughts running around in his head. His decision made, Arnold brushed Black Shadow from his mane to his heel, fed him new hay, made sure he had fresh water and departed for the house and the manual typewriter.

Beth met him with a cup of hot coffee and a kiss. When he told her that he needed to spend some time alone to sort out his thoughts and prepare an answer for her in writing, she showed him to the office. Beth gave him a quick hug and left the office, closing the door quietly behind her.

Arnold began to think and began to write:

First,

Dear Beth,

You can be assured that I, Arnold, will try my best to be honest with you. I will not keep secrets from you that come into my life from this time forward. I acknowledge that I have lived a confusing and complex life prior to this and there are some things that occurred that I cannot tell anyone about, even you.

These happenings are sad. Some were cruel and some are legalistic that still may cause harm to me in the future. I cannot be responsible for these situations because I cannot predict what may happen as a result of actions other people may take.

Beth, I believe I understand your situation; you need to have a surgical procedure performed to correct a certain condition that occurred at birth. I intend to help you in any way I knows how and will continue helping you for an extended time following surgery. This includes working on the ranch and taking care of whatever needs to be done until you are able to return and manage the ranch activities.

I hope to live with you during this time and share our lives in any manner you deem appropriate. Doing the right thing has many meanings, but it does not include causing you harm in any manner. I do not intend to be made wordless by sad events. I intend to help you deal with life and will not run when you decide to discuss complex subjects with me. We may not always agree with each other, but I will not be deceitful in dealing you.

Here, I'd like to discuss the subject of love. Due to a situation that occurred a long time ago —I was in a marriage that began with an abundance of love. This love discontinued for reasons beyond my control. The reasons, however, were not ones I could accept and continue to live within that marriage. — This may not be very clear, but all I can tell you about this situation follows: The negative emotional effects of the legal process from that period of my life have not been easy for me to forget or forgive even to this day. I still visualize a man, not myself, a stranger, entering my wife sexually. The violation stays in my head, and I cannot forget it or otherwise get it out of my consciousness. It lingers, frequently recurring in my mind. I fear the effect this may have on my future relationships.

It has been 2 years since my divorce was final. I have avoided developing serious relationships with anyone since that time. I am fearful of becoming committed to someone for any length of time. Having said that, I am struggling with the situation I face with you. I believe you are a special person with special needs, and I believe I can help you, but I am not sure I can love you the way you want to be loved. I will do my best not to hurt you. I hope to avoid causing you or myself any grief as a result of my past.

Again, I will be honest and tell you that I sometimes think of my past and sometimes walk and think of ways to deal with something I cannot fix. I must learn to forget it.

It will become important for the two of us to become aware of each other and our quirks. Therefore, we must discuss everything we can discuss, and I promise to be a good listener.

Arnold

After signing the document, Arnold made a copy and gave the original to Beth.

They sat on the couch, in front of the fireplace and she read what he had written. She read it a second time. This time loud enough Arnold could hear her. After that, they hugged for a long time.

"Arnold can you tell me more about your ex-wife?" asked Beth.

"I do not want to talk about her, not even mention her name. I'm trying to deal with the loss of that love and affection. I believe these two factors are fundamental to any relationship and are extremely difficult to live without especially when you once had both. For years I cried whenever a thought of her came to my mind, and now I get angry concerning the entire event and want to avoid thinking of her and all we went through. I went through two years of counseling to forget, but it has not worked. Now, I have implemented my own plan of action, that being to travel, camp out as much as I can and enjoy mother-nature at her best. I substitute mother nature for love and affection and sexual satisfaction. I only encounter people, enjoy whatever they bring to me and heal my wounds."

"What about living relatives, such as brothers and sisters, and possibly parents?" asked Beth

"I had a large family of 5 brothers and 7 sisters. Sickness and accidents have taken all of them leaving no relatives except uncles, aunts and hordes of cousins. They are fun loving and good people, but I do not want to share my life with them, or anyone, except perhaps you," replied Arnold.

"How can you afford to travel, Arnold, since you don't have a job and camp out, living by yourself and earning very little money?" Beth asked.

"I once had a job where I made a lot of money, Arnold said. "I made great investments and lived frugally. I enjoyed fantastic luck."

"I am very interested, Arnold. Please explain," Beth encouraged.

Arnold responded in a general manner.

"First, I worked for a long time at managing people, doing contract work, which was lucrative for several years before the Republicans and Democrats decided to ruin the economy and things went sour. Then, I purchased a nice investment as a venture capitalist. That has paid me handsomely for a long time and continues to do so today. I also inherited mineral rights on a farm in Oklahoma. Had I not encountered such legal expenses when my wife filed for a divorce, I would now be a wealthy person. Considering everything that has happened, I try not to worry about anything. I try to avoid making serious mistakes in the way I live, and I practice helping and loving people. All the while, I try not to be angry at the things that occurred in the past. For some reason, those events continue to haunt me."

Beth asked Arnold if he needed more money to live on than what she was paying him.

He responded, "No. I haven't spent the money you have already paid me."

"I can pay more if you need more." Beth said. "I understand that you have assets, but I do not understand how you can live without using any money. I admit that I do not pay you much. Do you enjoy this type of lifestyle? You have only purchased two pair of jeans since arriving at my house and not even a new shirt. Why?" she asked.

"Beth, I have spent hours and hours asking myself that same question and there is no answer. I've tried to eliminate emotion from my life, even remove the source of emotion and the occasions that cause it. I have failed. I still have feelings about many things. In order to deal with that, I travel alone and camp out and enjoy mother-nature and whatever God presents for us to enjoy."

Beth looked at Arnold and asked, "Do I cause you to become emotional?"

"I became emotional the first time I heard your story," replied Arnold.

"You cause me to become emotional too. I cannot avoid thinking of you and all that you have encountered in life. I want to play a significant role in changing your outlook in life," Beth admitted.

"I thought you were beautiful the moment I saw you," said Arnold. "I have not changed my mind even in the face of all you have told me. I want to live happily for a long time. I anticipate the future to be a good one and will strive to make it so."

Beth hugged him and Arnold hugged her back.

Arnold excused himself and went to the barn. He saddled Black Shadow and started to go for a ride. As he exited the barn, Beth came running to meet him and asked if she could join him.

"Come along," he said. "I know we will enjoy a ride together. It will clear our heads."

The weather was cool and both horses seemed to need exercise. Their gait was spirited, and they held their heads high. Black Shadow nuzzled Autumn Time and it occurred to Arnold that a romance may be in the offing. Stranger things have happened.

Beth and Arnold rode with a cool breeze blowing in their faces refreshing them. Soon Beth made a looping turn and headed to their favorite place. They were welcomed by a covey of quail and several cottontail rabbits. Listening to the quail, made Arnold think of the farm where he was raised in Oklahoma. He became nostalgic recalling good times. As Beth dismounted and spread a blanket on the grass, he thought it might be cool enough to warrant a small fire.

He began to gather small tree limbs and twigs and place them next to the blanket. When he started a small fire, Beth was pleased as the breeze was cool. Autumn Time and Black Shadow moved away displaying their natural discomfort with being close to smoke and fire. Arnold joined Beth on the blanket as they watched Black Shadow again began to nuzzle Autumn Time, he rose to mount her, and she remained perfectly still to accommodate her stallion. Twice more, Black Stallion mounted Autumn Time. The third time, he was erect and ready.

Beth made a note of the date and time for future reference.

"I hope Autumn Time enjoyed that," Beth commented.

"I do to. Sometimes once is not enough," Arnold replied.

"Just like men and women," said Beth lethargically.

The two of them lay close to each other on the blanket and began to think of their recent discussions. Feeling the warmth of the fire, they relaxed, dozed and dreamed.

Later returning to the barn, Black Shadow pursued Autumn Time, and it was a struggle to keep him away from her while Beth was riding her. They headed directly to the barn and quickly removed both saddles and bridles so the horses could be free to follow nature's direction.

Arnold found it hard to take his eyes off the mare or stallion as they each seemed to enjoy their coupling and mated again and again. He noticed Beth was as engrossed in this activity as he was. After a while, Arnold and Beth adjourned to the house.

Upon entering the ranch house, the two sat by the fireplace. Beth moved his hand to her breast as they snuggled. This touching was all the intimacy they pursued.

"When the time comes when we can really have sex, you will need to assist me because I have never had sex before, and I might be clumsy," Beth murmured.

"We can use a little practice," Arnold suggested and pulled her gently down on the rug in front of the fire. Arnold was patient and touch Beth everywhere, stimulating her desire and allowing her to enjoy the time.

"I'd like to experience the full pleasure of having an orgasm Arnold," Beth whispered in his ear. "You need to be prepared when it is time."

Arnold continued to touch, stroke and press her, drawing her along to completion. He found this experience to be very enjoyable though different. She cried out and clutched Arnold tightly. Her body arched in pleasure and all her words caught in her throat for a long minute.

When her body relaxed, she was happy and groggy. He would not forget that night in front of the fireplace.

In their distraction, they forgot to set up the coffee for the next morning and morning came too early for either of them. Arnold made a pot of coffee, poured a large cup for Beth and one for himself and went to the barn to check on the horses.

When he came back in, Beth helped him research her condition. December 14, the day of surgery, was fast approaching. He read through everything Beth had on the subject of hermaphrodites and sex modification surgery. He wanted clarity about what the expectations were for this kind of surgery. The subject soon tired both of Arnold and Beth. Beth suggested they go to the restaurant and eat dinner.

CHAPTER 22

That evening eating at the restaurant, Shoo Ann waited on Beth and Arnold.

"What can I get you?" she asked.

After they had ordered and she had turned the orders in for the cook, Shoo Ann came back to the table.

"I would like to buy a quarter horse and house it at your ranch. Would that be possible?" she asked.

"Do you know how to ride?" Beth asked.

"No. I don't know anything about horses, but everyone who comes in here talks about how much they enjoy their saddle pony," Shoo Ann said. "I think I am missing a lot of fun and want to learn how to ride. Do you know anyone who could and would teach me to ride?"

Beth looked at Arnold and asked, "Will you?"

Arnold looked from one woman to the other, then said, "Yes. I will, but how are you going to buy a quarter horse, pay for his feed, water and housing?"

"Also, do you already have a saddle and bridle?" Arnold asked.

"What is all that stuff?" Shoo Ann asked.

Beth and Arnold laughed, enjoying her innocence.

"I can work in exchange for the horse boarding expenses," Shoo Ann suggested. "I can cook and clean and make coffee."

Beth nodded. "I think that will work out well," she said.

"Is the horse going to be a him, or can it be a girl?" Shoo Ann asked.

"That is up to you. We will find whichever you want," said Beth.

"Make it a girl then," Shoo Ann decided. "Trying to learn about men around here is difficult enough. I do not want another male to try and understand."

Arnold snorted and Beth along with the customers at nearby tables laughed when they heard this.

Following dinner, Beth and Arnold returned to the ranch and looking around the barn began to plan where they would put another pony, saddle and bridle.

"We will make room," Beth said.

Before we had even entered the ranch house, Shoo Ann came walking through the yard and asked if she could take a riding lesson since she was off work and had nothing else to do.

"You can ride Autumn Time if Arnold will give you a lesson now," Beth volunteered.

"Do you really want to ride this late in the day?" Arnold asked.

Shoo Ann replied immediately, "Yes," and started for the barn.

Arnold followed her. When they got to the barn. Arnold showed Shoo Ann how to safely work around and handle a horse. She was very interested and listened closely. Arnold showed her how to put the tack on a horse by putting the bridle, saddle blanket, and saddle on Black Shadow.

He then asked Shoo Ann to lead Autumn Time from the barn and he brought out a bridle, saddle blanket and saddle.

"You go ahead and put these on Autumn Time, while I watch," Arnold instructed.

Shoo Ann did a remarkable job and needed only a little assistance. She had a good memory. Arnold was impressed and asked Shoo Ann if she knew how to mount the horse, to which she replied, "Yes," and jumped up on Autumn Time using the stirrup and sat in the saddle.

Arnold swung up on Black Shadow, and the two riders headed east away from the barn. Autumn Time followed Black Shadow and there was little for Shoo Ann to do except stay in the saddle and enjoy the movement of the horse beneath her. After a while, Arnold dropped back so that he and Black Shadow followed Autumn Time. Shoo Ann did not know how to guide Autumn Time, so the horse took the lead and wandered along a route she was familiar with. They ended up at Beth and Arnold's favorite place where the grass was green, and the spring ran among the trees. The horses paused, Arnold dismounted, and Shoo Ann followed.

Once they were off the horses, they sat down and discussed Shoo Ann's riding experience. Arnold told her how to steer the horse using the reins and how to hold them in one hand. They remounted their horses and returned to the ranch house with Shoo Ann in the lead, practicing her steering.

After they were done putting the horses up for the night, Arnold invited Shoo Ann to come to the ranch house and discuss specific details about the purchase and housing of the pony that she wanted to buy.

Beth invited Shoo Ann to stay the night and asked her when she worked at the restaurant again.

"Not tomorrow, but the next day," Shoo Ann replied. "I'd love to stay. Thank you for thinking of it."

Arnold was puzzled about where she would sleep because the spare room was packed with boxes and there was only one bed and a couch.

Beth volunteered that Shoo Ann could sleep with her. "Right now, we only have one bedroom set up," she said. "If we are going to have a guest for a while, we will need to clean out the other room and put a bed in there.

I have never slept with two women. I have no idea how that would work, thought Arnold.

Since neither woman invited him to join them, he prepared to sleep on the couch. The couch was pretty uncomfortable for a man of his size, and his feet hung over the end unless he curled up on his side. His mind also would not rest. He kept imagining what it would be like to be invited into the bedroom to see two women make love to each other, especially when one of them had both sets of sex organs and the other had a desire for both.

His sleep was not peaceful that night.

Waking early the next morning, he needed hot, black coffee and some time to himself to think. He decided to go for a ride on Black Shadow and drank his coffee on the way to the barn. Black Shadow was eager to run. A cool breeze blew in Arnold's face as Black Shadow swept through the countryside at a smooth gallop. Frost sparkled on the hills and the grass in the chilly morning. Black Shadow's stride was long and smooth. Losing himself in the power of his stallion, Arnold's heart and mind quieted. He felt at home on Black Stallion's back. He fit the powerful horse well. Weaving through trees and leaping over shallow ditches, the two of them seemed to be made of one muscle, strong, sleek, and male. He felt well. Atop Black Shadow, he was able to think that all was well, and that all would be well.

Arnold had no idea how far he rode. He wondered if he would find the boundary fence of the ranch. He held onto the dreamlike sense of wellbeing for as long as he could. Occasionally, he saw cows grazing in small bunches eating the mature grass before it was buried by snow.

Dreamtime is over, he thought, feeling the direction of his mind shift from living in the moment to wondering what would come next.

Arnold pressed Black Shadow with his knees and the two of them made a wide turn at a slightly slower speed and headed back in the direction of the barn and ranch house.

By the time the barn came into view, he had slowed Black Shadow to a walk. The horse was hot and sweaty, but his breathing was already returning to normal. Beth followed by Shoo Ann came out to the corral to greet him.

Beth wanted to know if he wanted some breakfast. Arnold said he did.

After Arnold brushed Black Shadow and fed and watered him, the three decided to go to the restaurant and enjoy a big breakfast.

While eating bacon, biscuits, gravy and sausage, Beth received a restaurant house phone call from Marc Evans, the man who represented the auction house. She took the call in Maggie's office and returned to the table after a short conversation.

"Marc intends to round up the cattle to sell early tomorrow," Beth said to Arnold. "They will load trucks the next day. He will arrive later today to mark the cows to be sold. He wanted to know who from the ranch would be available to confirm the identification of the cows for sale, and I told him you would be."

"When will he be here?" asked Arnold.

"He said about 1:00 PM," Beth said.

CHAPTER 23

From the restaurant, Arnold rushed to the bank where, leaving Beth in the truck he jumped out and went in to review the current cattle market. It looked active and rising.

Arnold quickly concluded that selling 300 cows and 200 calves was going to bring in a lot of money.

Perhaps, he thought, we will have some luck and get a good price.

Back in the truck, he looked at Beth.

"I estimate the total sale will amount to approximately $146,000.00 net to you. That is based on the price reflected in the current market of $300.00 for each cow and .40 per pound for each calf. The calves will weigh an average of 700 pounds each. The hauling expense and commissions will cost around 3% of that, or $4,300.00.

"That is a very good profit I think," said Beth.

"Now that the sale will happen soon, we need to schedule the artificial insemination with the veterinarian. We are already late for that. The calves will be born in August instead of May, which is preferred. We also will need extra hay for the young calves next winter," Arnold commented to Beth.

"Arnold, I did not think of any of that when we discussed the artificial insemination, and you spin out this information as though it was common knowledge."

"Lots of experience is all," Arnold said. "It is necessary to plan ahead and purchase the hay while it is available. It is best to have it in the barn before you need it. Also, we do not have a lot of time because your surgery is coming up in less than two weeks. I will need to be here when the hay is delivered. I don't want to be here tending to the hay delivery when I should be at the hospital with you."

Beth reminded Arnold that he could order the hay through Marc and the auction facility.

Arnold was relieved to know that and set about calculating how much hay they would need if the 200 cows deliver 200 calves all of them in need of feed for December, January, and February. This, he calculated would require 40 bales per month for three months, or 120 square bales of hay.

When Marc arrived at 1:00 PM to begin the process of sorting out the cattle to be sold, Arnold asked him about buying hay from him. Marc quoted a price of $300.00 for the 120 bales delivered and stacked.

"Where do you want them stacked?" asked Marc.

"In the barn on the north side." He showed Mark where he wanted the hay stacked. "Will it be okay if I am not here when it is delivered?" asked Arnold.

"Yes. That will be okay," Marc said.

Arnold turned to Beth and told her he did not need to be present when the hay was delivered by Marc's crew.

Then, Beth received a call from her physician scheduling a presurgical evaluation for the next day at 9:00 AM,

"Arnold, can we get to Pueblo for an evaluation tomorrow at 9:00 AM?"

"We can make it if we leave early tomorrow. I think we should use my truck since the farm truck is getting somewhat unreliable for long trips. We will also need to return quickly to round up and load the cattle. The December schedule is getting full," Arnold said.

The next morning, Beth and Arnold left early in the morning, leaving Marc separating cows for sale according to their directions. They loaded the truck for a quick trip to Pueblo and a return. The weather for December was good. The sky was clear, and there was no sign of snow. They arrived in Pueblo in time for Beth's appointment.

Arnold had to wait in the waiting room while the surgeon and his team evaluated Beth. The nurse said she could not let him be present since he was not family. This was disconcerting for Arnold and he demanded a detailed briefing from Beth's family doctor while the surgeon was present. The nurse agreed this was possible. He was skeptical and was concerned that it would not occur.

Beth entered the evaluation area and Arnold waited. Several hours passed with the nurse periodically keeping him up to date. After five hours had passed, the nurse approached him and said, "Beth's physician and the surgeon wanted to brief both of you in about 20 minutes."

Arnold agreed and waited, but not patiently. He began to fret and asked himself, how did he get into this situation? While waiting, he thought of his mother and father and the advice that they had given him over and over, again, "Do the right thing." Thinking of his parents and their admonition, Arnold relaxed and felt confident he was doing the right thing for Beth by being there for her to lean on. The nurse, physician, and surgeon arrived with Beth. Beth appeared calm. She grasped Arnold's hand and gave it a tight squeeze.

She smiled and said, "It's okay. We are doing fine. Sorry you had to wait so long."

The physician introduced himself, the nurse and the surgeon and proceeded to conduct a formal briefing. At this juncture, an administrative person with a new typewriter on a portable table joined their meeting and began documenting the conversation. The surgeon promised a copy of her documentation. Arnold thought the procedure was well planned and relaxed again.

The team of surgeons had decided to begin the procedure that day. The surgery would be conducted in three phases: phase one to begin on the first day, phase two in two weeks, and subject to satisfactory healing, phase three would begin two weeks later, and then Beth would be released if she was healing well, possibly one week following the last procedure. The doctor said that Beth would remain in hospital, the entire time with periodic physical therapy treatment to facilitate healing and emotional wellbeing.

"It is expected Beth will be released from the hospital about one week following phase three," said the hospital administrator.

"Do either of you have any questions?" the surgeon asked.

"When will I be admitted to the hospital?" Beth asked.

"In 30 minutes if you are ready?" The nurse said with a reassuring smile.

Beth and Arnold met privately for about 15 minutes and discussed the change of plans. Arnold agreed to remain with her following the first phase of surgery plus a couple of days subject to how well she was progressing then would return home and take care of the ranch with plans to return for phase two.

Considering all the work they had scheduled at the ranch, Beth said, "You probably will want to return tomorrow because the marking of the cows to sell will be in progress."

"I'll stay with you tonight. I'll see you after surgery and return to the ranch tomorrow for a couple of days then return for the next phase of surgery if all is going well," Arnold agreed.

Beth was groggy when Arnold visited her later that day but seemed to be doing fine. The surgeon and nurse briefed Arnold. They planned that she would start physical therapy scheduled the next day. Arnold ate his dinner in the hospital cafeteria and then rented a guest room on the hospital premise. The next morning, he when back to Beth's room. She was waiting for breakfast and was pale against the hospital gown. She smiled when he entered the room.

"It is okay for you to go Arnold. I feel mostly like sleeping anyway."

Arnold gave Beth a kiss and departed for the ranch.

When Arnold drove into the ranch, the process of marking the cows was in full swing. He saddled Black Shadow and rode through the herd confirming and taking notes about each cow and calf to be retained and those to be sold. This process took him all day to complete.

Several trucks arrived and the cows and calves were loaded. Since the sale would occur at the auction barn, he decided to attend. Mark informed him the check would be made out to Beth Howser with hauling and commissions subtracted from the total. He also said the check would be ready one hour after the last animal was sold.

Arnold was feeling very tired probably from the long day in the saddle coupled with the drive from Pueblo and the long day sitting in the waiting room worrying the day before.

He decided to eat dinner at the restaurant and retire early to rest both his bones and his mind. As he entered the restaurant, Shoo Ann waited on him and provided a good cup of coffee without him asking.

She asked what he wanted to eat and delivered it without delay. He informed her about Beth and his trip to Pueblo. Maggie was also interested, sat down at his table and listened to every detail. Maggie asked how he was going to work the ranch, sell the cows, haul hay and visit Beth.

Arnold replied, "I will handle it somehow."

Maggie asked if he wanted to hire someone to help. She volunteered the names of two cowboys who were familiar with ranch work, including hauling and stacking hay. Arnold asked if she had their phone numbers, which she provided.

Shoo Ann asked if she could use Beth's pony Autumn Time so she could practice riding horses. She said she did not have the money to purchase her own plus the saddle, bridle and blanket. He told her that would be okay as long as he was around when she practiced riding.

The next morning, Arnold saw that the loading of cattle for market was completed without incident and the hay was delivered and stacked in the barn. He decided he did not need more help so did not call Maggie's cowboys.

About mid-morning, Shoo Ann came walking across the barn-yard heading for the house when Arnold yelled at her from the barn where he had been relaxing on a bale of hay. She was jolly, wanted to ride Autumn Time and volunteered to put the saddle and bridle on. Arnold continued relaxing on a bale of hay and watched Shoo Ann saddle up Harvest time. Watching Shoo Ann pick up the saddle and put it on correctly was interesting. Her petite body looked as if it hardly strong enough to lift the saddle.

He suggested they go for a ride and practice horsemanship. Arnold mounted Black Shadow with only a bridle and no saddle. He sometimes preferred riding bareback on short rides. Shoo Ann enjoyed her riding lesson and wanted to continue for a longer time than he, however she agreed to practice putting the bridle and saddle on and brushing Autumn Time.

"I am thrilled with riding," Shoo Ann informed Arnold. "I've never been exposed to ranch life before. I have to work the dinner hour tonight and that will last until late but come after breakfast in the morning to look after the horses so you can visit Beth again."

CHAPTER 24

Arnold called Beth in the hospital. She was doing great but needed to talk about losing body parts. Arnold suggested they wait for that conversation until he arrived to visit her. They would pursue that subject while looking each other in the eyes. She agreed and they discussed the upcoming sale of the cattle, the purchase of hay and Shoo Ann learning to ride Autumn Time.

She told him her third phase of surgery would be the most difficult if they decided to remove certain reproductive parts, such as ovaries and fallopian tubes and that the decision had not been made yet but would be within a day or two.

"I'm leaning a lot about the female system of reproduction. I will be spending more time reading the material given to me by my physician," Beth said. "The physical therapy is demanding but good for me."

Arnold murmured encouragement.

Not able to completely ignore the subject that was haunting her, Beth again brought up the loss of her penis, genitals and associated parts and wondered how this would affect her.

"They told me that I am not a true hermaphrodite," Beth said quietly. "They said that the proper term for people like me is 'intersex.' There are different variations of intersex individuals. Some have obvious genitalia at birth; while, some develop genitalia at puberty."

"I know a little about this, but not very much. I need to learn more," Arnold admitted, listening carefully to what Beth had to say.

"Arnold. I have to tell you that I will never be able to have a baby. That disturbs me greatly," Beth said this hurriedly.

Arnold thought he heard her voice break on a sob and then there was a pause.

"I think I'll hang up now if you don't mind, and we can talk when you come to visit, as you suggested eye-to-eye and face-to-face."

"That is a good idea. Good night Beth," Arnold replied.

They hung up and Arnold sat feeling disturbed by Beth's conversation and bewildered about what he should do.

Arnold went to the restaurant to eat dinner and found Shoo Ann waiting tables. She told him Maggie was cooking and wanted to see Arnold before he left. The food was terrific and the coffee even better and he helped himself to much of both.

Ordering a cup of coffee to go he thought about relaxing in front of the fireplace at the ranch.

He could not stop thinking about the plight of people who were born with a deformity like the one Beth had been born with.

Medical science had yet to find a way to normalize human development. Arnold thought. The most one could hope for if you were born with a sexual abnormality was to be made somewhat comfortable or somewhat able to fit in.

He could see from Beth's experiences that even when physical changes were made without difficulty, adapting to a new body shape still required huge mental adjustments. He imagined that many times extreme stress continued for a long time.

Most people just wanted to be 'normal,' he thought, but sometimes reaching a state considered normal seemed impossible. What an experience for anyone to go through.

While sitting on the couch and drinking a glass of wine, he received a second call from Beth.

It was late, 11:30 PM. Beth was crying.

He heard her say through sobs, something about being depressed after her surgery, facing a lonely existence in the future. She was wondering if she made the right decision.

"Oh Beth. What alternative do you have?" Arnold asked.

She continued to cry, unable to answer the question.

Arnold listened intently and periodically asked a question.

He introduced the subject of the sale of the cattle and the delivery of the hay, hoping a change of subject would help her focus on something else.

This seemed to work somewhat, but not much.

"Do you want me to come and visit you?" He asked.

That cheered her up tremendously.

"I'll drive to Pueblo early in the morning." Arnold promised.

Arnold's conscience bothered him during the night. The feeling was so intense he wanted to call Beth and solve her problems for her, but he knew he could not solve her problems any more than he could solve his own, which he had been working on for years without success.

Arnold believed firmly that Beth was a good woman, a very good woman, but one with a lot of issues that are difficult to solve. He committed himself to exploring ways in which Beth and he could initiate a journey of understanding and love that would alter their life.

For some reason, Arnold found that he was no longer focused on his past, instead he was using his energy to help Beth face the future. But he felt hampered by his thoughts of Brenda and the Chaplain. He seldom received any communication from Brenda and that complicated the picture because he thought he truly loved her. How could he commit anything long term to Beth and love Brenda? he asked himself.

During his drive to Pueblo from Alamosa, Arnold tried to find something positive about his own life that he could think about.

He wondered if taking Beth back to Oklahoma would help. Perhaps if he retraced his footsteps with someone as good as Beth, he would see things in a different light and his thinking would change. For some reason, he began to plan a visit to the cemetery where his family lay buried.

What would that achieve? he thought.

He thought of each relative who had died, including his son, who died prematurely and who he missed every day. Lingering on these thoughts, his tears began to flow, and he stopped the car to dry them.

He drove on and noticed a truck stop coming up. He pulled in and purchased a cold drink. A clock hanging on the wall of the restaurant indicated it was only 4:30 AM. Pueblo was about 2 hours from the ranch. He calculated that he had another hour to drive before he reached Pueblo. He decided to eat breakfast and use some of the extra time to relax and arrive at the hospital at the more reasonable time of 7:00 AM. He was very tired. After he ate, he decided to sleep in the truck and set an alarm.

The alarm woke him at 6:30 AM. He got out of the truck, stretched and walked around to wake himself up. He washed his face in the bathroom at the truck stop. On his way back to the truck, he became aware of the falling temperature and the light snow falling.

As he began to drive farther north, the snow became heavier and the wind gusts buffeted his truck reducing his progress. He thought of the Snake River and he was glad he had decided to wait until spring to go camping. The temperature was 24 degrees.

Not my kind of camping weather, he thought.

He stopped at a gas station and called Beth to let him know he was on his way. She was curious to know if he had departed the ranch.

"Yes," he said, "and I will be looking at you in about 30 minutes."

She said she was going to go to physical therapy early so she would be free when he arrived. He could tell she had perked up and even sounded a little happy. Already, his trip was paying dividends because Beth sounded happier than any time since arriving at the hospital.

Arnold started driving again. His mind drifted over his past and the issues of his own he wanted to solve, including those that involved Brenda. A slight depression began to settle over him.

Why am I making Beth's sexual issues, my issue? He thought. Taking on responsibility for others is something I decided to avoid at all cost.

A different part of him, a better part, told him that 'providing meaningful help to a person who needs it and who cannot help themselves or find anyone to help them made life itself meaningful for him.'

He decided this inner voice was his conscience, reminding him that helping people was a good thing that meant a lot to him.

'Stop fighting the idea,' the inner voice said, 'give it energy, attention and substance.'

When he focused specifically on those words from his inner self, he began to feel better. Over the next few minutes he thought about the energy, attention and substance helping people required and the energy, attention and substance helping people gave to him in turn.

By the time he approached the hospital, he was in a good mood. When he stood in front of Beth, he was rewarded by her overwhelming happiness at the sight of him. Happy tears filled her eyes. She clung to Arnold as he bent over the bed to give her a hug. He felt important to her. She cried openly. Arnold sat on the bed and held her until she composed herself and wanted to talk…and talk…and talk.

Arnold listened as she shared her worries about the ranch, her future and the difficulties of staying in bed while she healed.

She buried him in questions.

"How long are you going to stay at the hospital? What is happening at the ranch? Who is taking care of Autumn Time? How much did the sale of cattle net her bank account?"

"Which answer do you want first?" Arnold asked only slightly teasing.

She responded quickly, "How long are you going to stay with me?"

"Probably until early tomorrow," Arnold answered. "The ranch is fine. The cattle were sold for $45,000.00 net to you; Autumn Time is being fed, watered and rubbed down each day by Shoo Ann who loves to take care of her, and you already know that you will receive the money by mail."

To this Beth smiled and squeezed Arnold's hand.

She commented, "I can hardly wait to get out of the hospital and back home."

They ate lunch and dinner together in the hospital and enjoyed each other's company, much conversation and coffee.

Arnold told her about his tour of the southeast part of the ranch, which he informed her needed some maintenance because the creek was being overtaken by weeds, small trees and brush.

"What do you suggest we do?" Beth asked.

"We should fence it off with an electric fence, place fifteen female and five male goats inside the fence and let them eat everything except the trees," Arnold suggested.

Beth looked at him with an expression of bewilderment.

"Have you ever done that before?" she asked.

Arnold replied, "Oh Yes! Goats eat everything. Then you sell them."

"Let's do it now!" Beth laughed, "so there are goats there when I get home."

"Better yet, we don't need them now because the undergrowth will not continue to grow during the winter months. We can wait until spring and you can pick out the goats you want," Arnold said.

Beth and Arnold talked for hours, happily discussing the habits of goats and the possibility of using goats to clean up the pasture.

Late in the night, Arnold departed for a nearby motel and needed rest. They agreed he needed to be back at the ranch the next day to be present when the cows were artificially inseminated.

CHAPTER 25

After climbing into the comfortable motel bed, Arnold lay with eyes wide open, his mind turning from the happy goodbye he had shared with Beth at the hospital toward contemplating the ashes of his marriage and his divorce. As if stimulated by the lonely room, all the emotion and hurt feelings as well as conversations with counselors, his parents and lawyers rose up in his memory as painful as if they had occurred only yesterday. The memories of the lawyers were the most disturbing because those men were brutal and uncaring, strategically intending to take his possessions. He had battled them, protecting his possessions and assets.

At the time, he had suspected that the lawyers had provided false information to his wife, soon-to-be ex-wife, Charlene, making him look like the one who had betrayed the marriage. In order to defend himself and correct the falsehoods, he had hired a private investigator to find the truth. This delayed the divorce for two years, but it allowed him to layout the facts for the judge and provide information critical to his own defense. His lawyer and the investigator performed extremely well as a team and developed a strategic position that reversed the initial findings of the court. The truth was painful. It clearly showed that Charlene had been meeting her lover long before the divorce was begun, while Arnold and she were married, and Arnold was unsuspecting.

Despite the truth coming out, a large sum of money was awarded to Charlene, but the amount was nothing compared to the award her lawyers had asked for in the beginning. Arnold felt vindicated and free, but wounded, after the long court battle. Unfortunately, his ex-wife's lover and confidant had conspired with her lawyer and reaped 90% of the amount awarded to her by the judge. It bothered him that to date Charlene's lover had not been punished. Charlene was living in poverty, working a part-time job, suffering from ill health and facing a dreadful future.

Although he felt bad for Charlene, Arnold could not accept the fact that another man was having sex with her. Even though he realized they were divorced, the idea of another man penetrating the woman who was once his wife, bothered him terribly. His lawyers and friends told him to get over it, leave it alone, make new life for himself. He was working on that, but he was still furious at Charlene's lover, and although he forgave Charlene her part in the destruction of their marriage, he would never be able to take her back or make love to her again. Her betrayal of him by sleeping with another man while she was married to him was too much for him to stomach. He would never trust her. He was having trouble trusting any woman. Deep in his soul, he knew he loved Charlene still but would never admit it to anyone.

Maybe if I secretly send Charlene a large sum of money, thought Arnold, since I have the resources, maybe this act would help my soul and let me sleep in peace.

Because he could not sleep, he left very early for the ranch. The drive from Pueblo took two hours. The sun was just rising as he drove into the ranch yard. He was groggy from the drive and from lack of sleep.

His mouth and eyes felt dry as dust. As he entered the ranch house, he smelled coffee and headed immediately for the kitchen.

There, he found Shoo Ann beginning to prepare scrambled eggs for breakfast. Shoo Ann looked exotic and delicate in her short ruby-colored quilted robe. Her legs and feet were bare, her toes curling against the cool floor.

Arnold walked close to her. Towering over her, he cupped his hands around her elbows and looked over her head at the stove. "What do you intend to do at this early hour?" he asked.

"Eat breakfast with you and go for a ride on Autumn Time," Shoo Ann replied, still stirring the scrambled eggs.

"Are you aware of the temperature out there?" Arnold asked. "How do you propose to stay warm?"

"I brought a heavy coat that will serve that purpose," Shoo Ann replied.

After breakfast, Shoo Ann got dressed and went for a ride. Arnold was anticipating a phone call from the veterinarian, so he made sure he stayed near the house and the phone. Within an hour, he received the call telling him the veterinarian and his team were on their way to the ranch to begin the artificial insemination process.

"I'm available," Arnold said. "How long will the insemination process take?"

The veterinarian thought he and his team could round up all the cows and vaccinate 75 of them today and complete the remaining 125 vaccinations the next morning. The 75 would be isolated from the herd overnight but the next day all the cows would be released at the same time. He insisted on completing the vaccination part of the process for all 200 cows within the same 24-hour period. Following this procedure would help ensure that two weeks later all the cows would be ready for the sperm.

Shoo Ann returned to the barn and when Arnold told her the veterinarian had called was full of all kinds of questions about insemination.

Arnold invited her to watch and assist with the procedure when it occurred in two weeks. She was excited by the opportunity to observe and wanted Arnold to talk to Maggie to ensure she could be excused from restaurant duties that day.

Shoo Ann started to leave the ranch for the restaurant but, she returned and asked a last question that had been bothering her, "Arnold, how does the veterinarian insert the sperm into the cow?"

"You will see in two weeks," Arnold answered.

"I'm going to go to the library after work and find the answers to my questions," said Shoo Ann. "I know it is a small library, but it does have many books."

"Shoo Ann, to add some interest to the research, you should look up how the veterinarian is going to inseminate heifers," Arnold said.

"What is a heifer?" Shoo Ann asked.

Arnold smiled. "Look that up in the library."

Shoo Ann left for work excited about her new research project.

After the 75 cows were in the temporary corral, Arnold concluded there would not be enough room to confine the 200 cows that were left for the next day. He discussed this with the veterinarian who told him he was going to use five chutes at a time thereby allowing his team to artificially inseminate five cows at a time. He explained that three of his staff would retain one cow per chute in a waiting area near each chute but not within the corral. The gate to the corral would be open tomorrow. After a cow was inseminated, and the paperwork done, the cow would be released into the corral, but would be free to return to grazing and would not be confined longer. Arnold understood and felt better about the capacity of the corral.

The vaccination of each cow was completed as planned within the 24-hour period favored by the veterinarian, and the cows were released into the pasture. Arnold circled a date two weeks in the future on the calendar.

Beth called and wanted an update of the insemination process. She also wanted to talk more about using goats to eat underbrush. They discussed the entire plan they had proposed the day before including installation of an electric fence to keep the goats in a restricted area. She asked about how to protect the cattle from mountain lions and reminded him that several cows that had been killed and partially eaten by the big cats. Arnold suggested they add llamas to the cattle herd. He said he would contact other ranchers and determine what the other ranchers did to protect their cattle from lions. Beth informed him her father had at one time used llamas for this purpose.

After they hung up, Arnold realized he was becoming more involved in Beth's ranching business than he had planned; however, for now, it was an enjoyable pastime for him.

Arnold recalled that he had not told Beth that the banker had called confirming the wire transfer of $45,000.00 to her account. He thought it would be uplifting to Beth to know this information, so he called Beth back right away and told her. She was grateful for the good news.

"Do you want your pay?" Beth asked.

"I would be very grateful for it," Arnold replied.

"Why don't you bring a book of checks with you the next time you come to visit, and I'll pay you," Beth said.

Later that day, Beth called again to give him an update on the progress of her surgical repair.

"Yesterday," she began, "the surgical team, three of them, began skin-graphs to cover where they removed my penis and testicles. They included pubic hair that is the same color as my own pubic hair. I was very impressed with the result," Beth added.

Arnold thought she sounded upbeat and happy.

"My surgical counselor visited, and we discussed several facts that I needed to be aware of, such as, I will be sterile and can have sexual intercourse in a normal manner after three weeks. We also discussed some facts that I really didn't need to be aware of, such as, I can participate in anal intercourse after three weeks as well. I was surprised by their candor."

"My surgeon believes the surgery previously planned as the third phase would not be conducted because it was determined that it was unnecessary for now and may never be necessary."

She told Arnold that the surgeon and Beth's doctor were considering an early release date for her because she was progressing better than expected.

"I am struggling with the term "intersex" though," Beth confided. "And I am not thrilled with the possibility of growing whiskers."

Beth could not see the grin on Arnold's face through the phone cord when he asked, "Do you plan on shaving before we have sex?"

"That is not funny," Beth complained and soon hung up the phone.

As Arnold looked at a calendar on the kitchen wall, he realized Christmas was rapidly approaching. He also looked at a roadmap to plan a return to Oklahoma to take care of personal business. He considered flying to Oklahoma from Pueblo and decided against that because the winter weather was going to make travel messy and dangerous and because Beth needed rest, not work. He decided to stay where he was and do the job he had agreed to do.

Feeling a bit restless, Arnold grabbed a coat, his 30-06, and a little food from the refrigerator. He walked to the barn and saddled Black Shadow adding a saddle bag for the food and his coffee pot. He rode out of the ranch yard into a cold, but very refreshing wind. He decided to look around the creek area some more and decide whether his recommendation about adding goats was a good idea.

Black Shadow ran with such a smooth gait that Arnold felt as young as a 16-year-old boy dreaming in the sun on a summer day. In a very short time, he was looking at the sparkling water in the creek. A yellow leaf floated by every so often between the creek's banks where the grass had turned brown. He could hear the water gurgling below him. Locating a beautiful spot among the trees and next to the water's edge, he pulled on Black Shadow's reins. The stallion stopped and carefully crossed the creek to the clearing. Arnold dismounted and thought that here he could safely start a fire.

He retrieved matches and some paper along with coffee, some hot dogs and his coffee pot from his saddle bags and proceeded to build a fire. Soon the fire was large enough to place his coffee pot over the flame. He pulled a blanket out of his saddle bags and laid it next to the fire. He looped Black Shadow's reins over a nearby tree branch, sat down on the blanket and cooked a couple of hot dogs.

This is a king's life, he thought. What could be better than a burned hot dog without a bun, hot coffee, a cool breeze and his saddle pony standing nearby? Life could not be better.

Apparently, he relaxed more than he realized because he was startled out of sleep by Black Shadow's snort and the sound of his hooves striking the ground. The cry of a mountain lion calling for his mate reached his ears.

Arnold rose quickly because Black Shadow was becoming more agitated over the cry of the mountain lion. He reared up on his powerful back legs dragging Arnold forward as he grasped the reins. The stallion's nostrils flared wide and his eyes rolled, searching the countryside. Arnold reached for his rifle. He had no intention of shooting the lion, but he did choose a dead tree as a likely target to shoot as a warning. He released three quick shots into it. The loud reports from the gun echoed and bark blew off of the dead oak tree as the bullets hit.

He realized it had been quite some time since he had discharged a rifle. It felt great, and he promised himself he would do it again soon. Black Shadow did not like this sound of a rifle firing so close any better

191

than he liked the sound of the lion. Arnold had to spend some time calming his horse with soothing talk and slow smooth strokes of his hand down the horse's head and body.

Arnold consumed another cup of hot coffee. Then, he took care of the ashes with creek water. Black Shadow calmed enough to take a drink and seemed to have recovered from the trauma of the gun shot. Arnold tightened the girth and mounted. Horse and rider began a leisurely trek back to the ranch house.

That evening, he called Beth and described his afternoon on the creek. She asked him to take her the next time he went. He promised he would.

Arnold decided to head to Maggie's restaurant for dinner and more coffee. It was late and he was as hungry for conversation as he was for food, a good excuse for eating dinner at the restaurant instead of cooking for himself.

CHAPTER 26

Arnold decided to drive the truck over to Maggie's restaurant to charge the battery a bit and eat dinner. Upon his arrival, he found several ranchers with their wives, eating and enjoying a night out. He joined them and soon became deeply involved in discussing how to keep the cows safe from mountain lions. The recommended procedure was to train the entire herd to migrate to a safe area each night and to have several male llamas serve as guard animals.

How are we going to train 200 cows to migrate toward the ranch house? That seems to be the safest place, Arnold thought.

He kept this idea to himself and continued listening and asking questions. He asked about goats, Brahma bulls, and which breed of cattle was the most able to protect themselves. Goats and Brahma bulls were ideas that did not receive support from the other ranchers. Many in the group finished eating and began to depart for their homes. Two ranchers remained for coffee, and they agreed it was best to leave the herd to their own migration pattern each day but to attract them with hay and water to a safe place.

On his way back to the ranch house, Arnold began to think of a way to accomplish this objective because losing five cows each winter season was too expensive. Acknowledging the cold wind that blew from the north, he knew he needed to decide which course of action to pursue soon because winter was already here, and the mountain lions were going to be hungry. He decided to load several bales of hay in the truck and unload them near the barn yard to see if the cows would migrate to the hay.

Early the next day, he saddled Black Shadow and rode to the where the cows had spent the night and drove them to the hay. For the next three nights, the cows did as he had hoped they would and bedded down around the distributed hay. Digging a trench, Arnold installed an underground water pipe from inside the barn where water was already available to a water tank approximately 100 yards into the pasture, making water readily available to the cows. They began bedding down next to the hay and water.

That was an easy fix, he thought.

Two weeks passed, and on December 23, the veterinarian called to confirm his arrival with his team to finish the insemination process. Arnold informed him that he would have a young lady attending because she wanted to learn what all was required.

"You might want to be prepared for lots of questions," he warned.

The veterinarian asked if he could bring his 14-year-old daughter to learn the business. Arnold approved without much thought. The veterinarian confirmed the sperm would be from the Hereford breed as they had previously discussed.

The veterinarian's team arrived early the next day, and the round up took advantage of the cows bedding down near the corral. Soon they were driving cows through the chutes for insemination. Shoo Ann and Christi, the daughter of the veterinarian, spent most of the morning watching each cow be inseminated.

After lunch, the ladies disappeared indoors while Arnold and the veterinarian's team continued to work. When they were done, Arnold marked nine months from December 24 on the calendar. September 24, 1957 would be a very busy time with all the calves arriving.

Perhaps having them all done at once was not smart planning. Sometimes all you can do is your best, he thought.

The veterinarian reminded him to monitor the cows and if they started riding each other in about two weeks, he might need to return for another insemination exercise. However, if none of this happened, he could consider this effort a success.

Once the insemination team loaded up and left the ranch, Arnold took off in the truck to visit Beth at the hospital in Pueblo.

When he arrived, Beth was in a festive mood, the Christmas season made everyone happy and cheerful. The nurses were talkative and energetic. The nurse's station and room doors were decorated, and there was a Christmas tree in the waiting room. Everyone was smiling. Arnold had purchased a couple of gifts for Beth and a couple she could give to her favorite nurse.

Beth asked about the artificial insemination process, and Arnold gave her a thorough description of the day from morning to night. Some of the nurses were from ranches and farms and listened in and asked questions of Arnold as he told about the procedure. This pleased Beth because she loved the interesting conversation that revolved around something other than wound healing and therapy.

"Arnold, I'll be leaving the hospital within a week," Beth said. "I will still need to have physical therapy two times per week for a month."

The last nurse wished them a Merry Christmas and left the room so Beth and Arnold could be alone.

Beth was eager to show Arnold where the surgeons had grafted new skin with pubic hair in place. She pulled the sheet down and raised the hem of her hospital gown to just below her breasts. The area requiring new skin was extensive extending from about six inches below Beth's waistline to about halfway between her vagina and rectum and about six inches down each of her legs through the creases where her legs met her torso. She was told this wide an area was required due to ligaments extending away from the testicles and penis that had been removed during surgery.

"I am very sore, but physical therapy is helping immensely," she commented as Arnold and she looked at the scars at the edges of the skin grafts.

"Is it too sensitive for me to touch?" Arnold asked.

Beth smiled. "Be gentle," she said.

Arnold carefully ran his finger over the soft skin of the grafts, avoiding the ragged and red edges of each graft where the stitches held the grafts in place and tiny dots of brownish blood oozed out of the suture punctures.

"I really can't feel much. The grafts are numb right now," Beth said.

Beth cover herself back up with her gown and sheets. They continued to discuss the surgery, her rapid recovery and the plans she had for when she got home. The more they discussed her plans, the more excited she sounded and the stronger her desire was to go home, maybe even tonight.

Beth rang for the nurse who quickly threw cold water on the idea of going home until she had been released by her surgeon. Arnold did his best to change the subject, but it took several hours of discussion to change her mind. He told Beth he would return early in the morning for breakfast with her and stay through lunch before returning to the ranch.

"I'm so glad you are here Arnold and extremely happy that you will be here tomorrow too. It is Christmas," Beth said softly. "I miss you when you are gone. Sleep well tonight. I am tired and will sleep too."

Arnold left her room, walked through the quiet hospital and crossed the dark parking lot to his truck. The night was cold and clear. The stars shone faintly competing with the city lights of Pueblo. He drove the block to the nearby motel feeling depression settle down on his spirits.

As Arnold entered his empty room and sat down on the double bed, loneliness overcame him. He realized this was the first holiday season he had spent away from Oklahoma and familiar surroundings. He had noticed a bar open in the motel when he came in and decided to go down there and see if he could buy a drink for someone to cheer himself up. There was no one at the bar so he went back to his room and laid down on the bed. He fell asleep almost immediately and woke early from a sound and restful sleep.

He returned to the hospital and ate breakfast and drank coffee with Beth, talking about the holiday and holidays each had celebrated in the past. They halfheartedly worked on a jigsaw puzzle that had been left in the waiting room until lunch time. They ate together in the hospital cafeteria. This was a treat for Beth who normally ate in her room.

After Arnold walked Beth back to her room, he gave her a hug and a chaste kiss on the forehead and wished her a Happy Christmas. Beth wished him a safe journey back to the ranch and with tears in her eyes she watched him walk down the hall on his way to the truck and home.

Arnold was eager to get back to the ranch. Once on the highway, he drove faster than usual, oblivious to the beauty of the mountains more visible now with the leaves off some of the trees and the clouds threatening snow.

CHAPTER 27

When he arrived at the ranch and had taken his luggage into the house, he dressed for riding and went out to check on Black Shadow. In the dim light of the barn, he saw Shoo Ann lounging on a bale of hay. She had thrown a blanket over the rough hay and was resting back on her elbows. Her legs were crossed at the ankles and stuck out over the edge of the bale. Autumn Time was saddled nearby.

"Hi Shoo Ann," Arnold greeted her. "Are you preparing for a ride or have you just returned?"

"I have the day off Arnold, and I'm getting ready for a ride. Do you want to join me?" asked Shoo Ann with a smile. She did not immediately move off the bale of hay but continued to lounge back on it watching Arnold saddled Black Shadow. She got up, folded the blanket, and put it into her saddlebag when he had finished.

They rode to the overgrown treed area where Arnold and Beth were considering putting in goats. Arnold could not decide if it was a good idea or not. As they passed the area, he tried to visualize 20 head of goats eating underbrush among the trees. He wondered if the mountain lions would cause havoc with the goats. He recalled that in biblical times goats were used for sacrifices along with sheep. He guessed his purpose was similar. The lions might eat the goats instead of the cows. The idea of putting goats in the fenced enclosure did not appeal to him as much as it had, and he began to search for an acceptable alternative.

Shoo Ann rode Autumn Time up along-side Black Shadow and interrupted Arnold's thoughts.

"Can we ride as fast as the horses can run?" she asked.

"Have you ever ridden a horse at a full gallop?" He asked.

"No," she replied.

Arnold suggested she tie Autumn Time to a tree with the bridle and to ride double with him on Black Shadow for one trip just to get the feel of a horse running at a full gallop. She thought this was a good idea. She dismounted, tied her horse to a tree, and placing her foot on his in the stirrup, climbed in front of him, just inside the saddle with him.

They started out this way slowly with Shoo Ann holding the reins and her feet in the stirrups with Arnold sitting close behind her, his feet hanging loose. Shortly, Shoo Ann encouraged Black Shadow with a nudge of her legs to run, and he ran. He ran fast, but with a smooth gait. The riders seemed to float in the air as the horse moved beneath them. Arnold's large hands crept over her thighs and settle between them in the warmth of her crotch. He held tight. She jerked slightly as his fingers pressed into her through her jeans but did not rein in the horse or complain.

Black Shadow settled into smooth gallop. Shoo Ann was breathing heavily now as Arnold massaged her. Her body arched back until her head almost touched Arnold's shoulder behind her. She still held the reins but for all intents and purposes, Black Shadow and Arnold were in control at that moment. Shoo Ann shuddered in release under Arnold's hands but made not a sound. They returned to the side of Autumn Time. Black Shadow slowed to a walk, circled, and came to a halt as Shoo Ann went limp against Arnold's chest. He lifted her down and steadied her as her feet touched the ground.

Shoo Ann looked up at him and with her black eyes narrowed on his face asked, "I think I am now experienced enough to ride alone at a full gallop, don't you?"

Arnold threw back his head and laughed.

Shoo Ann swung up onto Autumn Time's back and nudged her horse into a full gallop, heading across the land toward the ranch house. Arnold quickly followed on Black Shadow. The two horses galloped neck-to-neck back to the home pasture and the barn.

By the time they arrived at the barn, the day was well gone, and the sun was beginning to settle into the mountains on the western horizon. They rode right up to the barn door and dismounted. Shoo Ann reached up into her saddle bag, pulled out the blanket, snapped it open and laid it on a bale of hay. She reached over and grabbed Arnold's hand and pulled him to her, saying

"So…, you know how to play?"

Leaving the horses saddled and sweaty, Shoo Ann spread the blanket out on the bale of hay and turned to face Arnold who was right behind her. She reached up to his shoulders and pulled his face down to hers.

Arnold wrapped his arms around her, lifted her off her feet and as she clung to him, unbuttoned her jeans and pushed them off her hips and legs with his thumbs. If she was wearing panties, Arnold didn't know because if they had once been there, they were now gone, discarded with the jeans.

He set her down on the blanket and pushed her jacket off and pulled her turtleneck over her head. Then he looked at her pale naked body. She was delicate. Her breasts were small and her waist narrow, her thighs long and smooth divided by a narrow patch of black pubic hair. He touched her there, sliding his fingers along the pubic hair. He found she was wet from her ride on the horse.

Shoo Ann stood up swiftly, reached out and undid the zipper of Arnold's jeans. His erect penis sprang out, heavy, long, and large. Shoo Ann wrapped her hands tightly around his penis. Arnold gasped. She pushed his jeans down. Arnold stepped back and dispatched with his clothes in one swift move.

Arnold lifted Shoo Ann up against him. She wrapped her legs around his waist, guided his penis to the entrance of her vagina and pressed. She was hot and wet but even with that, Arnold had to push hard to enter her. Once he was inside, they both were still for a moment, exploring the sensation, staring into each other eyes, unsmiling.

Arnold bent, still carrying Shoo Ann and laid her on top of the blanket without withdrawing from her. He brought his body down onto hers as she arched over the bale. His hand grasped her hips and they moved against one another, their bodies heating in the cool air. Shoo Ann shuddered and moved her hips frantically against his, her pleasure peaking. A soft cry escaped her.

Arnold held himself firmly inside her as her body squeezed his penis in waves. He moved gently inside her, biting his lips to restrain his own desire to climax. She clung to him weakly. He nibbled at her neck and collar bones and breasts until she came back to herself and smiled up at him.

"You are mighty big and fill me up," she whispered.

Arnold began to thrust harder, bringing both of them to a final and satisfying climax.

Black Shadow and Autumn Time shifted from foot to foot, their saddles still on their backs, their reins looped around their saddle horns. Slowly they moved into the barn until they could reach a bale of hay for themselves and munched happily while their humans rested in the hay and then dove again into the satisfaction afforded to their human bodies this Christmas Day.

CHAPTER 28

A rnold was drinking coffee in the kitchen when he received a call from Darrel, his investment counselor in Oklahoma. Darrel was calling to give him a late Christmas present, great news about his recent investments. He said some decisions needed to be made regarding the amount of money accruing at the bank. The account balance was approaching the maximum that was insured by the FDIC, or $500,000. Darrel wanted Arnold to direct him to one of three investments he was recommending. One of the investments had over the past year, earned a 40% return due to a three-for-one stock split. Darrel believed the expected return for the upcoming year would be approximately 9%. The two remaining investments he wanted Arnold to consider were expected to earn approximately 7% with the potential to earn more than that.

"Transfer $300,000 from the bank account to the 9% investment," Arnold directed.

"You will most likely exceed the one million mark if your investments continue performing so well. Are there any other investments you might want me to look at?" Darrel asked.

"Would you coordinate with my real estate representative to quietly purchase oil and gas mineral rights in and around the farm where I was raised? You know Robert Gillian, right?"

"Sure, I know Robert. I'll coordinate with him. Do you want to purchase the oil and gas mineral rights along with the land? Are you only interested in the land?" asked Darrel.

"I'm interested in it all, the land and the oil and gas mineral rights," said Arnold.

"I will contact Robert right away because we anticipate the farm you were raised on is going on the market soon," Darrel said.

"For what price?" Arnold asked.

"I don't know yet, but I will call Robert and have him contact you later this evening," Darrel responded.

They hung up. Longing for home encompassed Arnold, a nostalgia so strong, it was overwhelming. He felt anxious because he wanted the family farm so much. He hoped there was a chance he could purchase it.

Within an hour, his phone rang again. It was Robert Gillian, his real estate representative, calling with great news. He told Arnold that the person who currently owned the farm he grew up on was planning to sell it as soon as the appraisal was returned to him.

"Can you give me an estimate?" Arnold asked Robert.

"$15,000.00 for the land only as is. No work will be done prior to closing. The owner plans to sell it at auction and will take the highest price bid on the day of the intended sale," replied Robert.

"The house had been destroyed by fire and was never replaced. There are two barns on the farm that were constructed within the last two years," Arnold said. "I believe there would be considerable interest in the sale as oil and gas reserves have been discovered ten miles west."

Arnold did not tell Robert he had already purchased that property when he was young and owned the mineral rights in that area 10 miles west.

"Prepare a cash purchase offer to be delivered on the sale date or purchase it earlier if possible. Use your negotiating skills with the owner and see if he will sell prior to the auction date. Buy it as soon as you can for whatever price you can negotiate," Arnold directed.

"Don't lose this opportunity Robert! Discuss payment of the purchase amount with my banker, Darrel. I'll call him as soon as we hang up," said Arnold.

Arnold called Darrel, but no one answered. He had just put the phone away when it rang. Picking up the phone, he heard Darrel say, "I thought you might call me because Robert rang me up earlier wanting to discuss the proper way to transfer money from your account to purchase the farm. I'm calling to confirm that conversation and I'll take care of the transfer. I'll probably attend the sale on the sale day if the sale isn't completed before that."

Arnold hung up and enjoyed a good breakfast. He made more coffee and went for a walk to the barn. It was snowing and there was a light dusting on everything. He watched the quarter horses and tried, without success, to determine if Autumn Time's pregnancy was beginning to show. The mare came up to him seeking affection and nuzzled his shoulder and back. He brushed her and rubbed her ears. She seemed to be content until he did the same for Black Shadow. Then, she nudged him for more.

"Don't be greedy Autumn Time," Arnold laughed and swatted at her.

He returned to the house for a refill of the good coffee in his cup.

I make a pretty decent cup of coffee, he thought happily.

His conversations with Robert and Darrell continued to circle in his head. He wanted the suspense over with. He wanted confirmation of the purchase of his old home place. He tried to remember his life on the farm. It seemed exciting and happy. He knew better, but he intentionally refused to remember any of the negative stuff that had happened at the farm.

Arnold decided he would start fresh with this new start at the farm. He vowed to make amends to whomever he thought he should. He thought that God perhaps was giving him good fortune so that he would forgive his ex-wife. His first thought in this direction was to learn the status of his ex-wife. If she needed help, he would provide help. However, he wanted to avoid emotion and avoid making unnecessary commitments.

Just help her and leave the rest alone, thought.

Later that morning, he found himself saying out loud,

"Whatever you do, just do it one time, then leave it and her alone regardless of everything else. Do not try to forgive her ex-lover because he was crooked to the core of his being and has not earned forgiveness."

He went to his typewriter and wrote it down, printed it out and put a copy in his pocket.

He called Robert and asked if he knew where his ex-wife Charlene was living?

Robert replied, "Yes, but she does not have a phone and I do not know her address."

"Can you get a message to her?" he asked.

"I can." Robert replied.

It wasn't long before he received a collect phone call from Charlene. She sounded rough and slightly suspicious. She wanted to know what he wanted.

"I want to know how you are doing, where you are living and how is your health. I want to know if you are eating right," replied Arnold.

Arnold could tell that she was caught off guard by the questions and her voice became clouded by tears.

"I am horribly embarrassed to answer your questions. I live in poverty with several Indian women and two poor white women. We have no money except welfare checks from the state. We eat sometimes. I have lost quite a bit of weight that I can't really afford to lose.

My lover, John, was killed in a car accident and was held for a long time in the morgue waiting for someone to pay for his burial expenses. They finally buried him in the pauper's grave," Charlene said, sobbing quietly between her sentences.

"Will you meet me when I travel to Oklahoma?" Arnold asked.

"Of course, I will meet you," Charlene said.

"I am interested only in your welfare and not in you as a friend or lover. That is over. Do you understand what I mean?" asked Arnold. His voice was rough with emotion

Charlene started to cry harder. "I understand."

"Please keep my phone number and call me each Monday morning and give me a status report on how you are doing."

Charlene agreed and they hung up.

He then contacted Darrel and asked if he had a way of investigating Charlene and her living conditions.

Darrel replied, "I already know of her situation. I don't need to or want to investigate her in any manner. I will tell you what I know, and that should be sufficient because I know a lot about her."

They agreed that Darrel could send this information by letter, and Arnold would not bother him with a lot of questions if he gave detailed information.

Arnold worried that he had started something he may wish he had not, but he wanted to clear his conscience and help Charlene out of the situation she had gotten herself into. It had not dawned on him until today that Charlene was an innocent victim in the divorce proceedings caused by her ex-lover and his conniving.

All during the proceeding, John had said it was Charlene who wanted the settlements. However, when John took all the money and gave Charlene none, it all became clear to Charlene. Sadly, it was too late. John had wasted the money before he died, and none could be found or delivered to Charlene.

Charlene must have become so disillusioned, Arnold thought. She has become a person without money or the means to get money. She lost her way and started living on benefits from the state, hardly enough to survive on. When Arnold realized this was the situation, his conscience told him to help Charlene. He felt relieved that he had made this decision.

If this turns out to be a mistake, Arnold thought to himself, I will somehow extricate myself.

CHAPTER 29

Beth was still in the hospital and Arnold found himself alone in front of the fireplace staring into the flames, thinking hazily about how he might finally be getting over the divorce and the wounded confidence that plagued him. Helping Charlene was helping him clear his conscience. He could think through his past more clearly, and he realized he had been penalizing Charlene when she had not been the real party responsible for the legal battle that strung the divorce out. This blame had to be laid at her lover's dead feet. John had lied to her. Charlene had apparently been incapable of controlling any of his actions.

Late that night or early the next morning, he went to bed and slept soundly. He woke late the next morning and staggered to the coffee pot to find it as he left it the night before, cold with coffee grounds, but no hot coffee. He rushed through the coffee making process and tried to wait patiently for a fresh cup. Before the coffee was through perking, Shoo Ann came in. She told him that she had completed breakfast at the restaurant and wanted to practice riding Autumn Time.

He offered Shoo Ann coffee and she sat down to drink a cup with him. He was enjoying her company and trying to wake up when the phone rang. It rang several times before Arnold answered it. It was Robert with news he had successfully negotiated the purchase of the farm, including all the oil and gas mineral rights for $20,000.00 cash to be delivered to the owner when he presented the affidavit of title. The owner wanted $3,000.00 immediately.

Darrel had gone to the bank and made that payment by way of a cashier's check. Darrel wanted the cashier's check so there would be a document of record in addition to the contract signed by the owner. The contract is in the mail to you for your immediate signature. They said good-bye to each other and hung up the phone.

Arnold was very excited. He decided to make more coffee.

The phone rang loud and clear then stopped. He thought for a moment that he had imagined it had rung. It rang again. Lifting the receiver, he listened closely to Robert who was calling him again.

Shoo Ann seeing he was busy with another call took her cup of coffee to the barn.

Robert let Arnold know that the neighbor living to the east of the farm he had just purchased would entertain a similar offer for his farm that consisted of 160 acres and included the oil and gas mineral rights. Robert described the property as basically land, no house or other outbuildings and it was partially fenced.

"Has the land ever or is it now leased by any of the oil companies?" Arnold asked.

"No." Robert replied.

"In that case, I'll authorize you to purchase the 160 acres plus the mineral rights for up to $20,000.00. Offer $5,000 less than the $25,000 asking price since there are no outbuildings, and the property is only partially fenced. If the owner declines the offer of $20,000.00, I'll pay the asking price of $25,000.00.

"I can reduce my commission to 2% if it is necessary," Robert volunteered.

For the second time that morning, the two men hung up.

Arnold's stomach was reminding him that he needed breakfast, so he drove the truck to the restaurant where Maggie took his order and delivered it without delay. He had been so preoccupied he had failed to remember that Shoo Ann was at Beth's ranch riding.

Two ranchers came in, sat down and ordered breakfast. One of them, recalling their previous conversation concerning mountain lions informed Arnold that he had lost two cows in the past week. The rancher said there was evidence of more than one animal attacking the cows. The men discussed possible solutions but did not come up with one they liked best.

Arnold finished his breakfast and ordered a coffee to-go. He departed with a strong desire to be alone for some uninterrupted thinking time. He decided the best way to achieve this was to ride Black Shadow to his favorite spot on the ranch.

When he arrived at the ranch house, he went straight to the barn and saddled Black Shadow. The weather was cold and there were a few inches of snow on the ground, but he didn't mind. Black Shadow did not mind the snow either and was as eager as Arnold to get out and explore. The wind in Arnold's face was exhilarating at first, but soon he had to tuck his chin into his coat and pull his collar up.

Giving Black Shadow his lead, Arnold became lost in thought. He recalled his conversation with Charlene and decided to periodically send her money provided she would go to her doctor for a physical exam, start living a different life tyle, move into an affordable apartment or house and become a progressive woman again. He had sent a letter to her through Robert, who had previously volunteered to assist him. The letter informed Charlene that he was planning a trip to the farm and wanted to visit with her. She had responded by phone as soon as she received the letter and seemed excited about the contents and the prospect of meeting with him. She told him that her parents were also discussing ways to assist her. That gave him hope.

Black Shadow knew where to go, and they arrived in record time at his favorite spot. At least it seemed like record time to Arnold at first. He had been thinking so hard he had not been paying attention to the passage of time and distance and was surprised to find when he dismounted that he had been riding for two hours. He sat down on the bank of the small creek. He saw that the snow had covered up the grass Black Shadow wanted to eat. The horse pawed at the snow and unburied some of the grass. Black Shadow drank some water from the icy stream. Arnold thought that his black stallion against the white snow was a beautiful sight and said to himself, life cannot get any better than this.

Arnold and Black Shadow wandered around the ranch without purpose for a while and then went back to the house. He was laying on the couch trying to take a nap when the ranch house phone rang again and interrupted the peace and quiet.

It was Robert again, informing him that the owner of the second farm, the one east of his latest purchase, was seriously considering the offer of $20.000.00 cash for his farm, including all mineral rights. This was good news and after they hung up, Arnold continued relaxing, starting a small fire for warmth and enjoying its crackle.

His thoughts drifted until he recalled that he had no plan for his own future. He didn't know where he was going or what he was going to do. Like Charlene, Arnold felt that he had, apparently, lost his directional compass after their divorce. He had come to this part of the country as part of his search for answers. The answers remained elusive but recently might be becoming clearer.

Christmas 1956 had come and gone, the cold wind from the north was bringing snow showers daily, and it was about time he developed a plan to bring order into his life.

First, he thought, I should act quickly toward helping Charlene. Next, there were the 200 cows on the ranch that require my attention, and the delivery of hay was critical. Mountain lions continued to harass the cows, even in their safe pasture near the ranch house and this would only become worse as the temperature decreased and food supplies for the predators became even more scarce.

Beth called while he was thinking over all these tasks and told him she was going to be released in two days. He assured her he would be there to bring her home. He also told her he was planning to fly to Oklahoma on business. She wanted to discuss each little detail. Arnold told her they could talk about it on the way home from the hospital. She reminded him how anxious she was to end her 29 days in the hospital. He told her he understood and would see her the day after tomorrow.

He put more wood on the fire and finally dozed off. The phone did not ring any more that day.

CHAPTER 30

Arnold went to the restaurant for dinner and was surprised at the number of customers, each one eager to consume good, hot food and coffee. Maggie had given Shoo Ann the night off, and she was very busy. She seemed overwhelmed and even inattentive as she waited on customers. Arnold ate the steak, mashed potatoes and salad that Maggie placed before him. She seemed distracted so he did not attempt conversation.

As he drove into the ranch and prepared to park, he noticed a light on in the barn and could see Shoo Ann brushing down Autumn Time. He went to the house, poured himself a cup of coffee and listened to the radio hoping to get the latest update of the news. He heard a commentator relay a story about oil and gas exploration in Oklahoma. Their projections were optimistic and left the impression of good things to come.

He went out to the truck to retrieve a little parchment covered book he kept with him in which he recorded people he met and the revenue he was collecting on oil and gas wells. He noticed that it was snowing harder. He flipped through the book and located the name and contact information of a man in the oil lease business with whom he had previously done business. He thought about calling this man for more details on what was being reported on the radio.

Robert Gillian called Arnold right then and wanted to know if he wanted to purchase more land in Oklahoma. Arnold told him he would not be satisfied until he owned the entire section where he had already purchase one half of one section. Robert told him the reason for his call was to inform him that the owner of the half section located adjacent to his half section wanted to sell his at the same price as he had previously paid. Arnold instructed Robert to enter into negotiations and, if possible, purchase the remaining half section.

Arnold felt exhilarated with this news. He calculated the revenue he would receive when the oil and gas explorers reached his section. Satisfied with the financial opportunities coming his way, he reclined on the couch and went to sleep.

Robert called early the next morning as Arnold was drinking a good cup of coffee. He had Charlene with him and urged Arnold to talk to Charlene because he had delivered a letter Arnold had sent to her.

Robert passed the phone to Charlene.

"Arnold, I promise to undertake the course of action you described in the letter as soon as you can help me with some needed cash," Charlene said.

"I'm scheduled to fly to Oklahoma in four days," Arnold stated. "I'd like to meet with you."

"I don't think it would be good to talk in the company of the other women I live with because they too are destitute with no future," Charlene replied.

"I understand," said Arnold. "Follow the instructions Robert gives you, and I will find an office where we can discuss everything privately."

Charlene handed the phone to Robert.

Arnold asked, "Robert. Can you provide an office where Charlene and I can meet? Can you also plan to be a liaison between the two of us for the first week? After the first week, Charlene will have her own place with her own phone and address, and you will be able to step out of your current role as go-between."

"I can do that," Robert said. "Do you want me to give Charlene the $1,000.00 check you sent for her?" He asked.

Arnold said, "Yes," and hung up the phone.

Within a few seconds, the phone rang again, and he picked it up to hear Charlene on the other end of the line in tears, unable to talk coherently.

"Thank you, Arnold," she wept. "Robert told me that he was going to put me up in a nice apartment at your expense. You are a good man!"

"Your welcome Charlene. Good night."

The next morning it was snowing hard and the temperature was forecast to fall more than 10 degrees below zero. Arnold set about getting ready to travel to Pueblo and bring Beth home. He checked the tires on the truck. He checked the anti-freeze. He stocked the truck with extra clothing, a couple of blankets, food and water just to be prepared. Driving in the mountains was not his favorite pastime, especially when it was snowing.

As he pulled out onto the highway, his mind focused on Charlene's situation and he was confident that by taking action to help her, he had discovered the cure for his own depression. He was anxiously waiting to take the action he had planned.

Since Brenda was still involved with the Chaplain in some way, he decided to put her to the back of his mind and divide his thoughts between Beth and Charlene. He was committed to a non-emotional, straightforward relationship with Charlene with no attachments. With Beth, that as another matter. He was not quite sure where their relationship would lead.

He arrived at the Pueblo hospital ahead of time and went to Beth's room. She was already packed, waiting to begin the checkout process. She hugged him when he walked into her room. She looked vibrant and cheerful and talked with determination about beginning a new life. She handed him two pages of instructions from the surgeon and the family doctor.

Looking at the number of suitcases she had packed, he went out of the room to get a luggage carrier. Upon his return, Beth's family physician was giving her last-minute instructions, and he added a few for Arnold.

Once out of the hospital, they traveled south on Colorado State Highway 25, which had been cleared of nearly all the snow except that which was currently falling. The pine trees were covered with mounds of snow, and snow covered every inch of the ground. When he saw a small cabin among the trees, he pointed it out to Beth and daydreaming out loud asked, "Wouldn't it be nice to stay in that cute little cabin in the snow and warm it with a large fireplace?"

"My ranch house is nicer than that cabin. It has more space and a nice kitchen in which good food can be easily prepared," Beth reminded him.

"You are right about that," Arnold agreed.

Beth scooted across the truck seat closer to him. She laid her head on his shoulder and asked, "What kind of business are you going to deal with in Oklahoma?" Arnold told her there were several projects he needed to tend to, including insuring that all the legal aspects of his purchase of two tracts of land, including the oil and gas mineral rights were completed properly.

He told her about Charlene too and about the action he planned to initiate to help her.

Concerned, Beth asked, "So you still loved your ex-wife?"

"I do not love her like I once did, but I care about her well-being and quality of life. This is one of those values my father and mother taught me, 'do the right thing.' I am financially capable of helping Charlene, so I do not want her living in poverty. It is the right thing to do to help her."

When they arrived home, Beth went to rest because coming home from the hospital was more activity than she was used to.

Arnold put his winter coveralls on and went out to check on the cows. It had been two weeks since the artificial insemination had taken place. He wanted to do as the veterinarian had suggested and determine if the artificial insemination was successful or if a second effort was required. He did not see even one cow humping another, so he concluded everything was progressing well. Beth could expect new calves in September.

Back in the house, Arnold was relaxing when the phone rang. He picked it up.

Robert was on the line, telling him that he was the proud owner of a very special section of Oklahoma soil.

"You paid $20,000.00 per quarter, including the mineral rights," Robert said. "Transfer of ownership will occur within two weeks."

"That is good." Arnold told him. I am thinking of having someone rent the property and undertake some repair projects. I'd like them to begin soon."

Robert assured Arnold there were several tenants he could choose from and promised to send him some names with qualification statements and work histories.

"Remember, I'll be there in a week," Arnold said. "How about you and your wife joining me for dinner and good conversation?"

"Ah. Arnold. My wife and I separated. Remember? She remarried a guy she and I were pals with for years. She married him two weeks after our divorce became final."

"I'm sorry Robert. I remember now. We can have dinner anyway." Arnold promised and hung up the phone.

Beth got up from her nap and she was one very happy lady to be home.

Arnold looked at the two-page document the doctors had given him more closely. He did not find travel restrictions among the instructions.

"Beth, would you like to make a trip to Oklahoma with me?"

She gave him a hug and seemed happier than he had ever seen her. She peppered him with questions:

"When will we leave? "

"How long will we be gone?"

"Where will we stay?" she asked.

Arnold answered each question in the order asked.

"Tomorrow."

"A week."

"In a motel."

"I'm going to ask Shoo Ann to deliver hay to the cows each day," said Arnold.

"Can she lift the bales in and out of the truck?" Beth asked. "Shoo Ann weighs less than a hundred pounds."

"I think so," Arnold replied. "I plan to have her show me that she can do it tomorrow morning."

The next morning, with her trial run at delivering hay a total success, Shoo Ann was all smiles as she waved to them as they departed for Pueblo and a flight to Oklahoma City where he had reserved a rental car from Avis.

They arrived in Oklahoma on time and stopped in El Reno, Oklahoma to reserve a motel room, eat lunch at a local café and proceed west to Calumet and Robert's real estate office. They also stopped at the First National Bank and withdrew enough money to cover their travel needs.

Beth teased Arnold and volunteered to donate enough money to meet her own expenses, but Arnold politely refused and informed her that this was his way of showing her how a true Okie would treat her.

From Robert's office, he called his contact in the gas and oil industry, a man named Wyatt Ore, to discuss the oil and gas leasing process. They met for an early dinner and interesting conversation. He informed Ore that he owned a section of land in Section 27 and wanted his opinion on how long he anticipated it would be before the oil companies would begin drilling in that area. Ore told him they had already core drilled in several areas and received very favorable results. He thought they would reach Arnold's section in perhaps one or two years.

"What do you expect the price per acre will be for leasing?" Arnold asked.

Ore did not hesitate to answer and said, "$40.00 to $60.00 per acre."

"Well then, I want to assure you that I am more than interested," Arnold said.

"I can understand your interest," Ore laughed.

The meal over, Arnold helped Beth up from her chair. She had sat quietly during the whole conversation. They thanked Ore for meeting with them and excused themselves, saying that they had other business to conduct.

Robert had informed Arnold of Charlene's new address and phone number, so he and Beth drove directly from the restaurant to her apartment.

Arnold called Charlene and told her they were on their way. She seemed to be excited.

Upon their arrival Arnold introduced Beth to his ex-wife, Charlene. Charlene gave them a brief tour of the apartment. She appeared to be settled in.

"May I invite some of the Indian women I lived with?" she asked.

"I suggest you avoid contact with them, make new friends, set your goals higher than living in poverty, find employment, attend church and live a good life," said Arnold

"I understand," Charlene sighed. "I've already applied for two positions and have been interviewed for one. I've seen the doctor for a complete physical. I received two prescriptions, one to help control my high blood sugar condition and a vitamin to increase the level of iron in my blood. I have your letters and would keep them for reference as I intended to comply fully."

"Do you need anything else?" Arnold asked.

"I would like to have a radio, but it is not a need," she replied.

Arnold took out his wallet and gave her cash to purchase the radio.

"Is it okay for me to give you a hug and a kiss in the presence of Beth?" Charlene asked, but did not wait for an answer and hugged and kissed him.

Arnold smile and they sat on the couch and discussed her plan for living a better life. Charlene cried a little then composed herself and at the end of the evening they all said good-bye with hugs and good wishes. Arnold was satisfied he had not revealed the depth of the hurt she had given him with their divorce. As he predicted, he felt better doing what was right. It felt good. He smiled at Beth as they headed back to the motel in El Reno.

Two days later, after talking to Darrell, Robert began discussions with two prospective farmers to lease the land and undertake several projects on each quarter. Beth and Arnold enjoyed touring the area. Arnold was particularly interested in the oil and gas exploration occurring 8 miles west of his recently purchased section of land.

When they stopped back by Robert's office, Arnold received a phone message from Wyatt Ore, the land man. He returned the call and found out that Wyatt wanted to meet him and discuss again and in more detail the leasing of Section 27.

Arnold, Beth and Wyatt met at a small café in Calumet where they ordered coffee. Wyatt presented Arnold with a contract to lease the entire section for $50.00 per acre. Arnold happily signed the contract and instructed Wyatt to deposit the entire $32,000.00 in the Calumet, First National Bank.

"I will gladly do that, and I am certain Darrell will be glad to send you a receipt," replied Wyatt.

They returned to Robert's office. Before Arnold left town, Robert wanted him to meet Charlie Anderson, who he recommended to take care of Arnold's land and undertake the projects he had mentioned. Arnold agreed to meet Charlie for lunch in El Reno at a local restaurant that both men were familiar with.

Once all three, Beth came along too, had ordered, Charlie said he could rent each quarter for $1,500.00 cash payable on January 1 of each year. Charlie wanted to bill Arnold for each project individually. He agreed to write to Arnold describing the work that needed to be done, the objective and the cost of materials if any, and they would negotiate the price for each project.

This arrangement seemed reasonable to Arnold, so they agreed, finished their breakfast and concluded the meeting. As they started to leave, Charlie asked if Arnold had heard the latest gossip.

"I have not," replied Arnold. "Is it interesting?"

Charlie replied, "Probably only to you. Did you know that Charlene is seriously dating Robert?"

"Very interesting," Arnold replied.

Beth and Arnold departed for the motel for their luggage before heading back to Alameda.

As they got into the rental car, Beth said, "I am thrilled I was able to come to Oklahoma with you and meet some of your business associates and Charlene."

Arnold gave Beth a hug and helped her into the rental car that would take them back to the airport.

CHAPTER 31

Arnold and Beth flew back to Pueblo. Everything was white with snow when they deplaned, and the temperature was well below zero. They needed all the clothing they could wear. The truck was covered with snow in the airport parking lot. They cleaned it off and drove to Alamosa.

They drove home without incident on the plowed roads and started a fire in the fireplace. Arnold sat back with Jack Daniels' in a glass to relax the muscles and settle the nerves. The trip had been rewarding, full of business, experiences and some emotion. Arnold was so pleased to start anew with his dream of buying back the home place in Oklahoma.

Beth had not really had time to settle in back home after her hospital stay before they had departed on their trip to Oklahoma, so she unpacked her suitcase and informed Arnold with a satisfied smile that she was not expecting to use the suitcase again for a long time.

Arnold fell asleep on the couch and was awakened by Beth when it was time to go to bed. Apparently, he needed sleep more than he thought because he did not remember the transition to bed at all. He awakened the next morning in bed with his mind working overtime.

He was optimistic about his new investment in the farm because he had reaped such great benefits for five years now from his other oil and gas production investments.

As he drank his coffee, Beth joined him, and Arnold could tell Beth was doing well. They discussed their plans for the cows and calves as they sipped their coffee. Beth then pointed out a lengthy letter from Charlie Anderson that was on the typewriter. Arnold said he didn't want to deal with too many different subjects this early in the morning. He preferred to slow things down and enjoy life more. They snuggled close to each other and watched the fireplace flames for entertainment.

Robert called later in the morning and wanted to know if his dating Charlene would interfere in any way with their business dealings. Arnold reassured him that he could not think of anything that it would affect. Robert told Arnold how glad he was that Arnold had introduced the two of them and indicated they were enjoying each other's company as their relationship blossomed into frequent visits.

"I might be rushing things," Robert said, "but time is of the essence at my age."

"I wish both of you happiness and a great future," Arnold told him. They changed the subject from relationships to real estate before hanging up, both satisfied that their business relationship was intact.

The next few months were occupied with the daily duties of tending to the cows in the deep winter. Arnold continue to give Shoo Ann riding lessons in the snow. He also taught her lessons about work on the ranch. Shoo Ann was eager to learn and welcomed each new experience with enthusiasm and vigor. Her small physical size did not hamper her work. She was strong and quick to undertake new duties. Working with Shoo Ann reminded Arnold of working with his mother during the times that his father was traveling on his job.

One day when they were delivering bales of hay to the cattle, Arnold asked Shoo Ann where she had been born.

"I was born in Indonesia where I lived until I was six months old, then my parents moved us to China, which is where my father was born before he moved to Indonesia. My mother was originally from Indonesia; however, my mother and father were Chinese."

"What religion do you practice?" Arnold asked.

"Basically Buddhism, but infrequently," she said. "I believe mostly in enjoying life's adventures, joys and excitement, but not in doing harm to anyone or to myself."

"Have you ever heard of Christianity?"

"Yes. Several times, but I do not really believe in their teaching," she replied.

"Do you believe in God?" Arnold asked.

"No. I believe that you follow paths of good behavior and avoid bad behavior and are reincarnated until you achieve perfection. Then all suffering is over."

Arnold then asked, "Who do you go to when you become desperate and want help?"

She looked him straight in his eyes, took both his hands in hers and solemnly said, "The only time I needed help was when my mother and father were killed with a hatchet, and I passed out with fear because I thought I was going to be next. But it did not happen to me. I went to live with my sister, Alice, who is two years older than I am. She and I lived together until I got transferred with other migrants to the United States. Since living in the United States, I have lived in New York, Chicago and now in Alamosa, Colorado. I love it here more than anywhere else."

The cold north wind became uncomfortable, so they got back in the truck and headed to the barn where it was more comfortable. Beth joined them and showed Arnold a letter he had received. The letter was from Robert who had been talking with a banker who inquired about his address. Robert wanted to know if it was okay to give the banker his address. Robert then concluded with a note that he and Charlene were doing great, and she was planning to move in with him around the first of the month. He would then cancel her lease.

Arnold, Beth, and Shoo Ann moved to the house and Shoo Ann soon left for work at the restaurant. Arnold went to the typewriter to respond to Robert's letter. He noticed he had mail from Darrell. Darrell informed Arnold that the price of oil and gas had gone up tremendously and his revenue checks were in excess of $1,000.00 each month. He suggested they invest at least 50% of that in mutual funds. Darrell went on to write that his conversations with oil and gas producers reflected a constant rise for the foreseeable future. He advised Arnold not to leave the extra cash idle when it could be making him more.

When Arnold called Darrell instead of writing back. He asked Darrell to contact Linda, his investment counselor, and said he too would contact her and give directions to invest in one of his recommended mutual funds. Arnold hung up with Darrell and called Linda. Linda answered the phone sounding happy and gleeful over some information she had just learned.

"Is this good news?" Arnold asked.

"Arnold, your portfolio is bursting at the seams and needs immediate attention due to the increase in both oil and gas prices as well as production levels. I'd say that is good news and a good problem to have."

"Fill me in Linda," Arnold said, "and then write it down and send a copy in the mail so I remember everything you say."

Linda happily complied, saying, "The price of oil and gas has tripled due somewhat to the Suez Canal dispute. Plus, the number of wells coming putting out oil within the area where he had invested had doubled and the forecast was unbelievable."

She paused then continued, "I had intended to call you earlier; however, I was on the phone with several people. We were trying to grasp the magnitude of all the news. My secretary is preparing a newsletter which I will send to you. Plus, I will include a letter that pertains only to you. This letter will be sent to you later today. I will include both letters in the mail I send to your banker, Darrell."

When Arnold told Linda that he had purchased a section of land that was eight miles from this current investment, Linda said, "Arnold. I must put the phone down as I am thinking they just announced the signing of a new lease in the area to which you are referring."

Within a minute or two, Linda returned to the phone and confirmed the news she had heard about the signing of the lease on his section.

Linda said, "I must hang up and collect my thoughts. I will call you later today."

Arnold put the receiver down and tried to relax.

Arnold began to calculate in his head an estimate of the amount of money he could possibly earn from the oil and gas business, including current earnings. He became confused and decided to wait for it to develop before he got too excited.

Beth came to the couch and sat down. She had an interesting expression on her face.

Giving him a hug, she said, "It has now been three weeks since the doctor told me to wait for three weeks before having sexual intercourse. So here we are, just the two of us."

Arnold gave a whoop, picked Beth up and carried her to the bedroom. Beth laughed startled at being picked up. She wrapped her arms around his neck to steady herself.

In the bedroom, Arnold set her down beside the bed and they slowly undressed in the half light coming through the curtains. They watched each other intently. Once they stood naked, Arnold placed his hands around Beth's waist and lifted her up on the bed. He stood between her legs and knelt there, carefully spreading her legs to view her new sex. He ran his palm down her belly to her pubis bone. No penis rose to greet him. The last time he had touched her, there had been a penis where there was now only skin and a triangle of hair that invited his finger to explore lower.

He carefully parted her folds to find the warm wet cleft. Slowly, experimentally, he slid his index finger into her vagina. Her vagina was deeper now, more developed.

Beth watched him silently. She was hot and warm but showed no sign of arousal.

He continued his exploration of her by running his hands over her inner thighs where the stitches had been and now only slightly raised scars remained.

He raised himself up and her with him. He arched her back over his arm.

"Are you ready," he asked? His voice sounding deeper than normal.

"Yes," she whispered.

He lifted her hips to his and pressed with his penis in search of the warm opening he had found there. He nudged against her and pressed steadily into the depths of her vagina.

Her eyes widened as he filled her. Her lips parted, but she did not speak. She held him tightly within her.

Moving one arm between her shoulder blades, he lifted her completely up onto the bed and covered her with his large body. With her sandwiched between his arms and his body, he grasped her buttocks and led her into the rhythm he liked best. Beth followed his lead and pressed back in imitation. Soon they were moving more freely against each other. Their movements gathered speed and force as they found they fit together perfectly.

"Arnold. You are very big inside me."

"Mmmm. You are very tight around me. Any pain?"

"None," she murmured.

Arnold was losing his concentration. With a single-minded determination like that of Black Shadow with a willing mare, he began to move with an automatic rhythm born of the natural desire to complete their coupling and release his seed inside this new woman. His big muscles strained and rippled beneath Beth's hands and she clung to him.

All night long they stayed locked together. Sleeping, then waking again to mate.

Early the next morning, Beth woke Arnold and reminded him they had no obligations that day before noon and proceeded to lay down over him, trying to match her smaller frame to his large one. After playing that way a few minutes, wiggling and stretching, she pressed him into her and sat up riding him as she would Autumn Time.

Arnold began to think he had died and gone to heaven, which seemed too good to be true, so he decided to just enjoy it all. The entire morning passed without interruption, except for hunger pains emanating from his mid-section. As he got out of bed and headed for the shower, he stopped by the kitchen and got a good cup of coffee for himself and one for Beth.

As he entered the shower, Beth accompanied him and together they explored her new crop of pubic hair.

CHAPTER 32

Business dealings in Oklahoma consumed Arnold. The purchase of land, leasing for mineral rights and investments occupied his mind. It was February and April did not seem that far away. He began to think of taxes and more taxes, mainly income tax. He asked himself, "What should I do with the latest purchases that might lower my income tax exposure?"

He called Darrell at the bank and asked him to think about his tax obligation and to contact Darlene, the accountant. He asked Darrell to set up a joint conversation between her, Darrell and himself.

Darrell said, "He would do that, but it would be the middle of next week before he would call him back."

"That will be okay," Arnold agreed.

"We are experiencing the heaviest freezing rainstorm in the history of Oklahoma right now, and many people have lost electricity with the temperature around ten degrees and the wind at 15 knots. Oh. You might also want to know that Robert and Charlene got married yesterday, and she moved into his house."

"That is just-right timing. They can keep each other warm in the ice storm, Arnold said."

With income taxes on the mind, as soon as he got off the phone, Arnold asked Beth what she planned to do about her income taxes.

"What are you referring to?" Beth asked.

Arnold was startled. He realized that they had not talked about income taxes before and a sense of panic began to set in.

"I mean quarterly income tax filings," he explained.

"I do not know what you are referring to. I know nothing about such a thing," Beth insisted.

"Have you ever filed quarterly or yearly income taxes?" Arnold asked.

"Never," Beth said.

"Have you ever retained a tax consultant to prepare and submit income taxes for you?" Arnold asked, trying to ferret out the situation.

"No. I do not know of a tax consultant in Alamosa, Colorado. What does a tax consultant do?" Beth asked.

Arnold was astounded that Beth had never done anything with her income taxes. This seemed unthinkable to him. He realized his life had suddenly become significantly more complex, and he needed a Jack Daniels.

He poured himself a drink and sat on the couch sipping. He thought of July 7, 1956 when he started his trip and drove west on U.S. 66.

This, he thought. This is not what he had signed up for. I am not searching for more responsibility and certainly not for more income tax experience.

To settle his mind, Arnold left the house for the barn and a ride on Black Shadow. He had not completed putting the saddle on Black Shadow when Beth arrived and asked if she could accompany him?

"Absolutely," he replied.

"Did the doctor approve you lifting a saddle?" He asked.

"No and I guess I had better let you do it," Beth replied.

Arnold lifted the saddle onto Autumn Time for her and tightened the girth. Both Arnold and Beth felt the cold wind hit them as they left the barn and were glad that they had heavy coats on. They were riding right into the wind. It caused their faces to redden and their eyes to water. They began to think a ride was not such a great idea. It was exhilarating though, and they laughed out loud through their frozen tears. They soon turned back to the barn to put the wind at their backs. This helped warm them some, but not much. They were happy to reach the hay-filled barn where the wind could not reach them.

As they ate dinner that evening, Arnold received a phone call from the accountant, Darlene. She told him she was calling Darrell early the next Monday morning and would like to have him on another line at the same time to contribute and answer questions. She told Arnold she had sent a letter by mail to Darrell and one to him that she suggested they review in detail as soon as they got it to prepare for the call.

Arnold promised he would be ready.

A couple of days later, Arnold reviewed the letter and discovered he owed $2,500.00 in Federal income taxes, and $1000.00 in state of Oklahoma taxes.

When Darlene called on Monday, Arnold asked Darrell if he could coordinate with Darlene and write a check for each amount owned. Darrell said that he would take care of both. Arnold was happy because he did not like to do business while being remote. Arnold thanked both Darlene and Darrell for their help and they closed their conversation.

He turned to Beth and said, "Let's look at a phone book and research tax consultants in Alamosa, Colorado."

There were none, so he called the banker in Alamosa and asked who he used for income tax preparation purposes.

The banker replied, "My secretary, Linda White, is the best tax consultant in Colorado. I'll have her contact you later in the day."

Arnold was pleased. Hearing this he had Beth sit down at the dining room table with him, put a pot of coffee on and asked her to tell him in detail what she knew about taxes from the beginning of her time running the ranch. He reached for a pad of paper for taking notes.

Beth said, "My mother died in March of 1951 and my father died in April of 1951, just 21 days following my father. I was 33 years old. We did not have a church or cemetery in which to bury them, so Maggie and I buried them on the ranch and placed rocks at the head of each. I'm so glad for Maggie's help. I was all alone otherwise."

Se began to cry as she remembered.

"I was by myself," she repeated.

Arnold hugged Beth.

"I am so sorry Beth. I think we should postpone the discussion about taxes until tomorrow," Arnold said.

Beth sobbed for a long time, all the while, hugging Arnold tightly and periodically attempting to talk, but she was not easily understood. She continued her story in bits and pieces.

"I was scared, confused and did not know who to contact. There were no funeral homes in Alamosa, no police, no fire station, and I was alone. I contacted the banker to witness the death of my mother and later my father since I did not know what else to do. Maggie heard about me trying to bury them alone and came down to help. That is why I love her so much.

We dug the grave as deep as we could, which was about three feet and put my mother in the grave. I did not learn until later that I should have dug the grave with the head to the east instead of the north. I buried my father and then dug another grave alongside my father's grave, facing the east, and reburied my mother in the right direction."

Arnold asked how she happened to learn the proper direction to dig the graves.

"I learned from a catalog," she said. "I also spread lime over the bodies so the animals would not bother either of them."

"How much lime did you use?"

"One sack for each," she said. "It must have worked because the animals have not even tried to dig them up."

Arnold complimented Beth on her resourcefulness and suggested they go to the restaurant and eat dinner. She agreed.

Arnold drove the old truck to the restaurant. The menu was usually the same from day to day, but on this day it was different. It included ham and beans with corn bread. The usual fare was available, but Arnold wanted the ham and beans with corn bread. He had not tasted brown beans in months, and it tasted excellent to him.

"What is the difference between brown beans and pinto beans?" Beth asked.

"No difference. Bring them both on."

He ate more than he should have and back at the ranch, he decided he needed to go for a walk. Beth agreed to go with him. They put on two coats each and bundled up in this way, they enjoyed the evening.

Beth resumed telling him what she had done regarding income tax preparation and submission since the deaths of her father and mother.

After thinking through all she told him, Arnold thought of Beth's many duties and considering her state of mind following her parents' death, he concluded she and he would need to reconstruct the history of her father's tax submissions followed by documentation of income and expenses incurred on the ranch since his death.

When he asked Beth about the amount of money that was made from ranch earnings each year, she said, "None."

"What have you been living on?" Arnold asked.

"We occasionally sell a cow or calf to neighbors, and we lived on that. The reason we had so many cows to sell this year is because I did not sell any from the time my father died until this year. This was due partly to a shortage of rain and little grass until two years ago."

Arnold relaxed because her answer simplified the income tax problem greatly.

When the banker's secretary, Linda, called him the next day, he was prepared. Beth and Arnold went to the bank and took care of Beth's past taxes in one hour.

The current tax obligation was a different matter, but one that could be handled, and Beth would be able to file her taxes on time. Having achieved peace of mind, they departed with an appointment for three days later to sign the current tax filing documents.

On their way home, Arnold happened to think of his Oklahoma driver's license and retrieved it from his pocket. Upon close examination, he discovered it was current until December 31 of the current year, which was 1957.

When Arnold did this, Beth said she did not have a driver's license and had never taken a driver test to get one.

"How do you get liability insurance on your pickup truck?"

She replied, "I have never had insurance on the pickup, and the license plate my father purchased in 1950 is still on it."

Arnold was stunned that Beth did not have a license or a current tag or insurance on her truck.

How could she not have known about these things? he thought.

However, he kept his mouth shut until he had time to think about how to correct the situation.

The next morning, he went to the restaurant for breakfast, leaving Beth to sleep in. Shoo Ann was waiting tables. When she brought his coffee, he asked if she had a current drivers' license.

"Yes, but I do not own a car because I do not have the money to afford one," she said.

Do you have a driver license manual that Beth can use to prepare for the driver test?" he asked.

"I sure do, and it is current because I recently renewed my license."

"Where did you go to get your license renewed?" he asked

"You need to take the test at the Department of Motor Vehicles in Alamosa. They will mail the license to you provided you give them a $2.00 fee," Shoo Ann replied.

Before Arnold left the restaurant, Shoo Ann brought him her driver license manual.

"My good deed for the day is going to cost you a minimum of one hour of your very best time. I like your size big fellow," she said with a wink.

"Thank you, Shoo Ann. I will deliver soon and thoroughly," Arnold replied with a grin.

As he drove to the ranch house, he told himself to avoid asking Beth any further questions until he got the situations that had surfaced fixed.

Linda called on the ranch phone and Arnold answered. She said Beth's tax forms were ready for her review and signature.

"Because she sold a lot of cattle in '56 for a large sum of money and had very little to deduct in expenses, Beth will need to write a check for approximately $1,000." Linda informed Arnold. "When she comes in to sign the form, Beth needs to be ready to accompany the submission with a certified check to the Internal Revenue Service for $1, 000.00 if she wants me to file the tax forms for her," she told Arnold.

Arnold said they would be in her office in thirty minutes if that was okay with her. Linda said that was fine. Beth and Arnold drove into Alamosa that morning and took care of the tax situation.

On the way home, Beth was so happy she proclaimed Arnold "King for a day" for helping her take care of this problem she knew nothing about.

"With you around," she told Arnold, "I am learning a lot about business."

The accountant from Oklahoma, Darlene, called Arnold that afternoon, and they discussed his recent purchase of a section of land, the significant increase in the sale of oil and gas and the anticipated increase in sales the following year. She said she had explored ways to avoid income taxes that could otherwise cause him pain and discomfort and was going to recommend a tax shelter if Arnold wanted to do that.

Arnold said he was open to suggestions, but he would like to think about ways to reduce his tax liability that would help people rather than just throwing money away. That would make him happy. She agreed to send him information via mail. Arnold could review it and call her back or respond to the mail.

Darlene also told him about recent news coming in about oil and gas production in Oklahoma. The price of crude oil and natural gas was expected to rise steeply, which she predicted would more than double his income for the next year. She said she and Darrell had reviewed their latest receipts and deposits for the past two months, and their usual deposit of $4,000.00 each month had increased to $5,000 for the last month. If this continues, she said, you will need to talk to Darrell and me to avoid account balances that are not covered or protected by the FDIC.

He promised he would call Darrell soon.

Arnold sat back and reflected on his recent increase in income and tried to think of the best course of action for him and his future. He called Darrell to discuss the increase. Darrell confirmed the increase in deposit amounts and was waiting for instructions. Darrell informed him that his bank account had reached almost $40,000.00. Therefore, he had some time to make a decision. Arnold was surprised by the amount since his Federal and State of Oklahoma tax liabilities were already paid, leaving him a handsome balance.

For a poor guy traveling across the country earning his keep by working on farms and ranches, Arnold was becoming wealthy.

CHAPTER 33

Since his finances were doing well and he had solved Beth's tax problem for this year, Arnold began thinking about camping in the Snake River in Wyoming. One cold morning, he retrieved his atlas from behind the seat of his truck and traced the route he would most likely take.

Beth joined him on the couch with a cup of coffee in her hand. When he told her what he was planning, she did not show much enthusiasm about camping under the open skies in such cold conditions. He clarified that he was thinking of waiting until Spring, at least three months away. She still did not seem enthused, and although she snuggled up next to him on the couch, she politely excused herself from the trip planning and pulled out a book to read.

Arnold thought it would be best to purchase a nice new pickup in which he could sleep and not have to worry about aggressive animals bothering him. He suggested this idea to Beth.

"Camping in the rough still does no appeal to me," she said.

"Maybe I could trade in your old pick up and pay the difference. That way when we part ways, you will have a new truck without payments," Arnold suggested.

"Part ways!" Beth cried. "What do you mean by that comment?" She put her book down and looked him straight in the eyes.

"I'm sorry. I didn't mean it the way it sounded," Arnold apologized.

"Are you planning on leaving?" Beth asked. He saw there was no easy way to make up for his hasty comment.

"Beth, I promise you, I am only planning to go camping," he insisted.

"As long as you return, I can live with that, but you did not say it that way," Beth said.

Going back to his planning, he thought, there is no chance of winning that discussion.

Darrell called later in the morning and expressed his opinion of five different investments he had been monitoring. He had sent Arnold information on each and thought the material should be there soon.

The information came the next day and was interesting. The earnings were great and the risk minimal. Part of the information indicated the potential for stock splits and continued growth while other stocks reflected growth but no stock split. Arnold called Darrell back and asked him to clarify the outlook for each investment in the long term.

Darrell was not enthusiastic about the stock split investment when compared with the other four. When asked to prioritize, consistent with the investment philosophy he consistently applied to any stock purchase, Darrell recommended two that were, in his judgement, better than most and one was superior to all the others.

Arnold told Darrell to make a decision for him within the week and let him know which investment and the amount. Darrell informed him the commission would be less if he purchased as much as 100 shares of any one of the stocks he suggested.

After finishing the discussion with Darrell, Arnold began to think that he was working harder than he wanted to. He wanted to travel and be free of worrisome responsibilities, and he wanted to enjoy beautiful scenery, fresh air and sunshine. Then, he came to his senses and became more realistic. He concluded, he should do both, work and play.

He decided to visit a local Chevrolet dealer in Alameda discuss the purchase of a new pick-up with a trade in of an old one. He did not like the choices available and asked how long it would take to order one similar to the one he had described. The dealer answered, three days with a nice down payment. Arnold asked if an out of state bank account was a problem. The car dealer said it was not a problem.

Arnold ordered a V-6 pick-up with automatic drive, cover on the back, top-of the line radio system in a deep blue color. The dealer asked for $1,000.00 down and wanted the remainder upon delivery.

When he got back to the ranch, he received a call from Darrell informing him that he had purchased 1000 shares at $20.00 per share, which came to an investment of $20,000. Darrell then remarked quickly that he had talked to the banker and he approved this with you paying him back the $20, 000.00 overdraft that he would cover for Arnold.

"The reason for this hurry-up approach is that it is expected that the Amigen stock will significantly increase in value when it is announced they had a breakthrough in two of their medicines," Darrell explained.

"I think it is a good idea," Arnold replied. "The amount purchased allows for the least among of commission to be paid."

"The Amigen stock has earned a return of .09 percent in the last year," Darrell stated.

They ended the call and Arnold calculated his net worth. It was approximately 150K and growing. He concluded to himself again that he could easily afford to do both, work and play.

Over the next couple of days, Arnold decided to simplify his business, so he called Darrell and Linda and told them he wanted Darrell to assess his investments and increase each one consistent with the oil and gas deposits that occurred each month while retaining a $50,000.00 balance.

They both agreed to handle it and to send Arnold monthly statements updating him.

Having set this in motion, he contacted Charlie Anderson.

"Charlie, I've been thinking about converting the cultivated land of the parcel I recently purchased into grass for the purpose of developing an all grass operation. I've coordinated this with the Agriculture Stabilization Conservation Service, and the representative said he would send me information about the government programs dealing with this. What do you think of that idea?" Arnold asked.

"The idea is a good one. Not the best, but it is one I can live with," Charlie answered.

"Good. Thanks Charlie." Arnold ended the call.

Now that his business was in capable hands, ones that he trusted, Arnold returned to his plan to travel to the Snake River. He knew he had to wait until the weather was better for camping outside, and this had him walking the floor trying to be patient.

Although it was cold and the snow was deep, Arnold decided to dress warm and ride Black Shadow. This was always good for both of them. He rode Black Shadow to his favorite place among the trees along the brook that still ran between snow and ice-covered banks. Riding through deep snow was slower, but it was beautiful. Down in the creek bed the wind did not reach him. He squatted and cleared an area of snow so he could build a fire for additional comfort. He collected some sticks and lit the fire with a match. The aroma of burning wood cheered him. He stared into the flames thinking.

I started running from responsibilities the day I was granted a divorce, he thought. I promised myself that I would never make the mistake of getting married again. Since that day I've been relatively free, but I still feel that I am running from something. I'm not sure what I'm running from or why I'm running.

Black Shadow remained near Arnold. Sometimes he butted Arnold's shoulder with his nose as if to tell him something important. Then the horse would step away and graze for a while. Then he would return to nuzzle Arnold's shoulder again, testing the fabric lightly with his teeth. Arnold wondered if something was bothering the horse. To be safe, he took his 30-06 from the carrier attached to the saddle and loaded several shells into the magazine. To be pro-active, he located his favorite dead oak tree and fired two rounds into it. The echo bounced throughout the valley.

Black Shadow did not like the sound of gun fire. He reared up on his back legs and flared his nostrils. Arnold doused the fire and mounted Black Shadow for a fast, as fast as possible in the deep snow, ride back to the ranch house. Arnold enjoyed Black Shadows powerful stride, but he thought the horse was just glad to be back at the barn. Arnold unsaddled Black Shadow and removed his bridle. He brushed the horse down and gave him some oats and hay. After he showered at the house, Arnold suggested to Beth they eat dinner at the restaurant, and she readily agreed.

"What do you think about Shoo Ann helping out with the ranch work full time?" Beth asked as they drove to the restaurant. "Shoo Ann mentioned that Maggie did not think she could afford to keep her on at the restaurant. I think it would be great to have her help when you go camping."

"Where do you plan for Shoo Ann to live?" asked Arnold.

"She can live with us at the ranch. She spends most of her free time there anyway," Beth said, "I would welcome her assistance with the cooking. She can give me driving lessons."

They arrived at the restaurant and ordered their food from Shoo Ann who was waiting on their table.

"You can move into the ranch house and start working on the ranch Shoo Ann," Beth said. "When do you think you would like to start?"

"Tomorrow morning would be fine," said Shoo Ann.

"Tomorrow morning, I have an appointment to pick up a late Christmas present at 8:00 AM," said Arnold. "The dealership representative called today and informed me that I could pick up the new truck tomorrow."

Beth decided the next morning to accompany Arnold to get the new pickup. As they drove the brand new clean smelling truck out of the lot with the radio playing, Arnold said, "I think we should register this pick up in your name and address, insure it under your name and treat the vehicle as if it is your new pick up."

Until that moment, Beth had not showed any enthusiasm for buying the new pickup. She did not seem to either approve or disapprove of the purchase. Now, she finally exhibited some excitement and asked, "Is it really mine?"

Arnold assured her it was. She wanted to drive it, so, they changed places and went sightseeing, driving for the pure pleasure of it. Beth chattered happily saying how well the truck drove and how much she liked the color.

Once they made it back to the ranch, Arnold received a flurry of calls. Everything seemed to be good news. Linda, being true to form, sent Arnold a tax shelter that, upon review, could prevent him from paying the IRS such large amounts of income tax. She informed him she was not an investment guru and wanted him to know she was not making a recommendation but would continue to send Arnold information and he should proceed at his own risk.

Arnold thanked her for the help. He had explored many ways to avoid the tax consequences of earning large sums of money. He was not pleased with the results he had achieved on his own. He believed God had directed him to success. So, he looked for tax shelters that helped people. Whenever Linda sent information, he placed it in a drawer beside his bed.

Robert also called Arnold that day and wanted to know if he was satisfied with his land purchase. Arnold assured him he was pleased and was open to additional opportunities if a good one surfaced. Robert said there was nothing exciting available right now, but he would keep him posted.

"How is Charlene doing?" Arnold asked.

"She is doing well," Robert said. "She has a new job that she really enjoys." We, Charlene and I, purchased a new house and will be moving into it soon."

CHAPTER 34

Shoo Ann moved in and began working on the ranch. Spring finally seemed to be making an appearance, showing everyone the world would soon revive. Trees began to blossom. Grass began to show the tender green that makes it beautiful, and birds began chirping all around the ranch.

Arnold was pleased with his financial portfolio and that Beth seemed to be recovering well from her surgery. He concluded he should finalize his plans for traveling to the Snake River.

Arnold was looking at his maps one morning when Shoo Ann appeared from her bedroom and asked if she could accompany him on his planned camp out. She said she had discussed it with Beth, learned that Beth was not going and wanted to take the opportunity to go if he wanted her to.

"I think I can handle things," Beth said as she too entered the room from her bedroom and caught the tail end of Shoo Ann's request. "I think a trip would be good for Shoo Ann, and the time alone will be good for me too."

Arnold realized the weather was somewhat cool and perhaps early for camping outdoors in the Wyoming area, but since he planned to sleep inside the pickup, he thought, why not. Arnold agreed to let Shoo Ann travel with him, and they began packing for the trip.

Arnold loaded the truck with supplies, especially water and coffee, and food stuffs that were easy to prepare. He threw in an axe and a wedge. He was familiar with several campsites in the area along the Snake River. He knew he might need to cut firewood because many campers used the wood in the campsites but expected others to restock it. Arnold did not care. He liked to cut wood. Cutting wood was a manly occupation and made him feel virile. He and Shoo Ann checked to make sure that the cattle were taken care of and would need very little attention until they returned.

They left Alamosa before sunup two days later. It would take 11 hours of driving to reach the Snake River from Colorado. He and Shoo Ann took turns driving. It was a beautiful drive, and Shoo Ann was like a kid with a new toy, excited and extremely happy, looking at everything they passed. They passed through several national forests, wide grasslands where antelope grazed, and stopped near the Wind River Indian Reservation for the night

There were no camps available the first night, so they rented a motel room for two. They walked to a nearby restaurant for dinner. Shoo Ann only ate half of her dinner. In the motel room, she seemed quiet and reserved. Arnold made no advances. He merely went to bed.

Shoo Ann listened to the radio for a short time after Arnold went to bed. Then she said, "Good night," got into bed and relaxed into sleep.

The next day began with a healthy breakfast and promised total enjoyment. They could see the mountains in the distance. Arnold was eager to get even closer to them. As they approached the Snake River, they located one of the campgrounds Arnold had visited before. They found a secluded camp site and set up camp. Shoo Ann made up a bed in the bed of the truck. Arnold built a fire to break the chill of the evening and pulled two chairs from the truck and set them close to the fire ring. He hung a coffee pot from a tripod over the fire. The aroma of fresh coffee spread over the entire camp site.

As if following the smell of coffee, a couple of visitors soon stepped into their camp and introduced themselves. They were two sisters, Martha and Estelle Livingston, both schoolteachers from Canada. Arnold estimated that they were in their late twenties and seemed to be very friendly. Arnold invited them to join the party for a cup of coffee. They accepted quickly.

The sisters admitted they were concerned about wild animals along the river. Arnold invited them to join Shoo Ann and himself at their campsite if that would make them feel more comfortable. They disappeared and soon came back with their gear. At the time, he was not planning for them to join them in the bed of the truck, but that is what occurred.

When they all gave up to weariness and banked the fire for the night, the two teachers moved into the bed of the pickup with Shoo Ann and Arnold. In the cold night, their bodies moved together for warmth. Legs and arms became entwined. For Arnold, it was hard to tell one woman from another as they groped about. Since Arnold was the only man, the other three knew exactly which one he was, and they gave his body a lot of attention, taking turns engulfing his hard sex into their soft, wet warmth and exploring his body with their hands and lips. Finally, they all fell asleep, warmed by the sex and the nearness their bodies.

Arnold crawled out of his bedroll the next morning, stoked the fire, made a fresh cup of coffee and enjoyed watching the moon and stars before the morning light made them fade into the sky. The early morning hours were especially enjoyable. It was quiet. Birds were just starting to stir. Although he could not see them, Arnold knew the elk would be feeding. And, the sight of the snow-covered mountains was breathtaking. For a moment he was mesmerized by the presence of a mother deer and her fawn. He completely tuned out the crackle of logs on the fire.

I've stayed away from the wilderness too long, the thought. He did his best to take it all in, enjoy it and let it sink into his memory forever. He promised himself he would frequently recall this scene as a reminder about the magnificence and beauty of God's creation.

Despite the beauty and peace of the campground, Arnold was soon back to thinking about his investments. He turned on the truck radio and listened to the stock market report. Although, he was supposed to be on vacation and he knew he had left his investments in good hands, he wanted his own update on his stocks. He promised himself that he would soon do something about his obsession with financial success, but he did not know what to do or where to start.

Several minutes passed before the ladies joined him. He had started cooking breakfast. The smell of the coffee and bacon cooking on the open fire was enough to stir their appetites and cause them to crawl out of bed and join him. After filling several coffee cups, he realized his four-cup coffee pot needed a refill and began preparing another pot. He had not prepared for four people at the breakfast table, but he made the food stretch to all of them. It was enjoyable listening to the Canadian ladies tell of their teaching experiences and about their camping journey.

Arnold had purchased a brand-new camera for the trip. He decided to use it to record the beauty he was seeing. He knew he was going to need some luck because he had not used a camera in years. Shoo Ann came to his rescue. She took over the picture taking and looked to Arnold to be a professional as she snapped pictures of the mountains, the river, a deer, the campers and the camp site.

After they had all eaten, Arnold suggested they hike to and along the Snake River, perhaps do a little trout fishing and return in a couple of hours. He made up a fishing pole for himself. Everyone agreed. He grabbed his fishing pole and the group began to follow a trail that led along the riverbank.

Arnold could not resist the lure of the fast current of the river and began casting for trout. Luck was on his side, and he caught two 8-inch trout. The ladies commented that they had never tried their luck at fishing. He suggested they start now. Taking turns, they each cast into the river and patiently waited, but not for long. Shoo Ann was the first to catch a trout but was afraid to remove it from the fishhook. She made faces and didn't want to touch the fish. Her antics had them all laughing. Martha and Estelle took turns demonstrating their skill at trout fishing. They also enjoyed watching boaters float by on the river. One group included swimmers paddling along-side the boat and yelling with excitement.

They walked for three hours. They took lots of pictures and complained loudly of sore and aching feet. When they returned to the camp site, Arnold cleaned the fish and laid them in the cold water to keep for dinner. Marth and Estelle donated food to go with the fresh trout and conversed about living in Canada. This conversation caused Arnold to write down their names, addresses and directions to their homes. Arnold was already beginning to plan another trip because their description of their own country was so exciting. That evening the four of them sat around the fire, ate fresh trout, drank good wine and consumed lots of good food.

Toward evening, Arnold and Shoo Ann discussed finding another camp site farther north along the Snake River. Arnold and Shoo Ann invited Martha and Estelle to accompany them. The trip along the banks of the river proved rewarding because all along the way they observed interesting wild animals. A mother deer with two fawns entertained them. The deer played near them and did not appear frightened at their presence. They thought it was too early, or perhaps late, for bears to be mating, but the bears were mating uninhibited in full view.

Shoo Ann informed the group she had never seen two bears mating before this and would probably remember it forever.

Estelle said, "In Canada, we watch this occur daily."

"Oh Estelle, don't tell stories," Martha scolded.

After three days of camping, Arnold and Shoo Ann decided to break camp and return to the ranch, saying their goodbyes to Martha and Estelle. Martha insisted they visit Canada and offered their house phone numbers. Arnold wrote the phone numbers on a paper and put them in his pocket. Shoo Ann noticed his action and informed him that she was going to keep him too busy to look elsewhere so he would not need the phone numbers. He thought she was being very protective and perceptive. Their drive home was enjoyable because they had got their fill of Mother Nature's trees, mountains, rivers and lakes.

Arnold saw a restaurant and stopped to use their phone to call Beth to inform her that everything at the Snake River had gone fine.

"Is everything normal there? Are the trees and grass starting to turn green?" Arnold asked.

"Oh yes." Beth answered.

"We were not eaten by bears," he said, "but we did see some."

"I'm glad. Do you want to know what is in your mail or do you want to wait until you get home to know about it?" Beth asked.

"I would like to know the contents of any mail from Robert, Darrell, Charlie, Linda, or Wyatt regarding investments, the farmland, the bank account or the oil and gas leases," Arnold said

"No....wait. I have changed my mind. I don't want to know until I get back. I'm on vacation!"

About halfway home, Shoo Ann suggested they stop at a motel and rest their weary bodies. It was getting late. He saw a motel in a lovely valley that seemed to beg drivers to stop and enjoy. Shoo Ann caught sight of the same motel and they agreed it was time to stop for the evening. While filling out the motel's registration form, he asked the desk clerks if they could recommend a restaurant. The two clerks said that the Ponderosa served great steak, but not fish. Steak sounded good to him, and he asked for directions.

After dinner, at the Ponderosa, he asked Shoo Ann if she had any plans for the evening.

"My plans are your plans," Shoo Ann said as Arnold unlocked the motel room door.

They stripped their clothes off and then, because they were tired and stiff from driving, they did not do anything at first but lie together on the full-sized bed. Later in the night, after each had slept briefly, they turned to each other in the moonlight that streamed in the window above the head of the bed.

Arnold touched Shoo Ann between the legs, and she lit up like a sparkler, stiffening as she came swiftly and without warning. Arnold turned her over, set her up on her knees and entered her from behind while her body still quivered with pleasure. He soaked up the last waves of her climax then began to move in slow long strokes in and out of her warm vagina. His rough hands stroked her from breast to pubis as he moved, exploring her curves and dimples. She began to breath faster as his fingers lingered over her nipples and then dove down to circle her clitoris. His long strokes quickened, and he grasped her hip bones and shoved himself one last time deep inside her then held her tightly as he finished.

They collapsed on the bed and Shoo Ann whispered, "Very thorough. Very good. Just as you promised."

Shoo Ann fell right to sleep. Arnold lay for a while thinking about how Shoo Ann slept with both men and women. Beth had told him so. She had told him that she and Shoo Ann sometimes slept together as lovers. He didn't know quite how that worked, but it seemed to be okay with him. He could share with a woman. Both Shoo Ann and Beth were completely open and accepted pleasure from wherever it came. He knew that. He accepted that.

That morning, they began the final lap of their journey to the ranch. Thoughts of his business dealings in Oklahoma crossed his mind several times during the rest of the drive.

As soon as they arrived, he reviewed the mail and became immediately possessed by a need to travel to Oklahoma and take care of personal business. He made several phone calls to determine the urgency of the issues. He contacted Robert about real estate, the two sections of land recently purchased and leased. He called Darrell regarding his investments and the balance in his bank accounts. The investments rose to the top of his priority list. He contacted Linda regarding a tax shelter she had discovered, and he asked her to provide more details about it. She told him the detailed description of the shelter was 68 pages, so they decided to go over it when they met in Oklahoma. Linda agreed to set a meeting date once she knew when he would fly in. He promised to give her that information soon.

When he was about to leave the house for a ride on Black Shadow, Charlie Anderson caught him, calling to report that all the projects to convert cultivated land to grass had been completed with outstanding success. He also said the rain gods were cooperating and a light rain had been falling for two days. The grass was already beginning to sprout and grow. This news sealed Arnold's plans to return to Oklahoma very soon.

Finally escaping to the barn, Arnold saddled Black Shadow. As they rode out of the ranch yard, Black Shadow headed for Arnold's favorite place, the trees adjacent to the flowing brook, without any direction from Arnold. It seemed like the horse could read his mind. Black Shadow stopped walking and started eating grass right where Arnold had previously made a fire.

Arnold dismounted and removed his extra blanket from the saddle bags and spread it on the grass. He stretched out and began to dream about returning to Oklahoma. Many thoughts rushed into his head and he almost panicked trying to prioritize the most important activities. At the top of the list sat Linda and the tax shelter. His recollection of Linda was a mix of investment ideas and curiosity about her personally. Was it possible for him to get better acquainted with her, or should he avoid her? He wondered.

He tried to relax and watched Black Shadow, but he could not get business off his mind. He got up and put the blanket back in the saddle bag, tightened the girth on the saddle and swung up on Black Shadow. Black Shadow took off in a gliding lope at the first nudge of Arnold's heels. They sailed over miles of ground before returning to the barn where Arnold gave Black Shadow a drink and a much-deserved rub down.

As he entered the ranch house, the phone was ringing. He knew relaxation was not to be, not now and not soon. Darrell was calling regarding his latest investment and wanted to set up a conference call with Linda. Darrel got Linda on the line and they discussed a plan that included splitting Arnold's holdings three ways and then selling all of it publicly, which would take it out of the private holdings. Linda expressed her opinion that it was a good thing to do, and Darrell agreed. Darrell said Arnold would net, over $60,000.00. Adding that amount to the first investment that split, if sold also (which was planned) would net approximately $120,000.00.

Arnold informed everyone on the call that he would schedule a trip to Oklahoma soon, and he would send them mail confirming his arrival date. After everyone hung up the phone, Linda called Arnold and asked where he was going to stay. When he informed her that he had not made airline reservations yet and that he wanted to complete that before contacting a motel, Linda said, "You can stay with me if you like, I have an extra bedroom you can use for as long as you need."

"I will certainly think about it," Arnold replied.

After these calls, it occurred to him how much he trusted and respected the people with whom he did business in Oklahoma. What Linda suggested was definitely not business though, and that did not help matters. His mind was spinning with possibilities. He didn't know Linda well, but he wanted to.

After his work was complete, Arnold joined Beth and Shoo Ann for a glass of wine and conversation in front of the fireplace. He reminded them that he was going to Oklahoma on business soon. Both ladies wanted to go with him.

"Who will take care of the cattle and horses if you both go with me?" he asked.

They did not come up with any answers, so it was agreed that he should go alone. He had a second glass of wine which felt good going down

Later, he called the airlines in Pueblo and scheduled a flight for the day after tomorrow.

His flight departed early and arrived in Oklahoma midmorning as scheduled. He rented a car and proceeded to his usual motel in El Reno. He checked in and deposited his luggage to avoid carrying it around with him or leaving it in the car. He called Linda to tell her he was in town and had a motel already to avoid stringing her along without a response from him. He wanted to establish a time to meet with her and Darrell regarding his investments. This took priority in his action plan. Linda called him right back and informed him Darrell wanted to meet as soon as possible, so they agreed to meet in Calumet in an hour.

He was pleasantly surprised by Linda. She was articulate, knew her facts and communicated the projection of earnings along with the risks. She did not show encouragement or resistance, and he thought she was totally objective. Darrell presented the latest earning projections and agreed with Linda in her assessment of the future. Darrell said the latest account of Arnold's total investment, if he should decide to sell on that day, would be a little over 1 million.

Arnold instructed Darrell to sell provided he and Linda had a plan for the next steps to take. They discussed his overall investment strategies, and both agreed he should sell, retain the money in his account, wait for the stock to adjust in value after reflecting the split, then purchase about $100,000 more and wait to evaluate the effect of that purchase. Then, later decide whether to purchase additional stock. They each believed the stock would rebound after six months or so and strongly believed earnings would be better than average in the long term.

Arnold agreed with the proposed strategy, and they conversed about family and local news for a while longer. Darrell left, and Linda and he got acquainted and agreed to go to dinner that evening at 7:00 PM.

CHAPTER 35

Arnold drove out of Calumet into the countryside to look over his recently purchased land. It was summer, so the low rolling Oklahoma hills were a dry green. Tall trees grew in the draws and showed over the ridges in small clumps of three or four. He headed first for the section of land that was his home stomping grounds, the farm he had been born and raised on.

He turned in at the gravel drive that was the entrance to the farm. The road was lined with fences on both sides and ended in a turnaround where two outbuildings stood on one side of the circle and the foundation that had once supported his family's home could be seen on the other. The house had burned down and had never been replaced. The foundation was engulfed in tall grasses and weeds. A bed of irises had survived the fire and the years.

He got out of the car and wandered around the two barns. The stalls were dusty, and cobwebs drifted from the ceiling rafters. Arnold remembered riding his horse across the fields and along all the roads in the area. He had spent a lot of time on Smoky his sturdy cow pony.

Smoky was a bay of uncertain bloodlines. By looking at him, his father had guessed he was part Quarter Horse and part Morgan.

While the farm was completely different from the ranch in Colorado, this piece of ground was home, a place where he, his siblings and parents labored many hours, sweated through many hot and dusty hours loading hay and milking cows, worrying where their next dollar was going to come from. They had also played cards, checkers, tag and baseball; went on picnics; prayed; and fished for bass and catfish. He opened a barbed wire gate and drove across the pasture to a pond that was partially overgrown with cattails and stopped on the dam, rolling his window down, leaning his head back on the seat, letting past times visit. When he remembered the past, the present did not seem real.

He replayed his father's words, "always do what is right." He also recalled his father giving him a handshake and telling him, "all will be okay." His mother's advice had been "be calm and never quit," accompanied by a hug and a kiss.

Emotion welled up in him.

Hearing a noise, he glanced out the window of the car, and saw a car approaching through the gate he had left open. He recognized the car as the one belonging to Linda. He wondered why she was here.

He got out of the rental car to greet her. She got out of her car and handed him a to-go cup of ice water.

"Are you deep in thought?" She asked.

"I am," he replied. "Would you join me? Thank you for the ice water."

Together they leaned against the hood of the car.

They talked for several hours. Both had experienced painful divorces. Linda told him she was 36 years of age and had once been married, but it lasted only six months. The marriage had ended ten years ago. She had dated periodically with little success. Most of her dates were with fellas she encountered in the investment world or educational field. She found them as lonely as she, but with little imagination. She on the other hand had big dreams. She wanted to have children and travel.

Linda seemed to have moved beyond her bad experience and no longer held ill feeling about any of it. Arnold wanted to know how this could be. He listened intently as she explained that she had a great desire to live for the future, not the past. She told him that her future held promise and that she was working hard to make the promise come to life. She was working on a degree in finance and on a certificate authorizing her to perform financial counseling. She was in the process of becoming a licensed financial counselor. Linda told him that her goals were of achievement not dwelling on pessimistic issues and despair.

Arnold recognized that this conversation was fitting in the light of his recent daydreaming about the past and future. He wondered silently if he could do the same as Linda, except his effort would focus on becoming self-sufficient financially through investments.

Looking at the time, Linda said, "It is almost time for us to get dinner. We have been talking a long time."

"Do you want to see the farm first?" Arnold asked.

"I would love to," Linda replied.

Together they drove in his rental car down some barely discernable tracks that had once been two-track roads used to get around the farm. The pastures needed some attention. The fences did too. The hills were beautiful and peaceful though as the sun set. They came back to the main compound on a different road than they had started on. Arnold pointed out the foundation of the house, and he and Linda got out to take a quick look in the barns before the sun completely disappeared.

When they returned to the pond where Linda's car was parked, Linda got in her car, and he followed her to a steak house in Calumet. Their dinner was delicious.

The next day, Arnold met Robert who had informed him he was pursuing the purchase of additional land adjacent to the southern section that Arnold already owned. Robert drove his car, and they toured the additional land.

Arnold asked Robert if he recalled that the previous mineral lease for one section was $10.00 per acre.

Robert said, "Yes. That is what it was, but the lease price has increased significantly because of the many productive wells just east of you, and they are now paying $40.00 to $50.00 per acre.

Arnold quickly calculated that amount in his head to be about $110,000 income for the section.

"That would buy dinner for several people," Arnold laughed.

As they completed their tour, Arnold asked, "Robert. Why is the farmer selling this land?"

"The farmer died, and the kids want their money."

"I want to buy as soon as possible, Arnold said. "I will pay as much as $15,000.00 per quarter."

"I must make a couple of calls," Robert said.

Arnold called Beth and told her he had purchased another section of Oklahoma soil. She did not sound happy.

Arnold met later with Wyatt Ore, the man in charge of the oil leases and confirmed the lease price of $40.00 to $50.00 per acre. Wyatt promised to send Arnold a check. Arnold asked if he could deliver it to Darrell at the bank instead. Wyatt said he would.

Arnold called Linda and they scheduled dinner again. Over hearty chicken fried steak and later over beer, they talked about investments and their personal goals until the early morning hours.

It was 2:00 AM when Arnold returned to the motel. He was not sleepy.

As he laid on his bed awake, Arnold wondered why his rising income and his bright-looking future did not bring him more peace of mind.

He wished he could put the hurt and bitterness of his marriage behind him like Linda did. He wished he did not replay the humiliation of knowing that his wife had been possessed by another man willingly during their marriage. On this subject his anger remained very primitively male.

If I was a stallion, he thought, I would have some satisfaction from driving the other male away from what is mine with the physical force of teeth and hoof. Instead I fought like a modern man, not with my fists, which might have been more satisfying, but financially with hired investigators and lawyers. The satisfaction of preserving my hard-earned wealth was there intellectually, but it did not penetrate to my heart, that vital organ that kept the anger of betrayal alive.

Arnold's bitter thoughts were interrupted by the ringing of the phone in his room. He looked at the clock. It was very early, so early in fact he had not slept only tossed and turned in his bed. He answered the phone and listened to Linda tell him she was driving to his motel and wanted to go to breakfast in 15 minutes.

He gladly promised to be ready, got up, washed, combed his hair and looked at the clock; it was 4:30 AM. Breakfast at that hour was always delicious and the coffee would taste great.

He and Linda met at the restaurant adjacent to the motel and enjoyed breakfast very much. They were realizing that they had a lot in common and that time flew when they were together. Arnold was developing a great respect for her, especially in how she faced the future and in how she conducted business. He thought she would be very successful and wondered if she was not perhaps the right person for him.

They made plans to ask Robert and Charlene to eat dinner with them soon.

Before they finished breakfast, Arnold asked Linda if she had any debts that he could help her with since she was still pursuing her education and he was currently doing well financially.

"I have one more payment of $600.00 that is due in one year," she acknowledged.

"Would you be willing to let me pay that off for you now, so you are free of that debt?" Arnold asked. "I want you to know how much I appreciate your investment advice."

"I'd appreciate that very much," Linda said.

"Okay then. Let's head over to the bank and see Darrell. I'll write you a check and you can do with it what you wish. You can be free of that debt."

They drove separately to the bank in Calumet.

"Darrell, I'd like you to write a check for Linda in the amount of $600.00 so she can finish paying for her education."

"Since you are interested in helping people with educational expenses," Darrell asked, "would you be interested in supporting some other young school-age children in need of financial help?"

"I am a supporter of several children whose parents are in an income level below the poverty line, but not yet qualifying for welfare assistance," Darrell explained. "I provide aid to pay for school supplies, lunches, medical help, and such."

"I'd be happy to confidentially pay for those expenses provided you are the front for it all and nobody knows the aid comes from me."

"That is Fine."

"How much do you need?"

"Between a thousand and three thousand a year, depending on the number of students that attended school."

"I will fund up to the three thousand a year limit," Arnold said. "Write two checks, one to Linda for $600.00 and the other for $3,000.00 to accommodate the aid to the children's fund."

"Are you going to move back to Oklahoma soon?" Darrell asked.

"Not soon, but in the future." Arnold informed him.

Darrell informed Arnold they were monitoring the balance of his deposits.

"There might be a significant increase in the near future," Arnold said, "especially if they drill for gas and oil on the section recently leased."

As they left the bank, Linda thanked him for the support and friendship. They agreed to communicate frequently and pursue a long and meaningful relationship leading to a great future. They smiled at each other.

"I don't want to sound pushy, Linda," said Arnold. "I only gave you $600.00. Do you need any monthly support? I'm only interested in your welfare."

"Oh no," Linda replied. "I am financially independent, thanks to my parents who left me a half section of land I still own. It is leased for income. I also draw a nice salary each month as an investment counselor. Thank you for helping me with the education debt."

"I am very impressed with your abilities Linda. I want you to succeed and I think you will," Arnold said. "I need to tell you one thing about myself, which has interfered with my relationships with women before I…"

Linda placed her fingers over his lips and interrupted him.

"I have more than strong feelings for you Arnold. I want you to know just how I feel. I do not often become emotional about a man, especially one I know the way I know you. I intend to see this budding relationship develop into full bloom because I love you and want you to belong to me. I have prayed to my Lord and Savior that you would see it my way, and I believe you think the same, but I know of the hurt you have experienced. I will help you deal with it, if you will let me."

Linda kissed him very passionately and said, "I love you, and I want you to call me often and return to Oklahoma soon."

With that, Linda turned and got into her own car and drove away.

Arnold stood in front of the bank a little stunned and then got into his rental car and returned to the motel. His plane left in 5 hours, so he had just enough time for a nap and to pack.

269

CHAPTER 36

Arnold tried to rest. He lay on his back, eyes wide open, his hands behind his head on the pillow. Sleep was nowhere in sight.

He asked himself why he could not make a commitment to someone as nice and smart as Linda. I think and feel the same way about Beth, he admitted to himself. And, there is Brenda, Shoo Ann, Maggie, all of them desirable.

The answer is that I do not want to get hurt. I don't want to be exposed to the pain and wounded feelings that go along with relationships, he thought.

Arnold was already missing Linda and wishing he had not tried to discourage her feelings for him as he had. He called Linda with the intent of trying to explain his emotions. She did not answer the phone. He dialed again, and she did not answer. Thirty minutes later, he tried again. He let the phone ring ten times. Again, no response.

He gave it up, put his boots back on and packed his suitcase. He drove slowly by his property and out into the country to watch oil well horse heads pump up and down. He drove to the airport, dropped off his rental car and walked through the crowd that had gathered to board the same flight he was on. When he finally boarded his flight, he sat beside a beautiful woman who was in tears.

He asked himself, what have I done to deserve this?

As they taxied out of the airport terminal, his seat mate asked him "Have you ever loved someone who did not love you?"

"I find it hard to understand how a man could not love you," Arnold replied.

She did not answer, and he soon fell asleep only to awaken to her continued sobbing. He listened for the whole flight to her intermittent sobbing but did not try to help her. Her pain was intense, so intense he was afraid he would be pulled in and his own pain reawakened. When the flight arrived in Pueblo, he got up to let her out of the seat. He gave her a brief hug, wished her well and followed her down the aisle.

He tried to shake off the dreariness of the flight. He was looking forward to a nice ride on Black Shadow and a stiff drink of Jack Daniels.

His business in Oklahoma was booming, He made no new commitments. He was again a free man with few responsibilities.

He said to himself, "Arnold ole boy, keep it that way."

As soon as he returned to the ranch, Beth greeted him with a hug and kiss and insisted they saddle the horses, ride to their favorite spot on the ranch and spend some time together by the brook. She wanted to hear all about his trip and his new properties. After the heat and humidity of Oklahoma, Colorado felt refreshingly cool and dry. He could almost see the shade of their favorite tree and hear the water as it flowed slowly downstream.

As Arnold settled into the saddle, Beth swung her leg up over Autumn Time.

"I am finally able to ride comfortably," she said. "Happily, the scars of my surgery are not so tight, and the muscles are starting to heal."

He felt the pent-up power emanating from Black Shadow as he danced around eager for a run. He felt the magic of ranch life at its best. Having Beth beside him was thrilling and uplifted his spirits. The two smiled broadly at each other from atop their respective mounts. For reasons he could not explain, Beth communicated comfort, a feeling of togetherness that he had not realized before. He sat back and enjoyed the ride to their favorite spot.

When they reached their favorite location on the ranch, Black Shadow seemed to be nervous. He held his head high. His nostrils flared, and his eyes rolled from side to side. He refused to settle down. Arnold surveyed the area, looking for the danger that Black Shadow sensed. Soon, he picked out the stealthy movement of the ever-present mountain lion walking along a nearby ridge. He retrieved his rifle from its place alongside the saddle and fired a few shots at a dead tree. The sound echoed up and down the valley, shattering the calm quiet.

The lion disappeared. Black Shadow settled down. He did not seem to mind the sound of the rifle as much this time. Arnold concluded that the horse had learned the rifle did not harm him. Arnold and Beth dismounted. Beth spun around with her arms out and her head back smiling into the sky. They shook out their blankets and placed them side by side on the ground. They lay close to each other feeling very much like they had been apart for a long time when it had only been two weeks. They cuddled and kissed passionately.

Beth wanted to know the details of the Oklahoma visit. He explained that his business dealings were being handled well by those he had chosen to make good investment decisions. He told her about the boom in gas and oil production and how the amount oil and gas companies were willing to pay for land leases had increased in rural Oklahoma.

He tried not to get into too much of the detail of the business dealings and explained them in an abbreviated manner. He told her he would need to make periodic visits to ensure all was well. Beth seemed to understand.

Beth enquired about his ex-wife, and he told her he did not see his ex-wife on this visit, nor did he plan to in the future. Beth wanted to know if he had encountered other women on his trip whom he found interesting. Arnold explained he had been on a business trip, one that required his focus and attention and not one that offered social entertainment.

He wondered why Beth was so inquisitive. He wondered if she was jealous. Rather than raise the issue, he chose to remain silent for the present time. Beth informed Arnold she wanted to go with him the next time. He felt so comfortable and happy with Beth that for a moment, he began to think of making a commitment, something that he had been refusing to do. He realized that his long-held suspicion and distrust was becoming a serious roadblock to his own happiness.

"Beth. Do you think I am cheating on you if I see another woman?" Arnold asked.

"I would hope you would do the right thing," she said, "as you have so often said your father advised you."

"I do not claim any right to you or your person," she continued; "however, I would like to claim you almost as if I owned you. But that is not right. I merely think and feel that way. You have treated me as no other person has treated me, including my own parents. I am selfish in a way because I love you and I do not want our relationship to be lessened in any way, not the slightest. When you are on a trip, I miss you from start to finish. That is how I feel.

I know that you were hurt during your lengthy divorce and by the false accusations made during the legal proceedings. Please allow me to help by listening to all of it closely and pointing out alternative thoughts to oppose the negative feelings. I'd like to plant new thoughts in your mind that are good. Let's kick this darkness out, so it is no longer a part of your life and not worthy of one second of thought from you."

"I will try, Madam psychologist," he grinned, "to focus on our relationship instead of on the past because it is more pleasant to think about," Arnold promised.

"But what should I do when I wake up thinking angry thoughts first thing?" Arnold asked.

"Think of us. Think of me. Your mind can only focus on one thing at a time. Force yourself to focus on something other than your anger."

Again, Arnold promised that he would try.

The lion returned and Black Shadow reacted violently, pulling on the reins that were tied over a branch. Arnold began to survey the area again and simultaneously retrieved his rifle, injected a cartridge into the chamber and fired a shot into the same dead tree he shot at before, and then he saw the lion. He thought it must be a female returning to the location of her den or to her cubs. He thought they should leave the area and leave the lion to her family. Although he had decided to purchase a few llamas to protect the cattle, it was not his intent to interrupt the lives of the wild animals. That is when he saw a second lion, one apparently interested in the other. He and Beth watched, fascinated, as the two lions met, romped in the grass and began to mate.

Their ride back to the ranch house was more relaxed than the one over; it was most enjoyable. They took the saddles off the horses, rubbed them down, made sure they had food and water and set them free to roam in the home pasture as they pleased. Arnold complemented Beth on how efficient she had become at taking care of Autumn Time. He asked her if she had calculated the gestation period for her foal. She said the little one was not due for 5 months.

They wandered up to the house and as soon they opened the door, the phone rang.

Arnold looked at Beth apologetically and said, "I have to answer it."

It was Charlie Anderson asking how much in damage costs Arnold was expecting from the oil drilling operation that was beginning to occur on the west section of his land.

"The oil companies will pay whatever they pay for damages." Arnold said.

"This is covered in the mineral rights lease I signed.

"You tell me when damage occurs to the land, and I'll assess the amount of damage to the value of the land as it occurs and make adjustments accordingly."

Charlie grumbled an agreement and they ended the call.

Immediately the phone rang again.

It was Darrell wanting him to suggest a way to accommodate deposits that would frequently exceed the amount insured by the FDIC.

"The oil and gas wells are beginning to produce well ahead of earlier predictions, and I need instructions from you about how to deal with the excess," Darrell explained.

"I'll be calling you soon," Arnold said.

"But I need an estimate of the amount you expect to be deposited each month, now!" Darrell said.

"Up to $400,000.00 dollars," Arnold replied. "I'll call you soon."

He glanced over at Beth after he hung up. She was laughing as she leaned against the wall with her boots crossed watching him. He quirked an eyebrow at her in question.

"You are obsessed with the business dealings in Oklahoma," Beth groaned, "and they are obsessed with you."

Arnold return his attention to Beth.

"I think we should get some llamas soon since we saw those lions on our ride."

"I agree," Beth said.

Arnold placed a call to the auction house for assistance. Their response was immediate, and they wanted to know how many and when.

"We want three females and three males as soon as you can deliver them."

The auction house representative promised to deliver the animals as soon as possible.

"Are they vaccinated against disease?" Arnold asked.

"Yes. They are all vaccinated," came the reply.

He was pleasantly surprised.

"Beth," he said, "I know you think I am obsessed with the deposit situation in Oklahoma. So, I am apologizing in advance for the calls I am going to have to make but it is necessary for me to make some important decisions."

"I understand," Beth said, "and I'm sorry for becoming irritated over it earlier."

He realized his obsession with business was becoming worse. If something needed to be done anywhere, he felt the need to do it, now. He thought he had been improving, but apparently, he had thought wrong.

Maybe if I think of Wyoming and the Snake River camp site and being all alone in the open with no one to bother me — Dream on Arnold, Dream on, he told himself.

CHAPTER 37

The lion activity on the ranch concerned Arnold mightily all that night. The next morning, he mentioned it to Beth and Shoo Ann and asked if there had been such activity while he was absent.

"I saw one near the barn while you were gone and one along the drive," said Beth.

"I've seen two lions while riding Autumn Time," Shoo Ann added.

Arnold concluded there was reason for concern. After breakfast and coffee, he reached for his rifle. He said he was going to return to the same area where they encountered the two lions the day before, and this time he would not be shooting at a tree.

"I think you should not go alone," Shoo Ann said. "I'll go with you."

"Have you ever fired a rifle?" Arnold asked.

"No and I am not in a hurry to do so," Shoo Ann replied, but stuffed her feet into her riding boots.

"I think Shoo Ann should go with you." Beth agreed.

Arnold and Shoo Ann saddled the horses and rode out to everyone's favorite area by the brook but did not see a lion. Out of caution, they drove the cattle to the corral and distributed hay for them to eat. Arnold hoped they would have llamas by the afternoon to accompany the cows on their next journey out to graze.

Several hours later, a truck and horse trailer came up the drive in a swirl of dust and backed up to the corral gate that Arnold pointed them too. The trailer contained six fractious llamas who were swirling around in the trailer, banging the trailer's sides, and squealing. Arnold thought they looked like they had had enough of being in close quarters and were ready to disembark.

Shoo Ann and Beth came running out of the house and jumped up on the lower fence rails, hanging over to watch the llamas join the cattle. Arnold swung the corral gate open, and the auction representatives opened the back of the trailer. The llamas launched off the back of the trailer as soon as the door was opened and ran–bounced around the inside of the corral. The bounce, a stiff-legged spring made Shoo Ann and Beth giggle.

The cows moved away from them cautiously. The llama's wool was thick and shaggy, strands of it flapped around their legs and shoulders as the llamas moved. It grew in patterns of brown, white, and black. Dark almond-shaped ovals encircled their eyes, making the llamas look exotic. There was a puff of wool between the llamas soft-looking ears. A couple of the llamas had stars on their forehead. All of their lips looked pursed. When the llamas stopped running and bouncing, they stood on stiff legs, their ears pointing forward towards the herd of cattle inquisitively.

Arnold, Beth and Shoo Ann watched the llamas join the herd and were satisfied that they were doing the best they could to protect their herd from lions. They opened the far gates of the corral so the cows and their new llama protectors could migrate out to graze. Arnold hoped the llamas would eat the extra underbrush in the pasture.

As the three of them leaned on the fence watching the herd slowly move out to the wider grasslands, Shoo Ann asked how she could purchase a quarter horse for herself. Arnold immediately volunteered to pay for the horse, saddle, bridle and other gear she would need. She expressed her pleasure at the news by giving Arnold a big hug.

"When can we purchase the quarter horse?" Shoo Ann asked.

"Do you know the style of saddle you want?" Arnold asked.

"I'll show you in the house," Shoo Ann said. "I have it marked in a ranch catalog."

Shoo Ann showed him the one she wanted while Beth went into the kitchen to make a fresh pot of coffee. Arnold knew Shoo Ann had been thinking about this for some time. The catalog was well worn and wrinkled. The corners of several pages were turned down.

After he drank some coffee, he relaxed with a shot of Jack Daniels, picked up the phone and contacted the rancher that sold him his quarter horse. He asked if he had another one similar to the two he and Beth had already purchased.

"Do you want a mare? A young or an old one? Or perhaps a stallion? Do you know what you want?" asked the rancher.

"We want a mare, younger, but old enough to ride and one that had been trained some but not for cutting calves, just for pleasure riding and occasional work with cattle."

The rancher confirmed he had one, a mare that had not been bred but could be in six months.

Shoo Ann was excited almost beyond control. She assisted in coordinating the price and time for picking up the horse. The current owner promised to deliver the mare early the next day. Shoo Ann was extremely happy, especially when she learned she needed a name for her pony.

Arnold and Shoo Ann prepared to depart to buy her a saddle and gear. Beth asked to go along. They all got into the pick-up and joyfully rode to the farm store in Alamosa.

Shoo Ann could hardly wait for the others as she strode from the truck to the store saying she had already been shopping. That became obvious when they entered the store because the attendant recognized her and knew exactly which saddle to show her.

"What size of saddle are you going to purchase," Arnold teased, "a regular, small or large saddle?"

Shoo Ann asked the attendant what size she should purchase.

"This saddle should be large enough to hold your butt," the attendant said and to the surprise of Shoo Ann and Beth, he pulled out a measuring tape. When he put the tape measure on one side of her and stretched it to the other, he said "You have a small, but beautiful butt, and it will fit into a regular saddle."

Shoo Ann was pleased, and she craned head around as if she was trying to see her own back end. She said she had never had her butt measured before. There was laughter all around.

Shoo Ann purchased a bridle, two blankets, saddle bags and then asked if she needed a sheath for a rifle.

Arnold said, "Yes, and make sure you practice with it, so you are safe."

As the attendant loaded everything in the truck, Shoo Ann grabbed him and gave him a big hug. The attendant grinned from ear to ear.

Arriving back at the barn, Shoo Ann started to unload her gear and discovered she did not have a stand on which to put her saddle.

With a confused expression on her face she asked, "Where can I find a dummy horse?"

Arnold replied, "We will need to build one out of two by fours."

Shoo Ann exclaimed, "I sometimes think I do not have anything or know anything!"

Shoo Ann came up with several names during the evening while the three of them worked to build a saddle stand for Shoo Ann's saddle. Arnold suggested she wait a few days and let her experiences with the horse give her clues to the most appropriate name for the mare. Shoo Ann did not like the waiting, but she did.

As promised, Shoo Ann's new pony was delivered early the next morning. She was extremely pleased. She liked the horse's color, size and her demeanor. She led her to the barn and put her saddle and gear on and rode her out of the barn to show everyone she was ready and capable. Beth told her, now we can go riding together. Arnold suggested they ride to the restaurant and eat breakfast. This idea was accepted by all. Arnold and Beth saddled up Black Shadow and Autumn Time. The three riders and horses headed out of the ranch yard at a trot. They were all hungry and looking forward to Maggie's great food.

Arnold promised himself that he would only think about food and enjoyment and not about business in Oklahoma or camping in Wyoming so he would not be tempted to bring up these sore subjects to the two ladies.

CHAPTER 38

It was late morning when they arrived back at the ranch from the restaurant. Arnold received a call on the house phone from Linda.

"Arnold, I have been contacted by Darrell about a job working for him as a Financial Advisor/Consultant. This would be a significantly increase in salary and benefits for me. What do you advise?"

"That would certainly be a great position for you," Arnold said.

"I think I'd like it. How are you doing. I have not heard from you since you left Oklahoma," she stated.

"I've been extremely busy and had intended to call," he replied.

They chatted a bit longer and assured each other they would be in contact. As he hung up the phone, Arnold felt sad and disappointed in himself that he had not offered her more encouragement about their relationship."

Within an hour Darrell called wanting to discuss Linda and the position he had offered to her.

Darrell confirmed Arnold's support for Linda for the position under discussion. Darrell asked if he thought there would be a conflict of interest because of his investments. Arnold said he did not believe so.

Darrell replied, "Good. I will offer her the position. Do you have a recommendation for how much I should pay her?"

"As much as you can afford, and she can earn."

Darrell said, "Thank you. She will do great."

Arnold hung up the phone. As he finished the call, Beth asked that he and she go somewhere private and have a thorough discussion about her and his relationship.

Because of the way Beth said it, Arnold anticipated a serious discussion.

He agreed and suggested they go for a drive. They got into the pick-up and drove down a narrow unused two-track road to a secluded spot on the ranch. When he parked, Beth looked all around, then said, "I want to understand you, and I want you to understand me so we can commit to each other forever."

"Beth, you may not be able to understand me, and I may not be able to understand you no matter how hard we try. Because of something that occurred several years ago, something that I still think of daily and worry about by the hour, our confusion may last forever.

I am convinced you are a beautiful, intelligent and warm lady that deserves the best of all worlds, but I cannot commit my life to you because of the hurt I experienced before I ever met you, because of my divorce that was final not so long ago. I have promised to be good to you and to help you, and I intend to deliver on that promise."

There was silence for a while and Beth looked out the window without speaking.

"Beth, it is your turn."

"Arnold, you have been very, very good to me, and I do not want it to stop. I accept the fact that you have been burned badly by a divorce, and I have been burned badly by the occasion of my birth. More than anything, I would like to have a child, but being an intersex person, I am unable to get pregnant and deliver a baby. We both live with a heavy burden. I want you and I to join each other and commit to carrying the load we each bear without making it worse than it already is. My desires are plain and simple, uncomplicated and easily accepted if we trust God. If we do not trust God, the loads we carry will become too heavy for either of us."

Arnold looked at Beth. He knew Beth could see him become anxious and sad. He wrapped his long arms around her and tugged her across the seat to him in a warm hug.

"Beth, you are right, He said solemnly. "I will give this the most serious of consideration and get back to you."

"Arnold. This is not a business deal for you to get back to me. Can't you tell me now what you feel after being with me so long?" Beth asked.

He did not reply, but tucked Beth tighter against his side and started the pick-up and drove back over the bumpy little road to the ranch house wondering what was going to happen next. He could hear his father say, "Arnold, do the right thing."

"Beth. Let's go for a ride to our favorite place."

Beth looked confused.

"I can't explain, but I think and speak better when I'm on or near Black Shadow, and when I'm at our favorite place things seem clearer to me. I won't make you wait for my thoughts. Let's go now, as soon as we get back to the ranch."

They returned to the barn and began to put the saddle on Black Shadow and Autumn Time.

"Do you want me to take a thermos bottle of hot coffee with us?" Beth asked.

Arnold responded, "Please."

They rode across the pasture to their favorite place at a gallop. Black Shadow was working his magic and Arnold felt it throughout his body. His body relaxed. Soon he began to think more clearly and felt more able to discuss with Beth their relationship.

At the brook under the tree, Beth spread a blanket and poured a cup of coffee for each of them. Arnold tied up the horses. When he joined her on the blanket, she handed him a cup and looked him right in the eye.

She said, "Arnold, you are the greatest individual I have ever known, and I desperately want the two of us to always be together. Our relationship does not require marriage, but it does require commitment, one to the other, never to be broken except in death. You may travel, do business in Oklahoma, work on this ranch, manage your own financial resources and be the same with me as you have been from the beginning."

He replied, "I have one question I must answer, and you may help if you can. How can a man resolve the plague of hurt that hangs over him, as a result of his divorce from a woman he loved and cherished more than anything in this world? When I think of my ex-wife having sex with the man that tried, through the legal process, to destroy me, I become furious and burn for revenge. I do not blame my ex-wife for any of the legal issues; however, I cannot accept the fact that another man penetrated my wife's vagina numerous times. This is unacceptable to me and it haunts me daily.

For three months at an unbelievable legal cost, I did not sleep, work or relax for one moment. I lost 60 pounds that I could not afford to lose and looked like I might be dying of cancer. After the investigator I hired testified and the case was dismissed due to lack of evidence, my ex-wife confirmed the malevolent nature of her lovers' motive. She then experienced his death in a car accident. She now lives in obscurity and poverty.

Now, Beth, tell me what I can do to forget this nightmare that haunts me daily," Arnold begged.

Beth said quietly, "Go and visit your ex-wife, enjoy having sex with her, hold her and tell her you do not hold her accountable for the nightmare caused by her lover and wish her well. Then walk away and never look back.

You will have done more than any man could ever be expected to do and your conscience will be clear. If it is not feasible to enjoy having sex with your ex-wife, for whatever reason, regardless of how small or unimportant, walk away having tried your very best."

Arnold sipped his cup of coffee and continued listening to Beth. She remained cool and calm as she continued, "You are struggling with anger and hate and the wish for revenge, all of which is against your very nature with respect to a once cherished wife. You are weighed down with a beleaguered conscience that needs serious relief. Go and find relief. Release yourself from this past."

When she was done speaking, Arnold laid on the blanket with his head on Beth's lap. Beth was wise. She had survived much hurt of her own and seemed to remain untainted by hate and anger. He hoped he could make the right decision when it came to Beth.

They laid peacefully, each thinking their own thoughts on the blanket in the grass. It was late afternoon when they returned to the house.

Shoo Ann greeted them at the door with a look of concern, but she did not say anything. They followed her slender aproned form into the kitchen where the table was partially set, and she was finishing a dinner of meatloaf, mashed potatoes, and buttered carrots.

CHAPTER 39

It was almost a year since Arnold started his trek from Oklahoma on Highway 66 in the name of gaining experience. He reminded Beth that he had promised only to stay and care for her ranch until she completely recovered from surgery. Arnold felt some urgency about deciding his future. Beth felt that they should not be in a hurry to make important decisions just because of the time of year.

Over the next few days, Beth and Arnold enjoyed several in-depth discussions regarding his past and their future. They discussed the legal and financial issues of living together for long periods of time without marrying, including the complications involved in gaining assets over time without a contract to ensure that each retained the rights to the assets they earned. They discussed establishing a baseline of assets for each of them, keeping separate bank accounts, how to handle life insurance, and many of the other issues that couples with assets encounter. The conversations became detailed and complicated and they agreed to postpone these discussions until they decided what they wanted to do emotionally first.

Beth was clear about her desires for their future. She wanted the two of them to stay together, not necessarily married but committed to each other. Arnold assured Beth he understood what she wanted, and he would not jeopardize their relationship while trying to come to a reasonable resolution.

Arnold walked to the barn. When he had thinking to do, Arnold either repaired fences or saddled up Black Shadow. As Arnold took Black Shadow's halter down from a hook on the barn wall, Shoo Ann poked her head out of a stall she was cleaning and asked if she could go along if he was going riding. Beth, who had followed Arnold out of the house, also appeared and said that she wanted to go for a ride too. So, they decided to make it a party.

As the three of them paused to watch the horses over the gate, Arnold asked Shoo Ann if she had given her horse a name yet.

"No." she replied. "I have thought of several but nothing exciting has happened to cause me to identify the most appropriate name for her."

The young mare and the stallion were nipping, nuzzling, and sniffing each other. They seemed to be flirting. Arnold pointed this out to the two women.

"Black Shadow and your mare seem to be courting."

As the Shoo Ann pushed open the gate, Black Shadow rose up on his hind legs and mounted her mare. The lunge was powerful and unexpected. Neither Shoo Ann nor Beth were prepared for such action and screamed, slamming the gate closed. The loud audience did not interfere with Black Shadow as he continued his endeavor. As the three watched, Black Shadow dismounted without mating the mare twice more. Then, he remounted with an erection and began thrusting. When copulation was complete, the mare walked out from under him letting him slowly down to the ground. Both horses looked satisfied. Black Shadow looked exhausted.

"Does that action give you any ideas about a name for your mare?" asked Arnold with a laugh.

"I am not ready yet to name her," Shoo Ann insisted.

They postponed their ride, and Arnold saddled up the bay mare he had ridden when he first came to the ranch to give Black Shadow time to recover. He was going to repair fences and attached the saddle bag with his tools. Beth stayed to watch the horses and Shoo Ann went back to cleaning out stalls.

Out in the peaceful countryside on his own, Arnold could not get his mind off Beth and her comments. She knew he had promised to stay until the early Spring season and now it was months past that time. He did not feel pressured to be anywhere in particular because he had no formal plans except to travel, camp out, enjoy the scenery and enjoy whatever experience he happened to encounter.

His business dealings in Oklahoma were being managed well, income had increased significantly compared to the day he originally began his journey, but he was not yet able to rest in peace due to his own hang-ups. Many of his thoughts were angry thoughts.

As he dismounted to patch a stand of wire, he thought that in some ways, Beth was the perfect woman for him. She seemed the most understanding of his fear of responsibility and his need for freedom. She would accept a relationship without the formality of marriage. She wanted to take their time in deciding what to do. He did not intend to leave on the spur of the moment. But he was beginning to think he should leave soon. He decided to discuss this candidly with Beth.

After he had worked for several hours, he returned to the ranch and got cleaned up. Beth was sitting on the couch reading. He sat down beside her and broached the subject of his leaving.

"Beth, we have to talk about my leaving the ranch. We don't have to hurry, but we do need to plan."

Beth put her head in her hands and cried.

"I don't want you to leave," she sobbed.

He pulled her into his arms She wrapped her arms around him, and they sat on the couch in front of the cold fireplace and held each other until she calmed. Shoo Ann came in from the barn.

"What is up?" she asked.

"We must discuss how Beth is planning to run the ranch when I'm gone," Arnold said.

"You have taken on all the work, the fence repair, the care of the cattle, the barn repairs, the taxes, the buying and selling, ordering feed and supplies and the care of the horses," Beth almost shouted. "You tell me how I am going to manage."

"What about Jerry, the one who helped you when Shoo Ann and I went camping?" Arnold asked.

"Okay," Beth said, "let's talk about him. His name is Jerry Jackson. He is an experienced ranch hand and is willing to work, but he has no management ability. He does as he is told and nothing more. His initiative is limited to the projects given to him and nothing more.

"He probably won't work out then," Arnold agreed.

"Let's advertise for a rancher who is looking for work," Shoo Ann suggested. "I want to enquire at the restaurant and identify someone local with local references. Someone with ties to the community," said Beth.

They agreed to try that approach, and Beth agreed to write the ad and place it in the restaurant. Arnold suggested Beth decide how much she was going to pay this person and that started another debate.

"I cannot pay anyone a full-time salary. I don't make that kind of money," cried Beth.

"Anyone working full time would require several hundred dollars a month and at least $200.00 more than I am making," Shoo Ann chipped in.

"How much time do I have to backfill behind you?" Beth asked Arnold.

"Beth I am in no hurry, and I want to remind you I will not let you down." Arnold said quietly.

Beth got up and gave Arnold hug. She then asked tearfully, "Does that mean forever?" They went to bed and slept.

Early the next day Arnold received a phone call from Darrell asking him for permission to give his mailing address to the oil and gas company drilling the oil wells because they wanted to mail orders and monthly payments to him.

"I'll go and get a post box tomorrow and call you back," Arnold said.

Arnold went to the local post office and filled out the forms for a post box number. He was assigned box 283, Alamosa, Colorado. Arnold notified Darrell right away.

As he drank his morning coffee, he thought that he could not in good conscience leave Beth. He also knew that he did not want to marry Beth because he felt marriage should be reserved for a woman who could and desired to have children and raise a family.

Beth wanted children. She just could not have them.

He thought about adoption and was not opposed to it.

He found Beth just getting out of bed, still in her night gown.

"Beth," he said, sitting on the side of the bed beside her. "I propose we pursue a life together and try to figure out how to deal with any issues that will surely surface as they come. At first, I hesitated about revealing my financial situation to you because I didn't want to look dishonest. I am not a drifter with no money. I go to Oklahoma because I have real estate and mineral right holdings there. They, along with my other investments, are producing millions of dollars."

Beth was silent.

"Will this money be a concern for you in our relationship?" Arnold asked.

"Absolutely not," she said after a while. "We can live as we want and not overreact to the amount of money in your bank account."

"What do you mean by "your" bank account?" Arnold asked.

She thought and then said, "I mean the money we would have access to."

They discussed the operation of the ranch and Arnold asked her to estimate the value of her 4,000-acre ranch, the house, barn and other improvements.

"I cannot do that."

"Do you have tax assessment documents we can refer to?" Arnold asked.

She nodded and when to get them from her files.

Upon close examination, the tax papers reflected an assessed value of one and one half million. Arnold contacted the state revenue office. They informed him he should add twenty percent to determine the active market value. When he informed Beth of this information, he told her to add approximately $600,000 to the $300,000 and she had property worth almost 1 million.

Beth said, "I didn't know I had that much. If we get married, we can combine our assets and be comfortable."

Beth got dressed and they moved out to the kitchen to eat breakfast.

"Does my worth, change your thinking about what you want to do?" Beth asked.

"No." Arnold said.

"The lack of operating cash is a serious matter for me when I try to meet operating expenses and only receive income every two years from the sale of cattle. It is a big stretch." Beth commented as she forked her pancakes.

"How do you handle that now?" Arnold probed.

"I received short-term loans through the bank at high interest rates."

"Would you like to have a backup amount that you can draw on and pay back after a sale?" Arnold asked.

"That would eliminate a lot of worry," Beth confessed.

Arnold picked up the phone and called Darrell. He requested a wire transfer from his account of $40,000.00 to Arnold Barkley and Beth Howser at the Alamosa, Colorado bank.

"Now we can hire some help on the ranch when you are absent," Beth laughed.

Right after breakfast, they went to the bank and established a joint account from which to draw funds.

CHAPTER 40

As soon as Beth and Arnold decided to pursue a committed relationship and the topic of assets surfaced, the business side of Arnold's brain began to work.

It was mid-afternoon and the chores on the ranch were completed for the moment. Beth sat reading beside him on the couch. Arnold grabbed a pad of paper and pen to write items down as he thought of them, but the very first thought that came to mind froze his pen. He had the sudden premonition that Beth might not have transferred the ownership of the ranch and motel and restaurant when her father and mother died. The question of Beth's ownership of the ranch needed immediate attention.

Beth looked up from her book at his sudden stillness.

"Beth. Did you ever change the ownership of the ranch after your father and mother died?"

"I never even thought that it needed to be changed," she answered. "I just kept living here and paying bills like my father and mother did before me."

She got up and went into the bedroom that was used as an office and came out with a file on the ranch.

Arnold soon realized that the paperwork on the ranch remained as it had for over 40 years. According to the documents he read, the ranch, motel and restaurant were owned by Beth's late father.

"Did you ever hire a lawyer for any purpose?" Arnold asked Beth.

"No."

"Do you care who I hire to perform legal work to change the ownership from your father to you?" Arnold asked.

"No. I do not want the restaurant and motel."

"We must discuss each of these issues with a lawyer," Arnold said.

Arnold's stomach was reminding him they we had not eaten in hours, so they adjourned to Maggie's restaurant for food and good hot coffee. Beth and Arnold continued to discuss the ranch ownership as they ate.

"You told me that you inherited the ranch from your father," Arnold reminded Beth. "How did that occur?"

Beth said, "There was no one else. What was I to do?"

"We will take care of this tomorrow," Arnold promised.

The next day they went to the Office of the Recorder of Deeds in Alamosa and confirmed her father was still the owner. They called the owner of the Auction house from their bank and asked him for a referral for a lawyer who was experienced in matters of real estate and transfer of ownership. The Auction house gave them three names and suggested the one that they found to be the most capable. His name was Walt Newbern. He was about 55 years of age with 35 years of experience.

Newbern worked out of Alamosa and agreed to see them that day. After a brief introduction and a few questions, Arnold and Beth were pleased with his suggestions and paid him the fee of $600.00 for handling the ownership transfer paperwork for all three assets.

As they departed Newbern's office, Arnold asked Beth what she was going to do with the restaurant and motel? She said, "I am going to sell them to Maggie for $10.00 and good and valuable consideration. Case closed!"

When they got home, Mr. Newbern called and asked Beth to place a value on the ranch and call him back when she had one. She and Arnold discussed how long Beth planned to own the ranch as the tax consequence would be affected one way or another. To place a high value on the ranch now would lessen the tax burden when she sold it and to place a low value on it now would raise the tax consequence when it was sold. Beth called Mr. Newbern and placed a dollar value of $400,000.00. He agreed that amount was reasonable and said the paperwork would be ready to go to a required hearing within three weeks. On their way back to the ranch, Beth and Arnold stopped at the restaurant and discussed the situations with Maggie and found that she was totally pleased with becoming owner of the motel and restaurant.

"I am the luckiest woman in Colorado," Beth concluded to the half empty restaurant. "I am blessed with having Arnold to guide me through these legal decisions."

Sitting back in her chair she reached for Arnold's free hand. They enjoyed the coffee Maggie brought them and the sunny afternoon.

Arnold raised the issue of the 20 horses Beth owned that were not producing income.

"I never did anything with the horses because my father loved them and had more than once refused to sell them."

"Are you particularly fond of any or all of them?" Arnold asked.

I'm fond of only two of them," she said. I've ridden them several times.

"When we get back to the ranch, point out the two you want to keep, and I suggest you sell the rest of them and use the money to build a new corral. What kind of horses are they? How much should you get for them if we sell them?"

Beth didn't know, so they decided to check with people around the community and try to come up with a decent idea as to their worth. The next day, Jerry Walker arrived for work. He was a local and knew horses. He said that horses were in demand and would probably sell for $200.00 to $600.00 each depending on their condition and age. He also recommended Arnold have the Auction house handle the sale.

Arnold was happy with his advice and scheduled the sale of 18 horses at the Auction house that very night. The entire group sold for $2,800.00. Beth was all smiles when she paid the Auction house for their services.

On the way home in the truck, Beth asked Arnold if he was always thinking of business deals?

"Always," he replied. "While sitting around a campfire watching the glow of burning logs, breathing the cool, clean air of the wild and open spaces, when fixing fences, when riding Black Shadow, the seeds of business deals germinate constantly in my brain. Then, I want to do something about those ideas."

Arnold said to her as they entered the house, "There is more for us to do, but first, I must take care of you."

They headed for the bedroom and Arnold undressed Beth and explored her newly created anatomy thoroughly.

He thought perhaps he could learn more about this woman who had survived for so long as a hermaphrodite. He wondered if she experienced the same sensation as other women during the sexual experience. But if he asked her, what would she have to compare to? He wondered if Beth ever or often experienced orgasms. He could tell that she loved being touched, but he would have to ask her the question about orgasms though because he could not tell. He knew Shoo Ann experienced orgasms frequently when they made love. Sometimes he thought she had an orgasm each and every time they had sex and sometimes there were multiple orgasms beginning early and lasting almost to the end of each experience. Feeling them made him feel extra good. He, however, did not experience this with Beth even when she seemed to be rising to a peak. It was never really a peak. Perhaps her experience of pleasure was just less dramatic.

Beth smiled up at him as she arched against him. His orgasm was intense and as they came down, their bodies cooled, and both slept the deep sleep of satisfaction.

The next morning, they drew the rough outline of the corral they were going to build with the profit from selling the 18 horses. They decided they would ask Jerry to start construction as soon as he could arrange purchase of the supplies. The lumber yard manager agreed to deliver the supplies, and Jerry agreed to use his tractor and post hole digging equipment. Within a matter of days, the project was completed and ready to be used, including a loading chute and holding pen for vaccinations.

While showing Beth the completed corral project, Arnold suggested she purchase 20-30 young steers and plan to sell them in the fall as there was plenty of grass now that the horses had been sold. Beth agreed, and they proceeded to contact the Auction house for their assistance. Within four days they owned 30 new steers. After examining them in the corral, Jerry said they looked good and they were assured they had all their shots. Arnold and Beth were ready for them to get fat and ready for the fall market.

By the end of the week, Mr. Newbern called and informed Beth she was the proud owner of the ranch and Maggie was the proud owner of the restaurant and motel. They decided to eat lunch at the restaurant and deliver the good news. Maggie was pleased and the food was delicious.

While they were at the restaurant and close to the post office, Arnold checked his mailbox 238 and found it to be full of papers and a note to see the attendant. Arnold identified himself to the attendant and asked why the note. He was told he needed a larger box and the man handed him another handful of envelopes. The mail was all related to his business in Oklahoma. He sorted through it and found orders to sign, a contract to read and a million flyers wanting to sell him everything.

CHAPTER 41

Beth and Arnold entered the ranch house just as the phone rang. Arnold answered it, and it was Robert on the other end.

"I've got some information for you, and I have to ask a question," Robert announced right after saying, "Hello."

"Hello Robert. What information do you have for me?"

"Charlene and I are separating," he said abruptly. "Will you talk to her?"

"I'll be there in a week. I'll talk to her then. I don't want to talk to her about this on the phone, and I can't get there any sooner."

Robert said, "Okay."

There was a long silence.

"So, what happened?" Arnold finally asked.

"I went out with the guys, became inebriated, encountered a woman that I used to know, and we had sex," Robert said. "When Charlene found out she went wild and informed me she was going to file for a divorce, which she has, as of today.

"How did Charlene find out?"

"I confessed," said Robert.

"Don't do anything that can be interpreted as retribution. Let me talk to her first. Are you sorry about all this?" asked Arnold.

"Yes, it will never happen again," Robert promised.

"Have you told Charlene that?"

"Yes. That is when she asked to talk with you. I guess she trusts you. She knows you and I have known each other a long time."

"Okay. I'll come and talk to her."

Robert thanked him and hung up.

Arnold hung up the phone but continued to look at the receiver for a moment. When he turned around, Beth was watching him. She came over and gave him a hug and said,

"As I said, 'Do your best.' When you get back, we can take a trip somewhere on our own."

Beth began searching for a ranch hand the next day, someone who could manage the ranch when Beth and Arnold were gone. She called all the nearby ranches and posted an ad at Maggie's restaurant. Beth and Arnold agreed that Shoo Ann was a reliable assistant, but not experienced enough to take over all the operation.

Arnold contacted the airlines and scheduled a flight to Oklahoma City for the next week.

That evening, he received a call from Charlie Anderson.

Everything was okay; nothing new, Charlie said. "However, I wanted to talk to you about a 4-H Club sponsorship. The leader of the 4-H Club in Calumet approached me about sponsoring some kids who cannot afford to buy calves to raise and show at the local and state level."

"What do they need?" Arnold asked.

"They need someone to buy a calf for them to raise and show," Charlie said. "I cannot afford to do this myself but would like to help the kids."

"How many kids are you thinking about?"

"Around 6 or 7."

"If you will keep it confidential, I'll pay the cost of the calves, their transportation, their feed, entrance fees and veterinarian services," Arnold stated.

"Can I tell the teacher at the school about the funding as long as I don't tell her who is doing the funding?" Charlie asked. "Her name is Mrs. Walker. She is 34 years old and not extremely attractive, but an extremely nice person with a heart of gold. She spends many hours with the kids. She barely makes a living on her schoolteacher's salary, but sometimes spends her own money to support the kids. She will be delighted that more children can take part. You will have to meet her sometime when you are in town."

"How can we help her in addition to the kids?" Arnold asked.

"Well, she rents a duplex in town and perhaps she could use some financial help."

"Is the duplex for sale?"

"Yes."

"Okay. I have an idea," said Arnold. "I'll call Robert and get back to you."

Arnold hung up and called Robert.

"Robert. Is the duplex the teacher, Mrs. Walker, lives in for sale?"

"It is, for $8,000.00."

"What would a person have to pay for it if he was a serious buyer," Arnold asked.

"The teacher has been offered the opportunity to purchase it for $8,000.00 with no commissions," Robert replied.

"Can you arrange for the schoolteacher, I think her name is Mrs. Walker, to purchase the duplex for as little as possible and arrange for someone to help her with the entire process? Can we pay the purchase price and closing costs, so it would be free to her? Arnold asked.

"Someone will have to buy and donate the duplex," Robert explained.

"Okay. See my banker and arrange for me to buy and donate the entire duplex anonymously and have the rent from the one side go to Mrs. Walker while she lives in the other side."

"The rent is $70.00 per month and the other side is rented." Robert told Arnold.

"Be sure to submit a bill for your services to my banker as well," Arnold said.

Arnold ended the call with Robert and called Charlie Anderson back.

"Charlie. It's Arnold. I've arranged to purchase the duplex, donate it to Mrs. Walker anonymously and for her as owner to receive the rent from the other half of the property. It is only $70.00 a month, but since she won't have to pay her own rent, that will give her some income. I'll have Darrell cut you a check for the kids' calves too."

"Arnold you are an angel in disguise," said Charlie. "Thank you."

The day before he left for Oklahoma, he called Charlene and informed her he was flying to Oklahoma to have a meeting with her to discuss her marriage to Robert.

"I'll be staying in the motel in El Reno. Would you meet me there?" asked Arnold. "I'd like to discuss this with no one else around."

Charlene agreed to meet him at the motel the next day, and she said that she was happy to hear from him.

Arnold's flight left Pueblo and arrived in Oklahoma City on time. He rented a car and drove to the motel in El Reno.

Charlene arrived soon after, and when she entered his motel room, his mouth went dry. He knew they were going to have sex. He could tell by the way she smiled, the perfume she was wearing and the way she was dressed. Her dress was short, and her legs were bare. She wore slip-on sandals. It looked like she could throw off that dress and discard her shoes in a second without fussing with buttons, zippers, buckles, or ties. He knew too…that he would enjoy it.

Part of him thought he could prevent the sex from happening if he thought long enough about her having sex with someone else behind his back when she was married to him. He tried conjuring up some resentment, but she smiled and began to undress. She was so familiar to him. She laid down on the bed naked, and all he could think of was the long ago past when they were young and newly married.

He could hardly contain himself as he approached her nude body, memories of the many times they had held each other swamping his reason. Charlene welcomed him with open arms and warm kisses. His hands filled themselves with her warm bare skin and the next thing he knew, three days had passed before they came up for air.

Oh, they talked some. They discussed many intimate subjects, constantly fighting against the urge to have sex and then succumbing. They relived moments of cherished love from the past, admitting to hungering for that love and regretting the betrayal and hurt that had destroyed their marriage.

Sometime during the 3 days, they discussed her planned divorce from Robert.

"What do you think I should do Arnold?" Charlene asked sleepily not raising her head from the pillow. She lay beside him, her nakedness covered by the white sheet.

"Do you love Robert?" Arnold asked.

She said "Yes."

"You must return to him, cancel any planned divorce and any further discussion on the matter and make your life with him. Consider this, you have had sex with me, but love him still. He feels the same way about you. He made a mistake."

After they said their goodbyes, Charlene left the motel and went to visit with Robert. Arnold was pretty sure they would be able to patch up their marriage.

Arnold was ravenous. He wasn't sure that he and Charlene had taken any time to eat in the last 3 days of love making. Maybe they had ordered room service…once. He felt empty of his resentment towards her and drained of his pain. He walked to the restaurant next door for breakfast, contacted Linda and set up lunch with her.

He went back to his room and took a nap. Sleep was another thing he and Charlene had neglected to do.

As Arnold drove into the restaurant parking lot where he had agreed to meet Linda, he saw that she was already there, waiting for him by the front door. She was dressed for work in a blue dress. She wore stockings and heels. Linda gave him a hug and he returned it.

Over soup and sandwiches, Linda informed him that she had met a gentleman through Darrell's investment dealings who was very impressive.

"He asked me not see anyone else until we have had time to get better acquainted with each other," she said. "I really think he might be the guy for me, and I am committed to that effort."

Arnold listened intently and did not break in on her as she spoke.

"I have known the gentleman for several months," she explained. "I am looking forward to both my new job, and my new guy!"

"I am happy for you Linda," Arnold lied.

Inside he felt that he had missed the boat somehow, but he also felt relieved that he had not messed up his great business relationship with this lovely, smart lady that he admired so much. He realized he probably secretly loved her and probably always would.

As they said their goodbyes at the door and were heading to their separate cars, Arnold called Linda back and grasped her arm.

"Linda, you have been a great friend to me, and you are a lovely lady. You are smart and kind and beautiful. Any guy would be lucky to have you. I truly wish you well," Arnold said and gave her a warm hug, a hug that she returned wholeheartedly.

Arnold drove out to visit his recently purchased land and talked with Charlie Anderson. Charlie was overseeing Arnold's participation in the Agriculture Stabilization Conservation Service Program. The organization encouraged farmers to improve the quality of the land on their Oklahoma farms by planting certain crops that put nutrients back into the soil. Charlie estimated it would cost Arnold about $1000.00 a year in income and wanted to know if Arnold would agree to have that amount taken out of his rental agreement.

Arnold agreed and told Charlie that he would suspend rental payments the first year of the program on each quarter.

Charlie was very pleased to hear of this. Charlie told Arnold that he had been watching the progress the oil and gas company was making toward the drilling of wells on his land. He said they had completed 4 wells and would complete 3 more within four months. This was good news to Arnold because it meant that the revenue would soon begin.

On the way to meet his airplane, he stopped to visit with Robert. Robert told him that he and Charlene had patched their relationship up and were having dinner together that night. Arnold grinned when he heard the news.

While in Calumet, Arnold also stopped in the bank to talk with Darrell. Darrell was glad to see him and wanted to discuss the donations for the poverty cases at the school. Darrell told him there were more people in need than he had originally predicted and wanted to know the upper limit of donations Arnold was willing to contribute.

"How much more do you need?" Arnold asked.

"Quite a bit," Darrell said. "I estimate approximately $6,000.00 would take care of it for a year."

"Approved," Arnold said.

"Also, the superintendent wants to initiate a program wherein he would recognize the winner and two runners up of a letter writing contest. The letter would be addressed to the governor telling him why students in Calumet were performing so well. The superintendent was thinking of offering a first prize of $100.00 and $50.00 each for second and third place."

Beating Darrell to the punch, Arnold suggested that he fund it and that Darrell take the amount out of his account or that he could write the superintendent a check on his account if needed. Darrell thanked Arnold for his generosity and reminded him that the oil and gas would start to flow in 21 days and large amounts of money would soon follow.

CHAPTER 42

Arnold finally got on his way to the airport in time for his red-eye flight. His airplane was on time and he headed for Colorado eager to see Beth and tell her about his newly found peace of mind. He was also looking forward to riding Black Shadow again.

It was very late when he arrived in Pueblo, so he did not call the ranch. He found his pickup in the parking lot and headed home. He began thinking of taking another vacation, one for just Beth and himself. He thought two weeks might be long enough for them to relax. Beth had told him one time that she had never been on a vacation. He would have to ask her where she would like to go.

When he got to the ranch, he went to the barn first and looked out at the horses grazing in the dark pasture. The sky was a sea of tiny stars.

The ranch house was dark except for a faint glow in the window of the room he shared with Beth. He figured Beth had fallen asleep with the light on.

As soon as he opened the door to the ranch house, he began to feel ill. A pair of well-used cowboy boots sat on the rug adjacent to the bedroom door. A low beam of light crept under the door. He crossed the room and pulled the door open slowly. He stepped in and observed two people in the bed. The naked rear end of a man arched over Beth. His head beside the pillow was not visible to Arnold.

Beth turned her head as the door opened and froze at the sight of Arnold.

"Jesse, maybe you should get up off me now and leave," Beth suggested after a short silence.

The naked man began to rise when a large, powerful arm wrapped itself around his waist and removed him from the missionary position he had held atop Beth. He was catapulted across the room ending up with his head in the corner of the bedroom with his feet facing his face. He looked with shock at Arnold.

Arnold recognized the wrangler from the sale barn, the same man who had delivered the llamas. Jesse was the name he remembered.

Jesse was trying to untangle his limbs and elevate his body to a standing position when he received a crushing blow to his lower back and then a wild chop to his rib cage. Jesse lost consciousness for a second before Arnold tossed him out of the room. He landed in the living room.

Beth screamed as loud as possible. Shoo Ann came running to the rescue. Later she told Beth that she observed a naked man trying to put his boots on backwards. Then, he gave it up and ran out of the house barefooted.

Shoo Ann entered Beth's bedroom to find Arnold and Beth staring at each other, Beth from the bed with the covers held up to her chin as if she were holding a shield and Arnold from the corner of the room where he stood breathing heavily his fists clenched.

"What happened here," Shoo Ann asked.

Arnold struggled to control his thoughts and words.

"What kind of a relationship do we have Beth?" asked Arnold. "There is nothing more insulting to a me, or any man, than to learn his loved one has allowed another man to penetrate her vagina with his penis or his tongue."

Probably both, he thought.

Beth sat silently, her face red and unhappy.

"Beth. I have loved you with everything God gave me, and I was willing to share it all with you, my money, my time, my love and my caring. And you, behind my back, when I was on a business trip, for God's sake, take up with the first cowboy that comes along."

Beth still did not say a word and just stared down at her hands clutching the bed clothes.

"Specifically, my question is this." Arnold spat. "Is this a caring and loving relationship we have, where we are meant only for each other, or is it one in which we care for each other but can also have sex with other people?"

"I thought it was a combination of both," replied Beth, "it is a loving and caring relationship one for the other, and one that allows each to have sex with others within reason as long as there is no interference between each person and their friend."

Arnold asked, "Do you really believe you can have sex with me and have sex with another man, and it will be okay with me?"

"I'm sorry you are offended Arnold. I would think it would be okay with you if I had sex with another man and still had sex with you and treated you with loving care."

"Well, I don't want you to have sex with another man while you are committed to me."

"Okay Arnold. I will not have sex with another man from now on as long as I can have sex with another woman. Is that okay with you?"

Shoo Ann, who was looking on, raised an eyebrow and looked from one to the other.

"I have agreed that is okay as long as I know the woman."

"Is it okay for you to have sex with another man?" Beth asked.

"Absolutely not," Arnold replied.

"Is it okay for you to continue having sex with women other than me?" Beth asked.

"Absolutely yes," Arnold replied.

Shoo Ann raised both eyebrows at that.

"Is that fair?" Beth asked.

"No, but I recognize your situation and believe it necessary to avoid objecting to you sleeping with a woman since the doctor said that would be necessary for you to enjoy sex. He said that sometimes women enjoy sex more with women than men. I don't understand why."

Beth replied, "I understand your feelings now. I will never have sex with a man again other than you. Please say that we can make this work."

"I don't think we can right now Beth," Arnold said. "I will pack my belongings and leave this ranch within 24 hours. I am sorry our relationship has ended in this manner."

Arnold looked at his watch and noticed that it was almost dawn. He departed the bedroom, drove off the ranch and sat outside the Alamosa bank until they opened. He then closed his accounts and took the cash over to the Chevrolet dealer and purchased a new blue and white V-8 Chevrolet Pick-Up with a horse trailer and a highway approved trailer hitch. The trailer was red and equipped with a feeder, a water trough and a ramp in the rear to make loading and unloading the horse easier. He asked that it be equipped with a temporary license plate. He waited for the purchase paperwork to be finalized and for truck and trailer to be ready. It took hours.

He returned to the ranch house pulling the trailer and found Beth in the living room staring off into space with tears still setting on her cheeks. No one apparently had noticed him drive up.

"Shoo Ann is in her bedroom and her heart is broken," said Beth. "I am extremely sorry for my actions and for not understanding how they would make you feel. Please forgive me," Beth said, getting up from the couch to stand in front of him with her head down.

Arnold bent over and lifted her chin so he could look directly into her eyes.

"Beth that will never happen, so do not ask me again please. You are a fabulous, beautiful and courageous woman. The sex you were having with Jesse is not something I can tolerate."

Arnold departed the ranch house for the barn and prepared Black Shadow for travel. He filled the trough in the trailer with water and the fodder rack with hay. Shoo Ann followed him out to the barn. As he came out of the horse trailer, she handed him a fresh cup of hot coffee, smiled sadly and said, "Arnold. I love you, and I love Beth. I do not want you to leave. Beth is sick about her actions, and I believe Beth will never violate your trust again. Please forgive her and give all of us a second chance."

Arnold set the coffee cup down on the bed of the truck and walked over to Black Shadow who was tied to a post in the middle of the runway. He untied the big stallion and led Black Shadow into the horse trailer. He secured him and stepped out to lift the ramp that doubled as a back door for the trailer. He shot the bolt home to secure it. In his mind's eye, he could see Beth sitting on the living room couch crying, unable to fully understand his anger and hurt.

Beth came into the barn as he was throwing his suitcase into the back of the truck. Shoo Ann salvaged the coffee cup from the bed of the truck and heading back to the ranch house, left the two of them alone. Beth approached him tenderly and hugged him. Arnold stood still for the hug but did not return it.

"Arnold, I was afraid to come out here. I am finding it difficult to live with myself, and I respectfully ask for the opportunity to discuss our situation with you. I know that what I did was wrong, and I am embarrassed. I assure you this or something like this will never occur again. I will do anything you ask to earn your trust again. Forgive me for what I have done and tell me what I need to do."

"I am forgiving you but, I am going back to Oklahoma. I am going home."

"Please don't shut me out completely. I received a call from my doctor who wants me to set up a six-month checkup next week. He suggested you accompany me."

"I had planned to see you through your entire recovery, but since the appointment is only a check-up, it probably will not require my attendance. Good-Bye Beth. Good luck."

Arnold swung his long legs into the cab of his new truck, closed the door, turned the truck and trailer around and headed out the drive towards the highway.

Autumn time raised her head over the fence and whinnied when she could no longer see Black Shadow. Black Shadow's whinny could be heard answering as the new red trailer turned onto the black top.

CHAPTER 43

It was late August when Arnold arrived in Oklahoma. It was hot, hot, hot. He had driven across the corner of New Mexico and the pan handle of Texas, stopping at Clayton Lake, New Mexico to sleep and let Black Shadow out of the trailer. The lake was a beautiful blue against the high desert landscape. He hobbled Black Shadow so he could wander but not run off and gave him some hay. Then he tied the big stallion to the trailer at dark and slept in the open nearby. He started early the next morning and arrived in Calumet six hours later. Instead of going to a motel, he went to the farm he had grown up on, the one he now owned. He settled Black Shadow in the fenced pasture, so the horse had access to the old barn for shelter and pitched a tent for himself in the lean-to off the barn.

He was pleased with his decision to return to Oklahoma so far. His anger at Beth had subsided some. He realized he had not understood Beth very well. She was such a nice person he had decided they could deal with whatever surfaced as it came up. Before he found her with Jesse in bed, she and he had not discussed or even thought about what they thought about one partner having sex outside their established relationship. When he thought of Beth having sex with another man, he did not like it. But he was having sex with various women, and Beth did not even question it. So, the question remained: what was right?

He drove over to Roberts office to see if Robert and Charlene wanted to join him for dinner. When Robert found out Arnold was staying at his farm instead of at a motel, and staying for good, he offered Arnold the use of a desk in his office so he would have access to a phone. He also gave him a key to the building.

Charlene, Robert, and Arnold met an hour later at a local restaurant for dinner. Over salads, Robert told Arnold that he and Charlene had decided to have an 'Open Marriage.'

"I don't know much about such an arrangement. Can you educate me on the concept?" Arnold said.

"In an Open Marriage, either party can enjoy sex with someone outside the marriage agreement and the other partner would understand and not object," Robert explained.

"Since I'm not married," Arnold said, I do not have to be concerned with that situation, unless I participate in sex with someone who is married.

"Would you enjoy a situation where husbands and wives agreed to swap partners?" Robert asked.

"I think it would be better not to get married and avoid the controversy," Arnold replied.

"Well Charlene and I are going to participate in an 'Open Marriage' arrangement and see how it works for us," said Robert.

Charlene grinned at Robert and then threw a grin at Arnold across the table and tapped his leg under the table. Arnold was not sure if he received the right message, but he thought it might be nice to sleep with his ex-wife again sometime without being worried about Robert shooting him. He cherished the memory of the 3-day tryst they had shared recently.

That very evening, Arnold called Charlie Anderson and asked if he wanted to lease any or all the properties he would be closing on in the morning. Charlie agreed to lease the three sections and wanted to evaluate each of them before he made any recommendations regarding improvements. Charlie acknowledged that the quality of each section was somewhat better than his current holdings. Arnold told him he was more interested in the earning projections of the oil and gas leases than in agriculture production. Charlie agreed with that thought and told him he would need to be patient. Arnold assured him he was.

"While I have you, Charlie, would you be able to provide a status report on the 4H club activity you are funding?" Arnold asked. He was curious about the charitable activity.

"Yes, of course," Charlie said. "Mrs. Walker is available tomorrow afternoon."

The next day, Charlie and Arnold met at Mrs. Walker's place to talk about the year's 4H activities.

"I've already arranged for 7 twelve (12)-year-old boys and 8 eleven (11)-year- old girls to purchase, own, and care for steers located on one of Charlie's farms. The children are planning to show the steers at the state fair in late September," Mrs. Walker said.

She drove them out to view the steers that were held in a corral on the farm.

"Tomorrow afternoon, the 4H club will be meeting to perform their weekly check-up on each animal. That is why they are corralled right now. The veterinarian will also be present. Would you both like to attend that meeting?" Mrs. Walker asked.

Charlie and Arnold agreed that they would like that.

As they got back in the car that Mrs. Walker's drove them over in, Charlie got in the front seat and Arnold took the back.

"Thank you, Charlie for your support of the 4H program," Mrs. Walker said.

"I am 'Mrs.' to the school kids but to you and Arnold, I am Betty," she continued with a grin at each man. "Please call me Betty."

"Betty, I am Arnold, a single man and one interested in very attractive women," Arnold replied from the back seat.

Betty let Charlie out at his car and drove on to Arnold's truck.

As he was getting out, she turned to look at him and laughed, "I do not fit in that category, but if you have time while you are in Oklahoma, I can entertain you like an original Okie."

"I'd like that," Arnold replied. "Where and when."

"Tonight, my place at 7:00 PM," she suggested.

"I'll be there." he said.

Betty gave him the address to her duplex.

Arnold showed up at 7:00 PM on the dot with a bottle of wine. Betty was impressed. Arnold was impressed with Betty as well. She was wearing a tight pair of jeans and a tank top that showed off most of her firm breasts and slender tanned arms. Their eyes locked as they opened the wine and made a pretense of visiting while they drank a glass each.

Truthfully, Arnold thought, we are so busy drinking in each other, we can't pay any attention to the good vintage.

Arnold had not even been there a half hour before they had moved in close to each other on the couch and began to kiss. His hand went right to the lower hem of her tank top and pulled it over her head, mussing her light blonde hair. She wore a silky bra that closed in the front with only one clasp. He had that undone in no time and engulfed her soft warm breasts in his big hands. She arched back as he explored her nipples with his lips.

He reached down to undo the snap on her jeans next. She lifted her hips to help him get them off over her hips. Her panties came off with the jeans and she pushed them off her feet and sat naked before him. He pulled her over onto his lap and explored ever bit of her smooth skin while he was still fully clothed. She moaned as he spread her legs with his hand and stroked her there. He studied the contrast of her vulnerable naked body against his jeans and plaid shirt and recognized his own dominant position, clothed, muscular, and male, to her more vulnerable, naked, soft, and female. Possessive desire welled up in him, adding fuel to the heat that burned in him.

He lifted her up in his arms and placed her on the sofa while he removed his shirt and undid his own jeans. She watched him steadily as he revealed his stiff penis. He parted her legs, knelt on the couch and placed himself between them, entering her swiftly holding the rest of his body away from her, He watched from above as her eyes widened then closed as she arched her hips up toward him, making room within her for his length. He grasped a firm smooth buttock in each hand and worked himself deep inside her. He set up a steady rhythm of enter and withdraw. Her hands reached up to him blindly, trying to reach him and draw him down to her. He held himself away until she was frantic and on the verge of climaxing. He steadied her hips in his large hands as her hips began to undulate, demanding release against his hips. He let her pleasure peak without lowering his chest to hers. Her body arched and her heels dug powerfully into his buttock as she shuddered with release.

He could hold out no longer and followed her into completion, pressing her body down into the couch as his own body arched powerfully, spilling his seed.

It was her turn to explore him then. He lay still as her hands moved over his shoulders, chest, waist, back and buttock down as far as she could reach. Her lips moved over his face and neck.

"Umm. You are big and hard and male...bristly too," she murmured against his chin. "It is hard for a plain Okie woman to restrain herself with you inside her. Not fair at all."

His only response was to harden within her a second time and this time their love making took a slower longer turn.

"I think I like love making Okie style," Arnold growled at some point in their mutual quest to know every inch of each other.

Betty and he showered together, sat down to eat cold chicken sandwiches at the kitchen table and finished off the bottle of wine he had brought and open another from her pantry. Arnold concluded that he was partial to Okie women.

Later in the evening they talked about the school children she worked with. They seemed to be her single interest in life.

"I know who my secret benefactor is," Betty informed him sweetly over a glass of wine, "the one who assisted me financially in the purchase of this duplex, who funds the 4H activities including the purchase of the steers, and who is always ready to help with many other expenses."

Arnold stayed silent and watched her over the rim as he rotated his own glass of wine around in his fingers.

"Charlie is very good at not answering me when I raise questions about who is behind the funding I receive, but I knew all along that it was someone with a good heart behind the generosity. I knew it was not Charlie or Robert. So, I kept quiet until I knew for certain who it was. Today, I listened when you talked about your love for children in school who deserve a chance in life. I have decided that our benefactor is you."

Arnold smiled.

"Betty you and I could start a larger chartable effort if you would promise to keep everything confidential. I think we could help these kids and possibly their mothers, assuming they are good mothers." Arnold said.

"It would be the answer to many prayers. I can keep a secret. I promise. What do you want me to do? Just ask, and I will do it if I can," Betty said.

They began to discuss the actual needs of each family she knew about. Repairs to family homes seemed to be the most important need because all the families had difficulty keeping their houses warm in the winter. Betty and Arnold tried to estimate the amount each family needed to make immediate improvements in their living conditions. They prioritized that list according to the amount each family would need in descending order.

"I know experienced carpenters and utility workers who could be hired to do the work if there was money to draw from to pay everyone," Betty said.

"Would you be willing to sign off on completed projects and forward the bills to Darrell, my banker?" Arnold asked.

"I can do that," Betty said.

"I'll discuss this with Darrell. He would pay each worker when he saw that you had signed off on the project. I'll set up a meeting between the two of you so you can hammer out the process."

"How will we notify the mothers of each project?" Arnold asked. "Will they feel they had been left out of the decision-making process if we do the estimating and planning?"

"I'm having a 4H parent meeting in two days and could explain it to them then and find out who wants to be involved. If anyone objects, I can keep track of them and let Darrell know," Betty offered.

They sat thinking their own thoughts for a minute.

"Arnold, I've done some research on you." Betty stated after a while. "I know your background. You are an Okie too. I believe you are a good person. You are knowledgeable in many things and willing to share your knowledge. You are always helping people, and many don't even know about your assistance. I hope to help you enjoy living in Oklahoma again.

I cannot express my gratitude enough. These kids need a sponsor, and you have fulfilled their dreams. I wish you could meet their mothers. I say mothers because every one of them is being raised by their single-parent mother, and not one of them has any money to spare." Betty took a breath and then continued in a rush while she still had Arnold sitting there quietly.

"One last thing for you to know before you depart Oklahoma…I have not had a sexual relationship with a man since my husband was killed driving a tractor over eight years ago. I will never forget you. You are the only one who seems to care about me."

Betty choked a little from emotion at that, but continued before he could say anything in response, "You have given me great pleasure and much needed warmth and satisfaction. The world can be very cold on your own. Please let me know when you are in Oklahoma again."

Arnold hugged Betty as he left her home. He told her that he was staying in Oklahoma this time and promised to call her again. "You can reach me at Robert's office. He lent me an office and phone to use while I'm camped at the farm with no residence."

One week later, he was meeting with Linda, Robert, and Charlie to go over all his investment and real estate holdings when he received a call from Beth on Robert's office phone.

"Arnold, I'm sorry to bother you," Beth said into the phone. Her voice sounding a bit like she was underwater to Arnold.

"What is up? Beth." Arnold asked.

"I received a diagnosis from the doctor that I don't understand. I thought everything was fine, but my doctor says I have to have surgery again in two weeks."

"I thought you were doing fine, and you only needed a checkup," Arnold said.

"The doctor hasn't been really clear, but it involves internal bleeding that he thinks is going on because of some swelling I am having. He demands that my significant other be there during the surgery. You are the only significant other I could think of. He knows you were with me when I had the last surgery."

Arnold was thinking about what could possibly be wrong so he did not respond right away, and Beth must have taken that for hesitation on his part.

"Arnold, I might die," she wailed.

"Beth. I'm leaving first thing in the morning." Arnold assured her. "Do not be afraid. You will lick this thing like you have licked so many other challenges in your life. I know you will. I'll meet you in Pueblo. What motel shall I meet you at?"

Beth got a hold of herself and said that Shoo Ann was dropping her off at the Mountain Inn in Pueblo, and she would wait for him there. She hung up.

"Beth in trouble?" asked Linda.

"Yes." Arnold answered, lowering the phone. "She has some kind of internal bleeding and needs another surgery urgently."

"I'm sorry," said Robert. "She is a nice lady."

"Go on old man," said Charlie. "We can take care of things here as we have before."

Arnold put his head in his hands and prayed. Beth was such a tough woman inside. She had lived so long an outsider, unable to fit in with men or women all because of a birth defect. He respected her immensely.

She had messed things up between them, and Arnold know she was sorry and wanted a permanent relationship with him. He did not for a minute suspect that she had made this illness up to get him back though. He was going to see her through this crisis. God willing, he would be back to Oklahoma soon, his home.

www.ingramcontent.com/pod-product-compliance
Lightning Source LLC
Chambersburg PA
CBHW051609100726
47898CB00001B/294